"Michelle Hébert's well-crafted debut novel crackles with magic, mystery, melancholy, and a mind-blowing twist. She shines a sensitive spotlight on mental illness and its impact on self, family and friends. This tale is a wry reflection on life, death, grief and healing."

Jane Doucet
author of Lost & Found in Lunenburg

"*Every Little Thing She Does is Magic* is a beautifully crafted coming-of-age story about a young woman's journey towards the acceptance of her family. The novel is upbeat with a focus on trust and love and a surprising narrative twist that is skillfully woven into the story."

Atlantic Books Today

Every Little Thing She Does Is Magic

Michelle Hébert

Vagrant PRESS

Vagrant Press is an imprint of
Nimbus Publishing Limited
3660 Strawberry Hill St, Halifax, NS, B3K 5A9
(902) 455-4286 nimbus.ca

Nimbus Publishing is based in Kjipuktuk, Mi'kma'ki, the traditional territory of the Mi'kmaq People.

Editor: Stephanie Domet
Editor for the press: Whitney Moran
Cover design: Heather Bryan
Typesetting: Rudi Tusek
NB1670

Library and Archives Canada Cataloguing in Publication

Title: Every little thing she does is magic / Michelle Hébert.
Names: Hébert, Michelle, 1968- author.
Identifiers: Canadiana (print) 20230585906 | Canadiana (ebook) 20230585957 |
ISBN 9781774712740
   (softcover) | ISBN 9781774712955 (EPUB)
Subjects: LCGFT: Novels.
Classification: LCC PS8615.E30385 E94 2024 | DDC C813/.6—dc23

Nimbus Publishing acknowledges the financial support for its publishing activities from the Government of Canada, the Canada Council for the Arts, and from the Province of Nova Scotia. We are pleased to work in partnership with the Province of Nova Scotia to develop and promote our creative industries for the benefit of all Nova Scotians.

To my father, Gord,
who had great taste in music and beaches,
and enduring faith in me.

I see what you did there, Papa.

This book deals with themes that include grief and mental illness. Please visit *michellehebertwrites.com* for a full list of content notes.

PART I
The Fool

Sun Comes Up,
It's Tuesday Morning

Tuesday, April 18, 2000

There were three other times in my life when I'd woken up in a strange bed and didn't know where I was or how I got there. One brought me back from the dead. One made me hope that if I was dreaming, I wouldn't wake up. And one almost destroyed me.

It was always the smell that woke me. This time, it was bleach against flannel sheets. I never used bleach. Bleach reminded me of bad things, like hospitals and my mother.

The sheets were cool. He hadn't been there. He hadn't just gotten up to use the bathroom or get a drink of water.

I was alone.

An amber streetlight glowed through a low window, and I turned my face toward it. Moving my head took a lot of effort, as though it was no longer part of my body. *Maybe it's not*, I thought. *Maybe I'm dead.*

The thought cheered me a little.

A shadowy figure appeared in my periphery, and I startled, clutching the covers against me until I realized, with mingled relief and confusion, that it was Simon Le Bon from Duran Duran.

The bedside lamp wasn't where I expected it to be, and my hand fluttered through the darkness until it found a switch. The light dispelled any question about where I was. Corey Hart was peeking around the corner at me. Sting stared at me from the ceiling over the bed. And there by the window, crowned with a halo from the streetlight, was Prince.

I was in Paradise. Paradise Valley, Nova Scotia. My old room, with my old posters. My old life. My old ghosts.

Never had I been so disappointed not to be dead.

The corner under the eaves where I'd done my spells and read tarot cards looked like I'd been gone six minutes, not six years. The door to the old wardrobe was ajar, and I saw the sleeve of one of the Benetton sweaters I'd worn in high school. A ghost cloud of Love's Baby Soft and incense clung to the same carpet and curtains that had been there since 1987. There was no updating things in this house. There was no outgrowing or letting go.

My collection of Care Bears sat on top of the wardrobe, next to my old Cabbage Patch doll. The sight of its apple cheeks and yellow hair jolted me into the present.

Where was my baby?

I jumped out of the bed and tripped over the suitcase I'd dumped on the floor hours earlier, banging my head on the low eaves. I cursed before remembering where I was, and then braced myself for my mother's admonishing, "Dear! Language, please!"

My eyes darted around the room as I clenched and unclenched my hands. Relief: Pixie was curled up on the floor under the window, on a little nest of blankets and pillows I'd made for her. I tiptoed over. She smiled up at me, her big blue eyes filled with laughter. Pixie was always happy to see me. Unlike her father.

My stomach growled as I bent to pick her up. I hadn't eaten since before I left British Columbia. It'd been afternoon there, so how long ago was that? I shook my head. This was one of those practical applications of math that teachers always blathered on about.

I wrapped Pixie in a receiving blanket and put my finger against my lips to urge her to be quiet. She blinked happily at me. We crept down the attic stairs from my bedroom, out into the hallway past the closed bedroom doors, to the stairs that led to the main floor of the eighty-year-old house I'd grown up in. I learned at a young age which floorboards squeaked and where not to step to avoid waking my parents. This information probably took up brain cells I could've used for those practical applications of math, but I really haven't needed math much since high school. On the other hand, knowing how to avoid my mother is always a handy skill, with many practical life applications, no matter what my age.

I moved silently down the stairs, but at the bottom I tripped over one of the shoes I'd kicked off the night before as I ran up to the attic. The shoe skittered across the floor, and I stumbled into the wall. I held my breath, hoping my mother still slept as soundly as she used to.

My hand slid along the living room wall until it hit the light switch. Twin tulip lamps buzzed to life, their shades swaddled in plastic. Opposite me, the wood-panelled wall above the Zenith cabinet TV was dotted with family photos, separated from the picture window by an orange macramé owl the size of a small child. Its blank button eyes followed me around the room.

The gold shag carpet discharged static electricity with every step I took. The July 11, 1987 *TV Guide* sat in the same place on the coffee table, and I knew every word on the cover by heart: *Two* Cosby *Kids Tell How to Shape Up While Watching Your Favorite Show.* An amber candy dish sat next to it, filled with potpourri that had once been deep blue and scented with lavender, but after thirteen humid Nova Scotia summers, the wood chips had faded to aqua and they smelled like dust.

I sank onto the big tan and orange floral sofa, loosening Pixie's blanket and burying my face against her hair. She smelled of all the baby soaps and lotions in her old room. She smelled of dreams. She smelled of the life I'd lost. With her blond hair, you'd never guess she was my daughter. She got that from her father. As I brushed the little tuft of baby hair from her forehead, I was reminded of the way her father did the same thing with a floppy bit of hair that always fell onto his face. I felt a peculiar mix of love and pain.

A light switched on in the hall, and I heard footsteps coming down the stairs. Panic swelled in my chest. I didn't want to have to face my mother with Pixie in tow. I kissed my daughter's head and made sure she was tucked in comfortably on the sofa. I wished I could keep cuddling her. Back home, we'd cuddle for hours while I read to her. I'd been in such a hurry to leave, though, I hadn't packed any of her books. I hadn't taken much at all.

My mother's scent reached the bottom of the stairs before she did—a blend of Jean Naté bath soap and lemon furniture polish . She appeared in the living room doorway, backlit by the high wattage hall light like she'd stepped on stage, tipping her head for me to follow her down the vinyl runner leading to the kitchen.

It was 5:30 in the morning here, but my body thought it was 1:30 (there, I'd solved it), so I wasn't sure if I should have breakfast or a late-night snack. My mother would decide for me. I sat in the chair that had been designated as mine since I was a toddler and watched her bustle around the kitchen, her pink slippers slapping against the linoleum. Most things in my mother's kitchen (including her, according to my aunt) were well past their Best Before date, because she hoarded food as if she was planning to survive an apocalypse—which, as a matter of fact, she was. The preservatives in her stockpile could probably protect the entire human race from the ravages of nuclear fallout. God knows, preservation's what my mother's all about.

She placed a china cup filled with steaming tea in front of me. In this house, there was only ever tea, and always in a china cup—only riff-raff drank tea from mugs.

Wiping her hands on her green velour robe, my mother stepped back to look me over. It had been late when I'd arrived unannounced from the airport, and I'd hurried up to the attic without giving her time to properly size me up or ask questions. Now she was taking stock.

"You look tired," she said.

I stirred sugar into my tea and avoided meeting her eyes. "Of course I'm tired. I travelled across the country."

"You should've told us you were coming. I would've come to the airport."

"It was a last-minute thing."

"Your hair's a mess." She clucked her tongue and reached over to fluff it out. I swatted her hand away.

It's not like she looked so great, either. Her face was thinner, and her blue eyes were even more anxious than when I'd last seen her. There were threads of silver in her black hair now, but the style was the same she'd had for decades. Her diminutive size that once made her elfin now emphasized her middle-aged curves, but she still fit into the same robe she'd been wearing since 1987. Nothing about her had really changed. Nothing was allowed to.

She sat down next to me, focusing on her teacup but allowing her eyes to glance at my face when she thought I wouldn't notice. She was having a hard time controlling her lips—I could see them starting to rise at the corners in a little smile, but then she'd set them firmly in a straight line. She repeated this expression as we sat with our tea, like she was performing some kind of *Jane Fonda's Workout for Lips*. This is what she wanted for so long, to have me back, but I knew she was confused about why I was here.

Our voices or the rattle of teacups must have woken my brother, because he stumbled through the orange plastic beads that hung between the steps to his basement lair and the kitchen, wearing a Spiderman T-shirt and too-short pajama bottoms that made him look more like an overgrown six-year-old than a twenty-eight-year-old man. His light brown hair stuck up in tufts and his big toe poked out of a hole in his sock. Seeing me at the table, he gaped.

"The fuck are you doing here?"

"Thom! Language!" my mother warned.

Thom grabbed a teacup and smirked at me. I ignored him as hard as I could.

"Is he with you?"

"He's not," my mother said.

Thom raised an eyebrow. "So, what, then? Did he leave you?"

I didn't actually know if he'd left me. Had I left him? I tossed my hair and tried to look insouciant. I failed miserably.

"I'm just here for a little rest, until I figure some things out." I poured myself more tea, wishing it were vodka.

"Oh yeah. Perfect place for that," Thom said with a snort.

Thom's pretty much always been an arsehole, but his bitterness at this point in his life was understandable. He'd been living in my mother's house, back in his basement bedroom with the Samantha Fox posters and black-lacquered waterbed, for over a year. Since his wife, Kim, left him after five years of marriage, breaking his heart and convincing him it was pointless for anyone in our family to try to be happy. She'd secretly been seeing some guy for two years (Thom referred to him only as "Dickhead") and they ran off together to work on a cruise ship, so I pictured Dickhead as Doc from *The Love Boat*. He'd always seemed fairly creepy; just the type that would make off with some small-town boy's wife.

Thom quit his job, sold their house, and moved back home to lick his wounds. He'd been licking his pain like a Tootsie Pop for over a year, and he still hadn't come close to the centre.

I heard a door close upstairs. My mother heard it too, her eyes lifting as though to heaven (but really toward the second-floor bathroom).

"We're all early birds today. She'll be so happy to see you!" My mother lifted the teapot and hovered it over my cup, raising an eyebrow in question. I shook my head.

"I'm going back to bed." I pushed back from the table, sloshing my cold tea onto the placemat. My mother got up with exaggerated weariness to fetch a tea towel, and I used the distraction to escape her avocado-green kitchen.

Pixie was still tucked up on the sofa, peaceful and untouched by family drama. I gathered her up gently, smiling as I nuzzled her cheek. She was too little to ask me difficult questions.

From the corner of my eye, I saw Thom leaning back on his chair to watch me through the kitchen door. My smile faded. I turned away from him and hurried back up to the attic, Pixie in my arms. I tucked us into the Care Bear sheets, and stared, sleepless, at the old posters around my room. A distinct scent of ocean overpowered the Love's Baby Soft now. It's funny how you notice the salt air when you've been away from it for a while.

I held Pixie close and watched the rising sun reflect on the ocean in the distance, like it had approximately 4,955 times since the world stopped for my family. I figured that number out while I stared at my Duran Duran posters. It was a practical application of math.

The Love Cats

The sky through the attic's eyebrow window was flat and grey and thick with fog. The painted wood floors were grey too, and the ceiling that had once been painted a colour called "Dove" was, after almost twenty years, more like a pigeon. I stayed in bed until all the tea I'd drunk demanded release and my belly growled. Pixie would be hungry too, when she woke up. Moving carefully so that I wouldn't disturb her, I pulled on some wool socks and dug in my bag for a flannel shirt to throw over the T-shirt and sweatpants I'd slept in. I'd forgotten how chilly April in Nova Scotia could be.

My mother and aunt would be at work by now, but the blare of the TV told me Thom was down in the living room. Mindful of Pixie, I walked quietly to the corner of the attic, where two plastic milk crates overflowed with my high school collection of mixtapes. My old Walkman was discarded behind them, and I slipped the headphones over my ears even though I knew the batteries would be long dead. Wearing headphones is a universal signal that you don't want to talk. I hoped Thom would get the message.

In the living room, Thom's six-foot frame stretched the length of the sofa, and he clutched a throw pillow against him like a teddy bear. He was watching Jerry Springer's guests yell at each other, although I wasn't sure how he could see over the pile of empty chip bags, dirty plates, and beer bottles on the coffee table in front of him. I slid around the corner without him noticing and speed-walked to the kitchen.

I grabbed a box of cereal and took it into the dining room, away from the din of the TV. The old walnut table was still piled high with photo albums, hot glue guns, and jars of glitter, and the chairs were overflowing with envelopes and shoeboxes of photos, so I stood, shovelling sugary nuggets of Trix into my mouth and blinking at the loud red, flocked wallpaper. One wall was covered with framed family photos. I set down my cereal and went to look at my favourite.

The vivid Kodachrome image showed my mother and her sisters standing in the backyard just before my parents' wedding ceremony in 1969. My mother wore a copy of Princess Margaret's wedding dress and a smile that outshone everything else in the photo. My aunts wore turquoise velvet—probably not the most comfortable choice for a humid August day, but my mother always got what she wanted and would've pretended not to hear any objections. A speck of ocean is just visible through the limbs of the lilac tree. You could see it here, too, from the dining room's picture window, which was why my mother always kept the curtains drawn. Even so, I could smell it and I felt the dampness against my skin. My mother always tried to block out the ocean, but that's impossible, because in our town, it's everywhere.

Paradise Valley is neither paradise nor a valley. It's a small Nova Scotia town on a downward slope (in more ways than one). The town often has a sulphury, gates-of-hell kind of smell due to the nearby pulp mill, and on a humid summer day, the whole place smells like a wet fart, or one of those home perms we used on our feather-banged mullets back in the '80s. The stench clings to clothes and furniture. It attaches to your hair; it seems to leak from your pores. No matter how far away from Paradise Valley I get, I feel the smell of the place cling to me like a scratch-and-sniff birthmark.

You can't tell how stinky Paradise Valley is from looking at the photo of my mother and aunts, though. You can't tell they're cursed, either, but everyone in town knew.

The curse. It's about time I told you.

Almost three hundred years ago, one of my ancestors—Rosamunde McQuinn—fell in love with a man who was betrothed to a woman named Cailieach, who was known to be a witch. Poor Cailieach (whose very name meant "hag") couldn't compete with Rosamunde's beauty. When Rosamunde gave birth to a baby girl, the witch stormed into the cottage and placed a curse on the baby: one of her female descendants would be stricken with such unimaginable bad luck that her very existence would bring woe to all those she loved. The curse didn't specify when this would happen, or what the bad luck would look like—would it be a lifetime of small misfortunes, or one life-altering tragedy? Cailieach decreed the only way to protect McQuinn girls would be to make them ugly: ugly name, ugly clothes—nothing outwardly attractive at all.

You might think a curse about vague bad luck is kind of feeble, but its power was in not knowing when it would hit, or what form it would take. As a result, generations of McQuinn women were paranoid, and generations of McQuinn girls were stuck with ugly names. Heptabel. Vertiline. Grizzela. Anous. Over time, as the curse travelled through centuries and onto another continent, it lost its power to terrify, and by the early twentieth century, the imperative to give girls ugly names faded into a tradition of choosing names that were merely unusual.

My mother, who was born on Victoria Day, 1948, was christened Queena Victoria. The name suits her, because she started out regal and sparkling but morphed into a small matriarch with a frequently dour expression. Queena holds court from the only comfortable chair in the kitchen and rules over her small dominion with an armada of denial, manipulation, and disappointed sighs. She thought being called "Mum" was too ordinary (and she hates being ordinary), so I've always called her Queena. I only call her Mum when I want to annoy her.

My mother grew up knowing she was beautiful, and she thrived on it. There's a big photo on the dining room wall, with pride of place behind the head of the table, of Queena being crowned prom queen of Paradise Valley Rural High, and another of her sitting in the back of a convertible in a frothy strapless gown, waving and wearing a sash that says *Miss County Exhibition 1965*. Bunny, of course, always called her "Miss Cunty Exhibitionist."

Don't be fooled by my Aunt Bunny Velvet's cuddly name—Bunny's as hard as year-old Christmas candy, but twice as sweet. In the wedding photo, she stands next to Queena, looking like a perfectly angelic maid of honour—not like one who'd taken all the sensible sweaters and skirts out of my mother's honeymoon bag and replaced them with tawdry lingerie and smutty magazines.

The youngest sister in the wedding photo was willowier than Bunny and Queena. Her wavy black hair fell to her waist, the ends fanning out slightly in the breeze, in contrast to her sisters' elegant updos. She managed only a half-smile, her eyes looking at something off-camera and showing an obvious dislike for the velvet dress. She couldn't wait to get out of it so she could put on a wild minidress and go to a real party.

I made up that last part, though. It was one of many stories I'd made up about my teenaged aunt when I was a child, trying to fill in the holes with what little I knew about her.

Her name was Nerida Kelpie. I never met her. No one talked about her.

I'm named after her. I'm also named after a dead cat. Queena's beloved pet cat died shortly before she married my father, Donald Love. The cat was named after her other great love, George Harrison ("He was the most spiritual Beatle, you know, dear."). Bunny got her a new kitten, but my father was allergic and it had to go live with my grandmother. My mother was heartbroken, but she knew it was either my father or the cat. Sometimes, when my parents fought, Queena would wonder out loud, to no one in particular, whether she would've been better off with the cat.

Queena learned she was pregnant with me not long after the kitten left. That's why I'm named Kitten Georgie Nerida. Most boys over the age of ten called me Pussy instead of Kitten, so my personal curse was to go through life as Pussy Love, like a small-town James Bond heroine.

"The fuck are you doing?" Thom said from behind me, making me jump. He stood just outside the doorway, chewing on a sandwich, a blob of mustard oozing dangerously through the crusts. Queena would kill him if it stained her pink carpet. I willed the mustard to fall.

"Jesus. Don't sneak up on me like that. I thought you were Queena."

Thom swiped at his chin with his sleeve, releasing a little flurry of crumbs from his stubble. "She's at the store. Been gone for hours."

I turned back to the wall of photos, adjusting the headphones over my ears and hoping he'd take the hint. He didn't. He walked over and stood next to me, jutting his elbow out to knock me off my footing. I steadied myself and shoved my elbow in his ribs.

"How long you staying?"

I shrugged.

Thom smirked. "Yeah, you'll never leave. Just like the rest of us."

"It's not the goddamn Hotel California." I pushed past him and grabbed a pack of batteries from the junk drawer in the kitchen before climbing back to the attic to feed and change Pixie.

My parents moved into my mother's childhood home shortly after I was born, because my grandparents moved out, not wanting to confront Nerida's memory at every turn. My father converted the attic to a bedroom for me when I was twelve, and Thom sulked until my father converted the old basement storage room into a bedroom for him. It was dark and dank and overrun with spiders, with an egress window that was just wide enough for Thom to slither his skinny ass through. It suited him perfectly. Thom's original bedroom was a rarely used spare room now. And next to it, closest to the stairs to my attic, was Nerida's room.

I stood in front of its door holding Pixie against me, tucked in her little sling. My heart pounded just like it had the times I'd snuck in as a child, when I'd been terrified but thrilled by the danger of doing something Queena had forbidden. I glanced over my shoulder to make sure Thom wasn't lurking nearby and opened the door.

The rest of the house was stuck in 1987, but Nerida's room was frozen in 1970—forever the messy bedroom of a seventeen-year-old girl. The curtains were drawn to block out the view of the ocean, but the room was still bright. Deep-piled gold carpet intensified the brightness of the yellow walls, yellow gingham curtains, and matching bedspread; it felt like I was stepping inside one of those big yellow happy face signs. Nerida had done her best to tone down the yellow, plastering the walls with psychedelic art and posters of Jim Morrison and Jimmy Page.

The air was stale and tomb-like, the way rooms get when no fresh air has been let in for years. When I was little, the room had smelled of incense and leather. I breathed deeply now, but that scent was gone. There was a faint scent, though, like suntan lotion and wet sand on a hot summer day. My eyes went to the window, thinking it must be letting in a breeze from the beach but, of course, it was closed. No one ever opened this window.

I wanted Pixie to see Nerida's room so she'd know her great-aunt had existed. I suppose I wanted Nerida to see that Pixie existed, too. I showed Pixie the photos tacked to the bulletin board: Nerida on a boyfriend's motorcycle, with her minidress hitched to a height Queena would never have dared, and Nerida in a swimsuit, gold medal around her neck, at a provincial swim meet. I lifted Pixie's plump little hand to touch the handful of gold medals hung from the edge of the bulletin board. I showed her the tall white boots and crocheted green poncho thrown onto the closet floor as though Nerida had just taken them off, and the row of colourful polyester minidresses and corduroy bell bottoms that hung above them.

There were school notebooks and a pile of 45s on the floor, and the Beatles's *Let it Be* was still on the turntable of the portable record player. Cherry Blossom wrappers littered the top of the dresser, next to a pile of makeup brushes and a little trail of powdered blush. The alarm clock on her nightstand had wound down and no longer marked the minutes since she'd left.

I'd always looked at the things out on display in the room like I was being rushed through a museum, knowing I'd get in trouble if Queena found out. Queena was at the store, though, and I wasn't as worried about being caught as I'd once been. I reached for the little knob on the nightstand drawer.

The drawer smelled of tobacco and dried roses. The petals of an old corsage crumbled when I ran a finger along them, the roses too dry and brown to tell what colour they'd been. There were a few crumpled tissues with bright pink lipstick blotted on them, some pencils, and an almost full pack of Export A cigarettes. There was a little pile of snapshots, too—the top one was Nerida and a group of teenagers at a beach party. One boy was playing a guitar, and Nerida, wearing a crocheted bikini top, rested her head on his shoulder.

At the very back of the drawer was something wrapped in turquoise silk. I pulled it out, careful not to touch anything else. The silk slipped away in my hands, revealing a deck of tarot cards, and my breath caught in my throat with a shock of kinship and nostalgia.

It'd been years since I'd held a deck, let alone read cards. I ran my fingers along the edges of the old Rider-Waite deck with the same joy and wonder you might feel at finding a hundred-dollar bill tucked in an old coat pocket. I hadn't known Nerida read tarot cards. I mean, I hadn't known much about her at all. I turned the cards over in my hands and shuffled them until a card jumped out, landing face first on the floor. The Fool. A card that meant leaving the past behind, with no clue what comes next. Seemed these cards already knew who I was.

In an instant, I decided to take them. It felt wrong to keep them trapped in the drawer forever—it was like trapping part of Nerida in there, too. I wrapped them in the silk and tucked them into the pocket in my sweatpants, nudging the nightstand drawer closed with my butt.

"Knock knock?" Bunny said in a loud whisper. I'd left the door ajar, and only her face poked through the opening.

I pulled my big flannel shirt around Pixie and kept my hand on my pocket, as if Bunny would sense I'd taken something.

"It's okay," she said. "I won't tell Queena. She's still at work. But you shouldn't be poking around in there."

"I'm not touching anything. I just...I don't know. I wish I'd known her."

"I wish you'd known her too, sweet thing." Bunny lingered on the other side of the threshold, holding the door so that she couldn't see much of the room. "You still look so much like her. Even as you get older."

I suddenly felt very old. At twenty-nine, I was almost twice as old as Nerida had been the last time she was in this room. She'd been gone my entire life.

"Why don't you come down to the kitchen?" Bunny asked. "There's pie. We could talk. We haven't talked in ages." Her tone was light, but her eyes darted around Nerida's room and a red flush was creeping up her neck.

I muttered that I was tired and skirted around her to sprint up the attic steps, dropping, out of breath, by the windowsill. Pixie was hungry, so I held her to my breast and brushed her blond hair with my fingers until we were both calmer. I rubbed her back until she fell asleep, and then I rubbed the deck of tarot cards, wondering if they could give me some clues about how to fix my life. I wished something could.

Is There Something
I Should Know?

The old tampon box where I stashed my crystals was hidden at the very back of my wardrobe. I picked them out, trying to remember the name of each one, and arranged the crystals around Nerida's tarot deck to clean away any negative energy. I considered surrounding myself with the crystals, too, to do the same, but I figured for that to work I'd need to bedazzle myself head to toe.

I ran a finger along the mixtape cases until I found the right one for my mood: *BOYS SUCK* written on the spine in purple glitter pen by my teenage best friend, Tiny. She'd made every mixtape in my collection.

Tiny's name was really Tina, but no called her that except for substitute teachers. She had the nickname because she was only five feet tall, although by high school her teased bangs added at least three inches. We grew up two streets apart and had been inseparable since we were six.

In junior high, we developed a kind of code to use during our nightly marathon phone calls, so that our mothers and Thom wouldn't know what we were talking about. We spoke in song titles, picking the song that best represented that day. Around the same time, we started making mixtapes for each other. We had certain rules for choosing songs for both tapes and "song of the day." There could be absolutely no country music (certain ironic exceptions were allowed, but the rules about this were complicated and could require a third-party arbitrator). In a nod to the Can-Con rules, we tried to have at least 20 percent of songs by Canadian artists, but never Rush, Trooper, or BTO, which we classified as "older brother music." Under no circumstances were we permitted to use disco music. ABBA was the exception—we both loved ABBA and agreed that we could each use an ABBA song only once in our whole life, in the direst circumstances.

There was only so much we could say to each other through song titles, so to further evade our mothers' prying ears, we started writing each other nightly letters that we'd exchange at our lockers the next morning. Each one was signed "YBFFNMW": *Your Best Friend Forever No Matter What.*

Except it hadn't been "no matter what," thanks to the curses.

November 1981

Tiny told me about the curses when we were eleven, in the fairy tale section of my father's bookstore.

Fact & Fiction was Paradise Valley's only bookstore, and it was my favourite place in the world—a magical labyrinth of book-filled rooms that took up two floors of the big Victorian house where my father had grown up. There was a room for science fiction, another for mystery, and another with floor-to-ceiling Penguins. There was a special area with rare books and first editions. There was a little section about birds that only my father and his friend Mr. Barker ever seemed interested in, with taxidermied owls and gulls staring down from the tops of shelves. The most popular room in the store was on the second floor—Thom and I called it the Smutty Paperback room. It was off-limits to us, but we snuck in as often as we could and giggled our heads off. To my father's chagrin, it was Fact & Fiction's bread and butter.

Thom and I had to go directly to Fact & Fiction after school every day, because Queena worked there, too, and she insisted that we always be where she could keep an eye on us. She never gave us a good explanation. She only said it wasn't safe to let us out of her sight.

Thom's best friend, Ed, and Tiny came to the store with us most days after school, so Fact & Fiction became our playhouse. The boys played Risk and Battleship in the little kitchen in the back, while Tiny and I let our Barbies do questionable things with Ken in the Barbie camper van in the attic. More often, we sat in the children's section, reading fairy tales and talking about what our own princes would be like. Tiny's would be dark and handsome and brave enough to slay any dragons that showed up in Paradise Valley. Mine would look like the picture of Robin Hood on the cover of my favourite vintage storybook. Robin Hood, kissing Maid Marian's hand, was fair and handsome, and Maid Marian, with her long, dark curly hair and an ethereal silver dress, looked a little like me—or, at least, what I hoped I'd look like someday. I looked at that picture for years, and I hid the book in the attic so that no one would buy it.

My parents gave Tiny and me jobs when we were eleven—we'd unpack boxes and shelve books in exchange for a modest stipend and all the sugar donuts we could eat. I was organizing books in the fairy tale section when Tiny arrived one November afternoon, out of breath.

"I have the biggest news ever." She grabbed me by the wrist and pulled me around the shelf, out of sight of my parents. "You know how no one talks about your aunt?"

"Bunny?" Bunny had lived in Montreal since I was born, and only came home for quick summer visits.

"No, Nerida. I know how she died."

The breath left my body as if Tiny had punched me in the stomach.

There were certain subjects that were off-limits with Queena, like Thom and me leaving home eventually, or the birds and the bees, or what happened to Nerida. Queena went into a funk for days if anyone mentioned Nerida's name, and then my father would get upset, because he didn't tolerate us doing things that upset Queena. No one had ever said Nerida was dead, though—not in so many words.

Tiny and I were a little obsessed with Nerida and the mystery of a beautiful teenager no one would talk about—we were fascinated by her clothes and music, and all the preserved minutia that hinted at the teenage years ahead of us. We liked to make up stories about what might've happened to her. Usually, she was running from bad guys, taking on secret identities to keep them off her trail, and that's why she couldn't come back. We imagined she was a glamorous badass, like one of Charlie's Angels. Nerida meant adventure and romance and mystery. Every time I walked past her room, I touched her doorknob as a way of saying hello, so that maybe wherever she was, she'd know we hadn't forgotten about her.

Tiny was watching my face for a reaction. "Do you want to hear more?"

I nodded. I didn't know if I really wanted to hear more. But I didn't *not* want to.

"My mother says it's because your family's cursed."

I propped myself against the bookshelf while Tiny explained about Rosamunde and Cailieach.

"That's what happened to Nerida. She drowned because you're all cursed. That's why your mother never lets you go to the beach."

Over the years, Queena had given me lots of reasons why we couldn't go to the beach. Sharks. Jellyfish. Hordes of crabs that would chase me and pinch my toes off. I felt dizzy, my idea of Nerida betrayed, my trust in my mother shaken.

"But there's more. My mother says your father's cursed, too." Little red circles had risen on Tiny's cheeks and her brown eyes sparkled with the excitement of a good story. "All the Love men die before they're forty-eight. People call it the Love Heart, because their hearts just stop or something. Maybe it's not a curse, really. Maybe they're just sick."

My father was in his thirties. If this curse was real, there already wasn't much time left. But the only health problem my father had ever had, as far as I knew, was the ankle he broke in Grade 12 during a high school hockey championship. He'd stubbornly insisted on finishing out the game, scoring the goal that led his team to win the championship. It earned him the nickname Stubborn Donny, which Thom and I eventually shortened to Stubby. At 6'3", my father was anything but stubby, but it was also a nod to the stubby bottles of Oland's Export and cigarette butts he left in his wake.

"Will Thom die too?" I asked, my whisper barely audible. Thom drove me bonkers, but I didn't want him to die.

Tiny looked stricken. "No! I mean, I don't know. My mother probably made it all up."

Tiny's mother, Marjorie White, was very religious. She didn't believe in things like curses or witches or zombies, except for Jesus coming back from the dead. If she told Tiny I was cursed, it must be true.

"You really heard this?"

Tiny looked me straight in the eye and crossed her fingers, the way we always did to let the other person know we were telling the truth.

I pulled the neck of my lopi sweater up to wipe my eyes. "Is there any way to stop it?"

"My mother didn't say."

"But why haven't I heard about it before?"

"It's probably one of those stupid things parents talk about that they think we're too young to understand."

The little bell over the door tinkled as a customer came in. I heard

Stubby and Mr. Barker laughing, their voices growing faint as they walked to the bird section at the back of the store.

"We should do something. You know, to honour Nerida," Tiny said. "We could make a card and leave it at the beach. That's the last place she was, after all."

I heard Queena's laugh join Stubby's, and the clink of teacups. Queena was always making tea for customers.

"You know I'm not allowed to go to the beach," I said.

"We could do it really fast. We'll be back before your parents even know we're gone." Tiny turned her back on my objections and sat down at a table in the children's section with some construction paper and broken crayons, to make Nerida a card.

———

Fact & Fiction was just four blocks from the waterfront park leading to the beach, but I'd only gotten a bronze in the Canada Fitness Test that year, and Tiny had received a badge for participation. Each time we stopped, stitches in our sides and out of breath, I'd glance over my shoulder to make sure Queena wasn't coming after us.

A seagull flew past, rising on a current of warm air as it coasted to the water. I was excited to be following it—to finally go to the water's edge. But as we got closer, my pace slowed, the invisible band connecting me to Queena growing taut and ready to snap.

Tiny stopped and looked back at me. "Hurry up!"

"I should've asked Queena if I could go."

Tiny rolled her eyes. "She'd just say no. Can't you make up your own mind, for once?"

She turned and set off, walking even faster than before. I followed, slowly. It was easier to do what Tiny wanted than to try to figure out what I should do.

The beach was empty, and I stood at the bottom of the steps, remembering Queena's warnings. I wasn't brave enough to go right up to the water, but the waves breaking on the sand were mesmerizing. They sounded as natural as my own heartbeat because even if I'd never been this close, I'd heard them in the background all my life.

The mustiness of the seaweed mingled with the ever-present stink of the mill, creating a smell so sharp I could feel it, raw, against the back of my throat. I followed Tiny down the beach, weaving around driftwood and trails of worn shells and rock shards polished into smooth beauty by the Atlantic tides. My footprints sank into the wet sand, springing back up and fading behind me like I'd never even been there.

"Tiny, look!" I bent to pick up a translucent blue stone and held it up to the light, certain I'd found a rare jewel.

"It's just sea glass. Haven't you ever seen sea glass?" She came over to look at it. "Blue ones are hard to find, though. You're lucky."

It was so beautiful. I tucked it and a clam shell in my pocket and trotted off after Tiny, beaming as I scanned the sand for more treasures. My joy was tempered by a nascent anger. How could my parents have expected me to live so close to this beauty without ever experiencing it?

We placed Nerida's card under a sandstone rock near the cliffs. Tiny had drawn a broken heart and some tears on the front, and I'd written, "Sorry about what happened, Love Kitten and Tiny" on the inside, because it seemed rude to say "Sorry you died." The glee I'd felt minutes earlier vanished, and the loss of my aunt and the glamorous world we'd imagined for her sunk in.

Our thoughts were interrupted by a horn loud enough to be heard throughout town—the signal that marked the end of a shift at the mill. People in Paradise Valley marked time by the rhythm of the tides and that horn's twice-daily blast. The horn meant it was time for my parents to close Fact & Fiction for the day, too. We'd stayed too long. I turned my face to the ocean one last time, trying to memorize the feeling of the salt air stinging my eyes and the smell of seaweed on wet sand. My hand closed around the sea glass and shells in my pocket. At least I'd have them to remember it by, if I never got to come back again.

We opened the store's back door as quietly as possible, but we almost knocked into Stubby. He set some teacups in the sink and turned to look at our windblown hair and pink cheeks. Tiny and I froze, expecting to be grounded on the spot.

"Time to put up the Closed sign, girls." He turned back to the sink.

Tiny gave me a look of encouragement as she went out the front door, and I flipped over the Closed sign. When I turned around, Stubby was waiting for me, looking stern. I'd never been caught doing something Queena forbade.

I burst into tears and ran up to the attic.

The attic was filled with boxes and old furniture from when Stubby and his mother had lived in the house. I'd made a snug reading corner with some armchairs by the front window. It was my love of that attic that led Stubby to convert our attic at home into my bedroom.

Stubby came up the stairs and walked over to where I sat on the windowsill, awaiting my punishment. He placed his hands on either side of my head, running them down my curly hair to smooth it. My eyes followed his to my feet, and I bit my lip. My sneakers were stained with red sand.

He brushed some dust off the seat of an armchair and sat down.

"Where did you and Tiny disappear to?"

I twisted the ends of my hair around my fingers, watching my thumb turn purple. The words rushed out before I could wish them back.

"Tiny said our family is cursed, and that Nerida died because of bad luck and that I probably have it too, and that you and Thom are going to die because of some heart thing."

My own heart pounded so hard my breath was staccato. A crow yelled in the bare limbs of a tree across the street. It was a cold, lonely sound.

Stubby leaned over, elbows on his knees, and took a deep breath.

"There's no such thing as bad luck, and there's nothing wrong with my heart." He reached for my hand, his eyes twinkling. "I'll be around for a long time. I'm too stubborn to die."

"Did Nerida really drown?"

Stubby nodded, his expression turning serious.

I turned to look out the window so he wouldn't see me gulping back a sob. Nerida wasn't coming back. I'd never get to meet her.

"Is that why I'm not allowed to go to the beach?" I asked, once I trusted myself to speak.

"Your mother was there when it happened. She thinks the beach is too dangerous for you and Thom. You know how she is. It's hard to change her mind about things." He poked at one of my books with his toe. "It's like how Sleeping Beauty's parents tried to protect her by hiding her away for sixteen years, but in the end, the witch still found her."

I ran a finger back and forth across the window, drawing an arc in the layer of grime. "So, no matter what I do, the bad luck will find me."

"That's not what I mean. I mean it's better to be ready to face what life will throw at you. At some point, we all need to deal with hard stuff."

"That sure sounds like a curse."

Stubby leaned over and rumpled my curls. "You're not cursed. You're just growing up."

"Same thing."

"The thing is, Kitten, you can't spend your life thinking about bad stuff that happened, or worrying about what might happen someday. You can't control those things. You've only got control over right this minute. And if you focus on right now, you'll find joy. Okay?"

I nodded, but I didn't really understand what he meant.

Stubby braced his palms against his thighs and pushed himself up. "Time for us to head home."

"Please don't tell Queena I went to the beach! She'll ground me!"

"Well, you shouldn't have gone off without telling us, you know. You made a decision, and there are consequences." He rumpled my hair one last time before heading down the attic stairs.

That night, my parents had the biggest fight I'd ever heard them have. Thom and I crept from our bedrooms and sat on the stairs to listen.

"Why didn't you ground her on the spot?" Queena's voice was wobbly but sharp.

"How on earth would we ground her? She's not allowed to do anything as it is! For the love of Pete, Queena, you can't keep them away from it forever. Every other kid they know spends their summers there. You used to love it, too."

Queena blew her nose. I pictured her taking the tissue from her bra. "The smallest decision can change everything forever. If I'd done things differently, Nerida would still be here."

"It's not about anything you did or didn't do, sweetheart. You can't keep the kids safe by doing everything for them. Next summer, I'll take them to the beach and make sure they know how to stay safe." Thom elbowed me. I elbowed him back. "Maybe you could come to the beach with us, too. You need to face it. You won't be able to move on until you do."

"I never want to see that place again!"

There was a screech of a chair being pushed against linoleum as Queena ran down to the basement, her sobs spreading faintly through the house through the furnace registers. Stubby got up and walked into the living room, and we heard the strike and hiss of a match as he lit a cigarette.

My mother's crying faded to silence by the time I got into bed. I reached under my pillow for the piece of sea glass and rolled it between my fingers, wondering about what Queena had said: *The smallest decision can change everything forever.*

Then I heard faint music from the living room—The Association's "Never My Love." My parents had danced to it at their wedding, and on every anniversary since. If they were playing that song and maybe even dancing together in the living room, the fight must be over. Somehow, though, I didn't feel better.

Stubby might not believe in the curses, but if Tiny's mother talked about them and everyone else in town knew about them, they must be real. I needed to protect Stubby from the Love Heart, and I had to keep the bad luck away from me. I'd read enough fairy tales to know that getting rid of curses would take something I'd never found in Paradise Valley—something rarer than a piece of blue sea glass. It would take magic.

Home for a Rest

Tuesday, April 18, 2000

I woke to a pounding in my head, a steady knocking that pulled me out of a dreamless sleep. I rolled over to stare at Prince. It felt like so much longer than two days since I'd left BC, as if time had stopped when Matt stormed out of our house.

The pounding wasn't inside my head. It was Queena, pounding on my door.

"Kitten! Kitten, are you awake? Thom's made breakfast. There's sausage—your favourite."

Sausage was not my favourite.

"I'm not hungry," I yelled back. I rolled my eyes at Prince. I bet he never had people yelling at him about sausage.

I could hear Queena and Bunny talking outside my door.

"Should we call Matt? Ask him to come?" Bunny asked.

I clutched the Care Bear blankets to my chest, my heart thumping at the thought of Matt. I wanted him, but I didn't. I had to protect Pixie.

"No. We don't know what's brought her back," Queena said. I heard her loud footfalls walking away, followed by Bunny's softer steps.

I held Pixie tighter and replayed the afternoon I'd left. Parts of my memories seemed to be glitching, like a tape getting caught in a VCR. I could remember all the things Matt had said to me, but the memories of what I'd said to him were all mixed up. Maybe I'd said something awful, and that's why he hadn't called. Maybe I'd never hear from him again.

My head was pounding, for real this time. I pulled the covers over my head and cried myself back to sleep.

———

Pixie was next to me when I woke hours later, her arms stretched toward me in her sleep. I reached over to her and saw that my own arms were covered in a sandpapery rash. My eyes caught my reflection in the mirror across the room—they matched my skin: red and horrible. My face was gaunt and pale. I couldn't even remember the last time I'd washed it. Did crying count as washing? Because I'd cried a lot—every hour I'd been awake, at least.

My skin burned and I couldn't stop scratching. Goddamn Queena and her goddamned bleach. I fed Pixie and cleaned her up, making silly faces at her to distract her from my vigorous scratching. She nodded off again, and I placed her carefully in the middle of the bed so she couldn't roll off. Then, with my Care Bears blanket wrapped around me, I headed downstairs.

Bunny and Queena were grousing at each other in the kitchen amid the clatter of pans and the opening and closing of the fridge door. Thom and Ed were slumped on the sofa, staring at the TV while Thom flicked through channels. Ed looked alarmed when he saw me, and shuffled over so I could sit down. I pulled my blanket around my head so I didn't have to acknowledge him. He'd come back to Paradise Valley shortly after Thom did, for reasons I'd never been interested enough to ask Thom about. I considered him as much a part of our leftover '80s furnishings as the amber ashtrays and wood-panelled walls.

Queena appeared in the doorway, wooden spoon in hand.

"Nice to see you out of bed, Miss." She waggled the spoon to acknowledge me. "I made meatloaf, Kitten. Your favourite."

Meatloaf had never been my favourite.

Queena came closer and lifted the edge of my blanket to look at my face.

"What's that all over you? What've you done to yourself?"

"I'm allergic to all the goddamn bleach you use on your sheets."

"Language! You sound like riff-raff. And there's nothing wrong with my sheets. Maybe you just shouldn't spend two days in bed. Here, let me have a look."

I slapped at her hand.

"Well, don't scratch it or pick at it. You don't want it to scar."

I glared at her and scratched my cheek.

Bunny came in and sat on the arm of the sofa, throwing a tea towel on top of Thom's dirty plates. Queena raised an eyebrow at her and nodded her head in my direction.

"Oh dear," Bunny said. "What happened to you?"

"I'm either allergic to Paradise Valley or Queena's bleach."

"Maybe it's all the stink up in your attic," Thom said. "When's the last time you changed your clothes?"

"Shut up."

"You shut up."

"Children, be nice!" Queena singsonged, as if we were toddlers.

"It could be stress, giving her that rash," Bunny suggested. "I've heard Oprah say that when you keep your feelings inside, they show up in other ways."

"Oh Lord, Bunny, you sound like a hippie." Queena reached for my face again, and once more, I swatted her away.

Thom settled on *The Joy of Painting* and put down the remote. We all perked up.

"Oh! Bob Ross. I love watching him paint," Bunny said. She squeezed in next to me so that I was sandwiched between her and Ed.

"After Kim left, I'd eat McChickens and lie on the floor and watch Bob Ross reruns," Thom said. "Lulled me into a trance. Happy little trees and all that shit. One time he was almost finished a painting and he dropped a blob of paint, and I was like, Oh no, it's ruined! Know what he did? Just kept on painting and turned that blob into a squirrel. Looked like it was always supposed to be there."

"No mistakes, just happy little accidents," Ed murmured. I'd almost forgotten he was there.

We watched Bob Ross paint a lake scene for the next twenty minutes, each of us soothed by the possibility of transforming our personal blobs into happy little squirrels.

PART II
That Which Blocks You

Love Stinks

Wednesday, April 19, 2000

The house was quiet, except for the click of the numbers on the old RadioShack clock radio as they flipped from 11:29 to 11:30. I crept down the stairs, touching Nerida's doorknob as I passed, and moved slowly heel-toe-heel-toe past Bunny's and Queena's bedrooms, smug that I hadn't lost my ability to move undetected through the house, like a ghost or a spy.

The only phone was the yellow rotary wall-mounted one in the kitchen, with an extra-long cord that drooped onto the floor. The cord had lost its curl through years of me stretching it to get around the corner to the relative privacy of the dining room for my nightly calls with Tiny.

I'd forgotten how long it took to call someone on a rotary phone, letting the dial click-click-click back to position before finding the next number. My heart rate accelerated when the ringing started. I imagined the phone ringing in the kitchen of our house in BC, its white cabinets and new appliances the opposite of Queena's vintage decor. I pictured it ringing on our phone in the den, next to the pool table. I tried not to imagine it ringing on the nightstand next to the side of the bed I'd left empty.

The answering machine message Matt had recorded years earlier kicked in, with my laugh faint in the background. It beeped and I panicked, realizing I hadn't planned what I'd say.

"Hi. It's me. Kit. Hi. Um, I thought I should let you know I'm okay, in case you were wondering where we are. Where I am. Maybe you're not, though. Anyway, I'm at my mother's, in Nova Scotia. Just staying here a while. It's probably for the best. So here I am. Anyway, maybe you could water the plants while I'm gone? Not the finicky one in the dining room, though. It likes being dried out. But I guess you should water it after a month or so. If I'm not back. I don't know." I stopped for a breath. "I don't know what I'm doing."

I hung up and rested my head against the phone. Why was I rambling about goddamn houseplants like I'd just popped away for the weekend? I'd probably never see those plants again.

I started to cry as I pictured the plants, existing without me.

I'd been napping too much during the day to be tired at night, so I sat on the wide windowsill, watching Pixie's beautiful sleeping face, listening for owls and waiting for some flash of divine inspiration. Nerida's tarot cards were next to me, the crystals shining around them in the moonlight. I picked up the cards and closed my eyes, longing for the calm they'd brought me as a teenager. If I could remember how to read them, maybe they could tell me how to fix things with Matt.

Even though it was after midnight on a damp April night, a summertime scent filled the room—like sand warmed by the sun. I felt a chill across my cheek, like someone had touched me, and I jumped, knocking one of the tarot cards onto the floor. I bent to pick it up and flinched because the image on the card was a little too on the nose—a heart pieced by three swords against a background of grey clouds and rain. The Three of Swords, which means heartbreak, loss, grief, and pain. Well, this was about Matt, obviously. I didn't need a tarot card to tell me about my heartbreak.

Tiredness swept over me. I could barely get myself to my bed, I was so drowsy. Maybe the fumes from Queena's bleach were truly poisoning me. I nestled next to Pixie and closed my eyes, but the image of the Three of Swords was burned into my brain.

She's Not There

Dear Kitty,

All these years, I could never figure out how to send you a message, but I just realized we speak the same language: tarot. I'm glad you took my cards.

My grandmother taught me to read tarot the summer I was twelve. I thought I was too old to need a babysitter, so she tried to make me feel better by teaching me something Queena and Bunny didn't know. She'd learned tarot from her grandmother, who everyone in town said was a witch. That was your great-great-great grandmother. So, sorry, kiddo, but you aren't doing anything new. Magic's in your blood.

When you used to read cards up here, I'd whisper hints in your ear, because I could tell you didn't trust your intuition. You need to listen to your gut—that's where the real answers come from. Trust yourself. I'm pretty sure you're not listening to your gut or much of anything right now, though. You seem kind of spacey.

The Three of Swords means way more than this guy you left. It's everything that led you here. It's what made you who you are and what's still influencing you. Loss. Heartbreak. It's a drag, but that's all of us in this family, babe.

I'll just sit over here while you rest your head, and I'll whisper to you what I think the Three of Swords is all about. That's one advantage of being on this side. Clarity comes easy. You have to work for it, where you are.

So, get ready for a really far-out bedtime story.

———————

You didn't know Queena and Bunny until everything had already happened. You just see them in relation to yourself, not as their own people. The Living are really self-centred like that.

You didn't know that Bunny wanted to be an artist, did you? She used to sit in the sand dunes, sketching or painting the sea. There's a couple of her watercolours in the little storage space behind the old chimney, over there, tucked in a box. She gave them to your parents as a wedding gift, but you wouldn't have seen them on the walls because they were paintings of the beach. And you already know how Queena feels about the beach, after what happened to me.

Bunny sketched a few nudes, too. I found her and her model together not long before I died, and she swore me to secrecy. Lucky for her, it's pretty easy for me to keep secrets where I am. Ha.

We were all pretty, but Queena took it seriously, like it was her job. She was little and curvy, like an oversized Barbie doll. Bunny was taller and more hip, but somehow seemed kind of awkward, too. I was a much later bloomer than my sisters. I'm not sure I was really done blooming when I...well, I was nipped in the bud, right?

Queena never cared about school, because she knew she'd get anything she wanted from life just by being pretty. And Bunny had her big artistic plans. I was the only one who wanted to go to university. I was trying to get a swimming scholarship, because my parents didn't have a lot of money for things like school.

We spent our summers at the beach when we were teenagers. We'd sit on those big sandstone boulders in our bikinis and lure boys to us like Sirens. Queena didn't like to swim because she wanted to keep her hair set, and she always wore these enormous hats to keep her nose and shoulders from freckling. Bunny didn't care about swimming either—she just wanted to catch some rays and show off her assets on the sand. Me, though, I loved the water. Do you know where my name came from? In Greek mythology, the Nereids were the daughters of the sea god, and they showed up in the human world as waves or sea foam. When I was a little girl, I pretended I was one of them, splashing and diving into the waves, and yelling at Queena and Bunny to watch me.

Queena married Donny in 1969, when she was twenty-one. He was some real hot stuff, with his sandy blond hair, blue eyes, and deep dimples. They were perfect for each other, since they were both so good looking and both came from families with curses. That was just something people laughed about, though. Queena didn't believe in the curse, and Donny didn't believe the thing about the Love Heart.

We didn't hang out as much once Queena got married. And then she got pregnant and spent the next five months barfing. I felt kind of left out, to be honest. So, let's skip forward and I'll tell you what happened on August 29, 1970, when Queena was nine months pregnant with you.

It was a Saturday. It was hot, but the wind was strong and cool off the water, and I bugged Queena and Bunny to come spend time at the beach with me. I told Queena she'd be knee-high in bottles and diapers next summer, and Bunny would be off at art school, so we should get as much beach time as we could. I didn't want things to change.

Bunny was supposed to come with us, but she ditched us to go meet a friend. She was always sneaking off and not telling us what she was doing. That drove Queena bananas because she was the oldest, and she thought it was her job to keep an eye on us.

Queena spread her blanket on the sand and lowered herself down, her legs splayed open with her big belly between them. I peeled off my T-shirt and jean shorts and ran out into the waves. The wind made the water rough, but I didn't mind. I loved diving into the swells.

"I have to get my hat from the car!" Queena yelled.

I could barely hear her over the wind and surf. She waved to make sure I'd heard, then turned to climb the stairs up the sandstone cliffs to the parking area.

I swam farther into the waves, loving how they lifted me. And it all changed so fast, because suddenly they weren't lifting me. They were pushing me down. They were pulling my legs in the opposite direction from my arms. I kicked, but I couldn't get anywhere, and the water was in a hurry to take me sideways.

You might think I was scared, but I wasn't. I was mad. Isn't that a gas? I was named after a magical half-fish, goddammit. I was a gold-medal swimmer. This shouldn't be happening. I was pissed off at the ocean. Ha. Imagine the hubris.

I managed to get my head out of the water for a second, just my eyes and forehead, and then one hand, waving at Queena, who was standing on the water's edge now, hat in hand, screaming at me. The wind took her voice, though. I couldn't hear anything but the water and my heartbeat, pounding against my desperate lungs like a funeral drum.

And then I didn't hear anything at all.

It happens really fast. You're alive and then you're not, and you don't even know you're on one side and not the other.

Your perspective changes, and all of a sudden it's like you can see everything. But all I saw was Queena, knee-deep in the waves with the skirt of her sundress spreading out from her like a jellyfish, screaming my name. Some boys came running. I knew them from school. They ran into the water, diving and searching and diving again, but I wasn't there. Not the part they were looking for, anyway. They never found that part. I like to think it went back to the Nereids. Maybe I'm seafoam now.

So, you and me, we missed meeting each other by a week or so. Poor you. Named after a dead cat and a dead aunt. What a drag.

———

You're allowed to go to your own funeral, if that's your bag. Mine was at the church, with a big picture of me in my white confirmation dress staring back at everyone, since there was nothing to put in a casket. The photo was a couple of years old because most recent photos of me were in bikinis or at swim meets, and I guess no one thought those were appropriate, given the circumstances.

My teachers sat together in a clump, passing a little bag of tissues back and forth. Guys I'd made out with at beach parties sat at the back, and my swim coach, whose idea of motivation was throwing his clipboard at us, sat with my team and cried inconsolably. Queena and Donny and Bunny and my parents sat at the front. They weren't crying. They stared straight ahead at the statue of the Virgin Mary.

The music sucked. You know that pile of cassettes you've got over there? You should make one with music you want for your funeral. You don't think of that when you're seventeen, and then you end up getting sent off to eternity by your Aunt Gladys playing "How Great Thou Art" on a screechy organ. It was so embarrassing.

My mother saved all her sobs for the reception. My father sat next to her, clutching her hand with one of his and holding a bottle of whiskey in the other. My mother didn't talk to Bunny and Queena that whole day, and she was always a little cold to them after that. I don't know if she blamed them. Hell, Bunny wasn't even there, and what was Queena going to do, nine months pregnant and a crappy swimmer? I didn't blame them. But they blamed themselves.

My sisters propped each other up at the reception, leaning against each other on wooden chairs in the corner of the dining room. People mostly left them alone, because their grief was palpable, and it made people uncomfortable to see a heavily pregnant person so heavy with grief. They didn't say much to each other, either, until most of the guests were gone.

"It was me," Queena said. She didn't have a black dress big enough to fit her, so she was wearing a sky-blue smock with daisies embroidered around the neckline. Even though she was numb with grief, she was so vain that she probably hated not being the best dressed, making her pain that much worse.

"What was you?"

"I shouldn't have given her a drive to the beach. It's like I lured her to her death."

"Don't say that." Bunny was wearing her hair loose for once, like I always did, and she clutched at the ends, pulling her curls out smooth. "I should've been there, too. I promised her I'd go and then I flaked out. If we'd both been there, maybe she'd have been okay."

"I'll never forgive myself. Never."

"I can't forgive myself either."

"I was only at the car for a minute. I came right back."

"Of course you did." Bunny linked Queena's arm in hers and leaned her head on Queena's shoulder. "It was an accident."

Queena shook her head. "No. It's me. I'm the bad luck. Like it says in the curse."

Bunny pulled her head away to study Queena's face. "Jesus Christ, Queena, you don't actually believe that shit?"

Queena just shook her head and went to tell Donny she wanted to go home. She stayed in bed for the next five days, until she had no choice but to get up, because you'd decided to be born.

You were a really cute baby. I sat next to you a lot while you slept, just like in those creepy prayers they teach little kids about angels watching over them. Teen Angel, that's me. Ha.

I don't want you to think Queena didn't care about you when you were born. She wanted you more than anything. But she was pretty numb when you came along, and not just from the laughing gas.

When she and Donny brought you home from the hospital, she put you in a bassinet next to the bed, rolled over, and turned her back on you. Bunny stepped in. She and Donny got up with you at night, and Bunny showed you off to visitors. She told them Queena was resting. I think she was glad for the distraction.

A month went by, and Queena hadn't gotten out of bed, so Donny took her to the doctor. She came home with a bottle of Valium. I don't know if the pills made her any happier, but they made her spacey. She still didn't pay a whole lot of attention to you.

Then Donny came home from his bookstore one day and found Queena in bed, staring at the wall, while you screamed your head off in the bassinet. You'd managed to wedge yourself under the bumper pad and probably would've suffocated if Donny hadn't come in. I'd tried to will Queena to roll over and do something, but my options for intervening are limited over here. It's a drag. Anyway, Donny got the doctor to come, and ended up signing the papers for Queena to go to the psychiatric hospital in Halifax. He sat on the edge of the bed, bouncing you on his knee as you glommed on his car keys (no one gave a shit about germs, but look, you're still here), while the doctor explained that Queena could go there to "rest" until she felt herself again.

When she came back home a month later, Queena wasn't like she'd been before that day at the beach, but she smiled sometimes and even laughed. She'd pick you up and sing to you.

She put on her lipstick and girdle and joined Donny at the store. She changed her hairstyle slightly to cover the little burns on her temples left by the electroconvulsive therapy. It's the same style she still wears.

That's around the time she started being really protective of you. She wouldn't let anyone else hold you, and she kept your crib in their room because she was scared to let you out of her sight. Everyone wrote it off as first-time-mother jitters, but things got worse when Thom was born. After he was baptized, there was a little reception at home, and your friend Tiny's mother—Marjorie White—well, I blame her for setting Queena off. In my head, I always thought of Marjorie as "Margarine" because of her greasy hair and oily personality. Anyway, Margarine patted Thom on the head and said, "Poor wee thing." She told Queena she was brave to bring a boy into the family, what with the McQuinn curse and the Love Heart. Double whammy, she said. After that, Queena was on constant alert for anything that could hurt you or Thom.

Queena isn't the same person I knew when I was on your side. I'm not saying it's all about me, because that sounds conceited, and Queena was always the conceited one in the family. Everything just got really heavy. She kept a close eye on you and Thom. And she never, ever, let you go anywhere near the beach, which was a real bummer. Sorry about that.

You were there for that part, anyway. And it looks like my bedtime story worked because you're sound asleep. I'll stay with you and Pixie while you rest, though. It's nice to have the company.

Love,
Nerida
xoxo

Every Day is Like Sunday

Friday, April 21, 2000

When Queena wasn't at work or asleep, she was in the kitchen. After work, she watched soap operas on the portable black-and-white TV as she got supper ready. In the evenings, she sat in her chair in the corner, reading *The News of the World* and *Soap Opera Digest*. All of which meant, if you wanted to use the phone, you had to do it in front of Queena. At least I knew she'd be there to answer if Matt called.

I'd been in bed for hours, holding Pixie as she slept and trying to figure out whether I should phone Matt again, or never phone Matt, or go back to BC, or just stay in the attic forever. The moonlight through the eyebrow window cast shadows of tree branches on the ceiling, beckoning like a witch's boney finger for me to get out of bed. I'd been in bed so much these past months.

I crept past Nerida's room, touching the doorknob on the way. Snores came from behind Queena's door, and I heard a laugh track from the little TV in Bunny's room.

Light spilled from the kitchen to the dark hallway, broken by Thom's shadow moving back and forth. I stopped short when I heard the phone receiver slam into its cradle, and I took a step back, thinking maybe I shouldn't intrude. Then again, I knew he'd intrude on me.

Thom sat on Queena's chair, resting his head on the table. He glanced up at me, looking defeated, and put his head back in his hands.

"You look like I feel," I said, opening a cupboard and searching for something that wasn't past its expiry date. "What's up?"

"Called Kim." Thom's voice was muffled by his arms. "Our anniversary's in a couple of days."

"Ouch. What'd she say?"

Thom slouched back in the chair and looked at me, his eyes puffy. "Didn't say anything. She never answers. Won't talk to me."

"How long's it been?"

"Since she went off with Dickhead. We talked once when we agreed to sell the house. Only heard from her lawyer after that. Sometimes I think maybe if I could talk to her, I could explain, you know?"

I closed the cupboard and sat down across from him. "What would you explain, exactly? Nothing's changed. You still think you're going to die young, right? And she's been with Dickhead for ages now."

Thom cleared his throat to try to make me think he wasn't choking up. "It's just, I was watching *Oprah* today and she was talking about people forgiving each other and getting back together, even after years. It could happen."

"It could happen." I tried to think of some other encouraging thing to say, but Thom and I had never encouraged each other much, so it was like trying to remember high school French when you're ordering dinner in Quebec. Besides, I didn't want to help him sort out his life if mine was still going to suck. Misery loves company and all that.

"You know what we need? Bed lunch. Disaster snacks," I said.

Thom gave me a half-smile and stood up. "Yeah. Queena was ready for Y2K so there's a lot. C'mon."

I followed him through the orange beads leading to the basement, past his dank bedroom, to the place where Queena kept shelves of Pop-Tarts and canned food, air purifiers and respirator masks, first aid equipment and books on propagating bees and ladybugs, as well as a year's supply of toilet paper. Thom pushed open the heavy door, and we stepped into our bomb shelter.

We had a family tradition of watching TV together on Sunday nights. That changed in November 1983, when we watched *The Day After*. We sat transfixed and horrified by the movie about life after a nuclear attack, with its relentless onslaught of charred corpses and radiation blisters. Queena never wanted us to watch TV movies, after that.

"This could really happen," she said during a commercial. "Reagan or the Soviets could push a button any minute and we'd all die horrible deaths like that."

Stubby popped open a beer. "Well, there's no sense worrying about it. You have to hope the people in power will have some sense. People like us don't have any control over the situation."

Queena knew there were some things she couldn't control, like inflation, or my hair, or Bunny (generally). Despite this, she firmly believed she could control our survival in the event of a nuclear attack.

She cleared everything out of the cold storage room in the basement and set about making an honest-to-God bomb shelter. Over the next few months, she researched and stockpiled everything we'd need to survive a nuclear winter. There was a shelf filled with batteries for the transistor and shortwave radios, and piles of garbage bags for us to stuff our contaminated clothes in. She filled jugs with water and kept an ample supply of Kool Aid and Tang, and bought apple juice in bulk so that we wouldn't get scurvy. She got a supply of ready-to-eat military meals at the Army-Navy store, and set up cots and a Coleman stove with a month's supply of fuel (I wondered, but didn't ask, what would happen to us after a month).

Over breakfast, she shared statistics about how long it would take nuclear fallout to reach Nova Scotia if the Soviet Union bombed New York or Washington.

We had regular bomb shelter drills—Queena required all of us to be inside with the door locked in under five minutes. Thom and I only tolerated it because she let us raid the food afterward. She even let us have sleepovers in there now and then.

"It's good to get used to it for when we'll need to be in there for months on end." With Queena, it was never *if* we'd need the bomb shelter, but *when*.

We tried to talk her into dismantling it after the Berlin Wall fell, but she wouldn't hear of it.

"You can take your chances with glasnost. I'll keep my bomb shelter, thank you very much. It won't be so funny when Armageddon comes and you don't have any toilet paper, will it?"

Even a decade after the Cold War ended, Queena still added supplies, but she wasn't great at remembering to rotate the food on the shelves. It wasn't unusual to find Laura Secord pudding cups from 1985, or rusty cans of sardines. The Soviets hadn't gotten us, but botulism might.

Stubby's contribution to the bomb shelter was an ample stockpile of alcohol. He figured he'd need it if he ever had to spend a nuclear winter with all of us in a small windowless room. When Bunny moved back, she made sure it was always stocked.

"My contribution to world peace," she told Queena.

Stubby's aging stash was mixed up with Bunny's newer bottles, so you were never quite sure if you'd get a fifteen-year-old bottle of Oland's Export or a brand-new bottle of vodka. I was willing to take my chances. I went into the dark corner where the liquor was stored and grabbed two bottles, blowing the dust off as I handed one of the vintage wine coolers to Thom.

Thom rubbed his eyes and hunched over, every bit of him drooping. "Wouldn't mind if a nuclear attack came, and we could start all over again."

"That's kind of extreme." I sat on the cot across from him and took a swig of the cooler. It was a little skunky, but not enough to keep me from drinking it.

"You know what I mean. A do-over. Big bomb to erase all the crap."

I opened a Fruit Roll-Up and wondered if that's what Queena had been doing, all along. Maybe she wasn't trying to protect us from a bomb. Maybe she'd been willing one to come get rid of the world she didn't want. Then she could start over, prepared for the future with endless boxes of Lucky Charms, an ability to predict radioactive fallout arrival times, and total control over her family.

PART III
That Which is Far Behind

Sisters of the Moon

1985

My father kept spirituality books of all kinds in Fact & Fiction's Mythology room, next to the second-hand bibles. That's where I found what I needed: books on the history of witchcraft. Books on magic. Books on tarot, and the use of herbs and plants. These were the things I'd use to break our family's curses and keep Stubby safe.

With the matchless resolve of a desperate eleven-year-old girl, I set about learning the art of witchcraft. Fact & Fiction didn't get a lot of books about it, so my progress was slow. But by the time I was fourteen, I had jars filled with dried plants from Queena's garden, and I started growing my own plants in little pots on my windowsills, learning how each one could heal or harm. I stole a stash of candles from a back room in our church, and I bought crystals from the health food store in Elgin, the university town just up the coast. I found a deck of used tarot cards with a how-to booklet at the Sally Ann, and I spent hours learning to read them in a corner of my room. Learning about plants and how to cast spells was tricky, but tarot cards seemed to come naturally to me. I didn't have to consult my guidebook to interpret the cards very often, because it felt like the answers just showed up in my head, almost like someone was whispering them to me.

I'd been practicing tarot for almost a year before I worked up the courage to share it with Tiny. Magic was the only secret I'd ever kept from her. I worried that if her mother found out, she wouldn't let Tiny be friends with me anymore and she'd tell all her church lady friends I was a devil worshipper or something.

On a Friday just before Christmas, Tiny stayed over at my place after the first school dance I'd been allowed to go to. Queena still didn't like to let us out of her sight, but Stubby had argued that I was fifteen and should be allowed to enjoy my teenage years the way she'd enjoyed hers. Queena let me go, but she sat outside the school gym in the car the entire time, watching for me to come out safely.

The attic was always draughty, so we sat on my bed wrapped up in quilts my grandmother had made decades before, eating snacks we'd raided from the bomb shelter. I picked at a loose thread on my quilt, feeling too awkward to look at Tiny.

"I need to tell you something," I said.

Tiny stuffed half a Vachon cake into her mouth and raised an eyebrow.

"Well, ever since you told me about my family's curses, I've been trying to figure out if there's a way to stop it. If Nerida died because of the curse, maybe Queena or Bunny or me could have the bad luck too, right? And my dad's getting closer to forty-eight. There's not a lot of time to stop the Love Heart."

"So, you really think it's true?"

"Maybe. Yeah. And, the thing is, for the past couple of years I've been learning how to do magic. Because I think that's the only way to stop the curses."

Tiny looked at me from under her poufy bangs. "Magic? You mean, like, the Amazing Kreskin?"

"No, I mean witchcraft. Spells and stuff. And I read tarot cards."

"Ohmigod. Did Bunny teach you? My mother said Bunny's a witch. She says she's, like, evil."

"She's not evil. She's just from Montreal. Anyway, no one taught me. I taught myself."

"Are you serious?"

I looked in her eyes and crossed my fingers to let her know I was telling the truth.

Tiny licked crumbs off her fingers and sat up straighter. "Show me. Do a tarot thing."

I went over to my wardrobe and took the tarot cards from the old blue-and-red Adidas bag where I'd hidden all my magic stuff. My face flushed under the expectation in Tiny's gaze. I nodded for her to come sit next to me on the floor, and she slipped off the bed, her quilt trailing behind her.

"Okay, think of a question. You don't have to tell me what it is, but focus on it while I lay out the cards. Ready?"

She nodded, and I placed ten cards in a Celtic Cross spread. Tiny sat wide-eyed as I went through the cards and explained what each one meant and what the overall reading was telling her.

"Ohmigod. That was so amazing," she said when I was done.

I felt my shoulders relax. "Do you want me to try a spell?"

"Can you do a love spell? To make someone like me?"

My eyebrows shot up. Tiny hadn't told me she had a crush on anyone. "Who?"

She blushed. "Do I have to tell you in order for the spell to work?"

"I'm your best friend." I leaned forward, eager to hear her secret. "Shouldn't you *want* to tell me?"

Tiny squirmed, avoiding my eyes. "Never mind, it probably wouldn't work anyway."

"Of course it'll work!" I bristled, insulted she'd question my magic. "Maybe not right away, but... Look, it's okay, you don't need to tell me his name. It'll still work. I promise."

I got to my feet and looked down at her, still hoping she'd confess. Tiny picked fluff off of her socks and wouldn't look at me.

"Yeesh. Must be a big secret then," I muttered as I plugged in the electric kettle to start making some tea to attract love. I sprinkled in hibiscus, ginseng, and ginger from little paper packets. Then, I started a candle ritual. I was shaking—I'd only done spellwork for myself, and never with someone watching me.

I focused my thoughts and created a sacred circle in the far corner of the attic, walking clockwise, and marking the quadrants with stones I'd brought from the beach. A scent of the ocean filled the room—warm sand and salt air—as it always did when I read cards or did magic. I figured it came from the altar I'd fashioned from a piece of driftwood. I lit a candle on the altar and stood in the centre of the circle, eyes closed, and focused my energy on the heat from the flame. I felt the warmth spread outward with each breath, until I sensed it had reached the edge of the circle. Opening my eyes, I clapped my hands together and whispered, "As I will, the circle is cast."

I handed Tiny a small piece of pink paper and told her to write down the things she wanted in a boyfriend. While she wrote, I took a pink candle (stolen from the church's Advent supplies), rubbed it with lavender, and hollowed out the bottom with a little knife. I packed the hollow place with dried rose petals and reached out for Tiny's list, stealing a glance at it as I set the candle on top. It said, *tall, blond, blue eyes, lives close by, good at Dungeons and Dragons.* The only person I could think of who met those criteria was Thom. I screwed up my face and looked at Tiny suspiciously. She chewed a strand of her long blond hair, her cheeks as pink as the candle.

I pushed the idea of anyone, let alone Tiny, finding my brother attractive out of my head, and lit the candle. We focused on the flame until our teenage concentration couldn't focus any longer.

I handed the candle to her as we cleaned up.

"It can take a while to work. You have to light it every night until it's burned down. But you need to hide it from your mother, okay? And you can't tell anyone."

"No way, I won't tell a soul."

She told everyone.

When Tiny slept over on New Year's Eve, we rented *Purple Rain* and Thom and Ed watched with us. Thom sat next to Tiny on the sofa and smiled at her. This was enough to convince her my spell had worked, and she told everyone at school about my magical powers.

Girls passed notes to me in class, asking me to do a love spell for them. Even the most popular girls, the ones who'd never given me the time of day before, started saying hi in the hallways. Soon, I was offering tarot readings in the girls' locker room while Tiny kept watch for teachers, until we furtively moved things to my house.

I got out of going to Fact & Fiction on Tuesday afternoons by telling Queena I had a job in the school library. In reality, I'd rush home to read cards or do spells for five bucks a pop. Thom knew I was lying about working at the library, so he told Queena he needed to stay at school, too, and then he and Ed came home and spied on me. I made him a deal: if he acted as lookout and promised not to tell on me, I'd give him a cut from each customer.

"I dunno. Queena'd be pissed if she found out you lied. Especially since you're home alone, burning candles in the attic. You could burn the place down. She'd freak out."

"If you tell her, I'll tell her about the girly magazines you hide under the mattresses in the bomb shelter."

"Shut up. I want a buck from each customer, or I tell her. Two bucks, actually—you're getting Ed as a lookout, too, and he needs a cut."

"That's extortion!"

"What's that mean?"

"Use the money to buy a fucking dictionary."

People wanted love spells, mostly, so Tiny jokingly referred to me as the Love Witch, and the nickname stuck. I taught Tiny to read tarot and some basic spells so that we could reach more people. It came naturally to her. With someone to join me, I got bolder. We tried more advanced spells. We'd slip outside just before dawn to create sacred circles in the backyard. We ditched our preppy neon outfits and started wearing black and bohemian clothes from the thrift store. I let my waist-length hair flow wildly and looked like a tenth-grade Stevie Nicks. We made witch's ladder bracelets, weaving feathers and coloured string together and tying nine knots as we cast spells to protect our friendship forever:

> *By knot of one, the spell's begun.*
> *By knot of two, the magic comes true.*
> *By knot of three, so it shall be.*
> *By knot of four, this power is stored.*
> *By knot of five, my will shall drive.*
> *By knot of six, the spell I fix.*
> *By knot of seven, the future I leaven.*
> *By knot of eight, my will be fate.*
> *By knot of nine, what is done is mine.*

This was all just a warm-up, though—something to help me build my magical muscles. It was the curse-breaker I was after, but I was waiting until I was sure my magic was strong enough. I figured I had plenty of time. My father was only forty-one.

Spellbound

June 1987

"**W**e need more tampon boxes," Tiny said. "Or maybe we need to open a bank account."

"We can't open a bank account without our parents knowing. Just fold the money smaller."

We'd earned over two thousand dollars since I'd become the Love Witch. It was way more than we made from working at Fact & Fiction on weekends.

"We should do this for real," I said as I hid my tarot cards and all evidence of witchcraft. "I mean, when we're done school. We could have a bookstore like Stubby's, or maybe take over his store, but with magic and folklore books and stuff. And there'd be a special room for readings, and I could serve my love tea."

"We could share an apartment, too," Tiny said, as she put Thom's cut of the day's earnings in an envelope. "We could decorate it however we wanted and watch whatever we wanted, and we could make pizzas with cut-up hot dogs on top."

"You're so weird." I pushed aside my crystals and sat on the low windowsill. "You know what? We should try to manifest owning Stubby's store someday, for our magic shop!"

"Totally!"

We sat opposite each other on my bed, cross-legged and holding hands. "Concentrate," I whispered. We closed our eyes, and both focused our intentions on having our own emporium of books and magic. We stayed like that until the mill's horn blasted to signal the end of a shift and broke our concentration.

"I hope it works," Tiny said.

"Me too." I turned to look out at the town. It didn't look bad in the summer, really. It was fine until you smelled it. "So listen...I think it's time. To cast the spell for my father."

"Wait, really? When?"

"I was thinking next week, because it'll be summer solstice. Our magic might be stronger then."

We spent the next week collecting the things we needed to make a poppet—a magical doll—to absorb the negativity and bad luck that attached to the Love men, and to Stubby in particular. Tiny melted down candles to get the wax to form the poppet's body, and I fashioned a little garment made of fabric from a worn-out blue flannel shirt my father used to wear when he did yardwork. The poppet had a shock of Stubby's own hair, too, pilfered from his hairbrush. When we finished making it, I could tell it was supposed to be him. It even smelled of him, like cigarettes and aftershave. I hoped it'd be enough to trick whatever evil forces were conspiring against his heart.

Summer solstice would happen at exactly 7:11 p.m. We'd planned to do the spell outside, in the little grove of trees at the back of our yard, but it started pouring rain at suppertime. I got the attic ready instead, lighting candles and throwing gauze scarves over the lamps for atmosphere.

Tiny bounded up my attic steps at 6:55 p.m. and stood, breathless, next to my bed, with something squirming inside her oversized paisley-print shirt. She lifted it, and out jumped a tiny black kitten.

"What the hell!" I backed away, my eyes wide. "If Queena sees this, she'll kill us! Stubby's allergic!"

"We can clean up really well afterwards," Tiny said. "I just thought, you know, since we can't do it outside, we needed a boost. My neighbours have a litter in their garage. Witches have cats as familiars, right?"

In folklore, cats serve as magical companions that help bewitch enemies. This cat—tearing around my room and playing hockey with a tube of Lip Smacker lip gloss—didn't seem bewitching. I was nervous enough about casting this spell, and now I had to worry about Queena discovering the cat and Stubby sneezing himself to death, to boot. But Queena was down in the bomb shelter doing her weekly inventory, and Stubby had gone to the beach with Mr. Barker to check on piping plover nests. I snatched the poppet away from the kitten's claws and prepared to start the spell.

Heavy rain beat against the skylight as I cast the circle around me and lit a candle on the driftwood altar. I held the poppet above my head.

"Hear me!" I stared into the poppet's button eyes and tried to ignore the kitten's mews of protest. "I have created you, and your name is Donald Love. You alone shall receive and absorb the negative intentions of the Love Heart now directed at my father. So it shall be!"

I blew my damp curls off my forehead and felt my shoulders slide away from my ears. Lightheaded from the adrenaline, I stumbled slightly as I set the poppet on the altar, gently and with love, as if it really was part of Stubby. I was sure the poppet looked different now. More solid, maybe—stuffed with protective magic. I felt bigger, too—tired, but more powerful. Less afraid. Magical. I was sure the spell had worked. I desperately hoped so.

Then I heard a thud, and Tiny shrieked.

The kitten had wriggled loose from Tiny's grasp and jumped on my nightstand, knocking a candle onto the floor. I stomped on the flame with my bare feet, leaving a scorch mark on the old floorboards.

The kitten bounded from one side of the room to the other in terror. Thom and Ed were at the top of the stairs. We hadn't heard the attic door open to warn us.

"The fuck are you losers doing? Why is there smoke?" Thom asked.

"We had a little accident." I leaned against the wall to inspect the blisters rising on the sole of my foot.

Tiny corralled the cat and wrapped it in her shirt. "I'll get this back to its owner before your mum comes up. Call me later?"

As Tiny and the kitten disappeared down the steps, Thom stood in front of the altar.

"You guys doing voodoo now? Jesus."

I placed myself between him and the poppet. "It's not voodoo. If you must know, it was a spell to keep Stubby safe from the Love Heart."

Thom snorted. "You don't really believe that shit, do you? It's so fake. Just like your so-called magical powers."

I clenched and unclenched my fists. "My magic is real. And what if the Love Heart is, too? That means you're going to die, idiot."

"Everyone's going to die. Nothing you can do about it. But I'm sure Stubby'd be very interested to hear about this little voodoo version of him you made."

"Don't you dare tell him."

"Yeah? What's it worth to you?"

I sighed. "Jesus. Fine. How much do you want?"

"Fifty."

"Fifty dollars? No way."

Thom shrugged and started toward the stairs. "Okay. Been nice knowing you."

"Thom! Fine. Fifty dollars. And you promise not to tell, right? Not Stubby *or* Queena?"

"I won't tell. Gimme the money now, though."

I ordered him and Ed to turn around while I got the money out of its hiding place in my wardrobe. Satisfied, Thom tucked the money in his back pocket and went downstairs. Ed paused at the top step.

"Is your foot okay?"

I blinked at him, wondering how he had the nerve to talk to me. "Yeah. Get out."

"I like the doll thing. It really looks like your dad. I think you're really good at this," he said.

"Oh, I get it. You want hush money, too? Forget it, nerd."

"No! I just...well, okay. Bye." He disappeared down the stairs and shut the door softly behind him.

I gave the poppet a little squeeze and kiss on the head before placing it on top of my wardrobe, tucked behind the Cabbage Patch Doll. I'd leave it there to collect any ill will being directed at Stubby, at least until he'd made it safely to forty-eight.

Two nights later, I sat on my bed after finishing my evening letter to Tiny. Outside the window, fog was creeping into town like it did most summer nights, as if the gods had decided they'd seen enough of our human dramas and pulled a curtain to block us out. There was a shuffling and a thump at the bottom of the stairs, and footsteps running away. I slid off the bed to see what fuckery Thom and Ed were up to this time.

Just outside my door was a little package wrapped in He-Man wrapping paper. I sat on the steps to open it, in case it was dog poo or some other nasty thing I didn't want in my room.

It was a Magic 8 Ball. There was a note taped to it, written in Thom's scrawl: *Not exactly a crystal ball, but you're not exactly a witch.*

What an arse. I mean, here I was, trying to find a way to stop the Love Heart that'd probably kill him one day. I gave the 8 Ball a gentle shake while I whispered my question:

"Is my brother a total dickhead?"

Signs point to yes.

Gone Daddy Gone

Saturday, April 22, 2000

I slept most of the day and cried at night, like some kind of weepy owl or depressed bat. Pixie slept more than usual, too, but at least that gave me an excuse to stay in the attic, away from my family's questions.

Four a.m. It'd be midnight in BC. I wondered if Matt was asleep. I'd only phoned him the once, but even if he was furious with me, I thought he would've called by now to make sure I was safe and doing okay, or to say goodbye for good, or to tell me he'd killed the houseplants—anything really. We'd never gone five days without speaking.

I sat with Pixie under the window, playing pat-a-cake with her hands as I made up a story about an owl that fell in love with a starfish. I raised to my knees to look out the window, so I could show Pixie the big pine tree where the owl lived. That's when I noticed the tarot cards. The Fool and the Three of Swords still lay out on the floor, but another card was laid below them, as though someone had started a Celtic Cross spread. I blinked at it. I didn't remember putting it there. It was a few inches from the deck, so it hadn't just slipped out, and it was placed quite deliberately with the others. I shook my head. Queena's bleach fumes or my weird sleep habits must be affecting my memory.

The card was the Five of Cups, in the position of the far past—a card that meant mourning, self-blame, separation, and feeling abandoned.

The Three of Swords was about Matt. If the Five of Cups was about the far past, it must be all about Stubby.

Pixie was watching my face, so I pulled a silly grin to make her laugh as I turned away from the cards and headed to bed. I rocked her to sleep in my arms, humming tunelessly to push the shadows away, until she nodded off. I nestled next to her, and I thought about the Five of Cups until I fell asleep.

Saturday, July 18, 1987

A pile of books clattered off the windowsill when someone whipped open my curtains. I woke with a jump, wincing as the early morning sun hit me straight in the eyes.

"Just me," Stubby said. He came over to sit on the edge of my bed. He wasn't smiling, and his eyes didn't twinkle like they usually did.

I winced again. I was in trouble.

That summer, I'd been taking advantage of the fact that my parents went to bed by 10:00 p.m. and were sound sleepers. I'd sneaked out to three beach parties since school ended, tiptoeing past my parents' room and out to meet Tiny and our drive, Rodger, before sneaking back up to the attic a few hours later. Last night, though, as I slipped in through the front door just after 3:00 a.m., Stubby was in the kitchen, chasing some Tums with a glass of water. I waited, frozen in the dark hallway, until he turned to put the jar of antacids back in the cupboard, then I escaped upstairs, congratulating myself on my stealth.

Now, I pulled myself up to sitting and held my knees to my chest, bracing for the impact of reality. He must have heard me. He must have seen me.

"Smells like a bonfire up here," he said.

I pulled my hair over my shoulder farthest from Stubby, twisting it into a braid that I hoped would smother the smell of driftwood smoke.

"Anything you need to tell me?"

I shook my head.

Stubby's eyes looked tired, and his face was pale despite his tan. My stomach twisted with guilt for making him feel so bad. I hated lying to him, but I didn't want to lose the little bit of freedom Queena allowed me. I hoped it would be like that other time he'd caught me sneaking off to the beach with Tiny—maybe he'd just rumple my hair and tell Queena to lighten up a bit.

"Time to get up. I'd like you to mow the lawn this morning. You were supposed to do it two days ago. And then, when Fact & Fiction opens at noon, you can come over and give all the shelves a good dusting. You and Tiny didn't get to it last weekend, since you showed up so late."

I nodded. My cheeks burned.

"I'll go fiddle with the mower and make sure the starter doesn't give you trouble. Maybe you'll feel like talking to me later."

I waited for him to rumple my hair, but he walked over to the stairs, stopping at the top to look back at me, a shadow of disappointment on his face.

"Make good decisions, Kitten."

He disappeared down the stairs and I fell onto my bed, blinking back tears of guilt. But guilt quickly gave way to indignation—maybe if Queena didn't watch every move I made, I wouldn't have to sneak around. Then indignation gave way to sleepiness, and I pulled the blankets over my head and dozed off again.

When I went downstairs two hours later, Thom and Ed were in the living room playing video games on the Atari. Queena was in the basement doing laundry. I decided the lawn could wait until after I called Tiny.

I switched on the AM radio in the kitchen to cover our conversation a bit, and spread Cheez Whiz on toast as Tiny interrogated me.

"You and Rodger disappeared pretty fast. Joanne said she saw you getting in the back seat of his car. So, what happened?"

"You know. Stuff. But nothing major."

I balanced the receiver between my shoulder and chin as I slammed the back window shut. Stubby was pulling the lawn mower's starter cord over and over, trying to get the engine to stay on, and all the racket made it hard to hear Tiny.

"Are you just not telling me? Or are you going to be Paradise Valley's oldest virgin?"

"Yes to both, probably." My cheeks flushed as I remembered how Rodger had touched me. "So anyway, what was last night's song?"

"How about 'Like a Virgin' for you?"

"Well, let's not forget the musical wisdom of Jermaine Stewart. 'We Don't Have to Take our Clothes Off to Have a Good Time.'"

Bon Jovi's "Livin' on a Prayer" came on and I reached over to turn up the radio, but stopped, hand raised midair, suddenly aware of the drone of the lawnmower in the backyard. Even with the window closed, it seemed unusually loud, as if the volume on the rest of the world had been abruptly turned down. I opened the window again to see what was happening. The lawnmower was roaring down by the shed at the bottom of the lawn, but Stubby wasn't there.

The hairs on the back of my neck tingled. I dropped the phone to my side as I opened the window wide and leaned against the screen for a better look.

There was a mound on the lawn behind the mower.

I flew out the back door and across the lawn while a dozen explanations tumbled through my head. Maybe he'd tripped. Maybe the mower had chopped his foot off, like those War Amps commercials always warned could happen. I wondered why he wasn't yelling for help.

Stubby was wearing the T-shirt Thom and I had given him two Father's Days ago—the blue one that said *Rad Dad* in big red letters.

It smelled of gasoline and grass and Aqua Velva. It smelled of comfort and love. He clutched the fabric over his chest with one tight fist. I switched off the mower, and the world became unnervingly quiet.

Stubby's eyes moved to meet mine. They were scared and confused, and maybe a little stubborn, like he was trying his best to refuse whatever horrible fate was being handed to him.

I scanned his body, hopefully, for broken bones, bee stings, anything fixable, but the only signs that something was wrong were his hand clutching his chest, and his face, pinched and twisted in pain. My body went cold in the July sun, and I thought my own heart might stop.

"No! No no no no. Stubby, no!" My voice sounded too loud and my words came out as a wail. I half-sank, half-fell next to him and struggled to lift his head and shoulders onto my lap. They were as heavy as stone, but I held him gingerly, like a bird with a broken wing. "What happened? Are you okay?"

"I've been better." He tried to wink, but it turned into a grimace.

"You'll be okay. I'll go get help." I was scared to leave him, though, and my mind raced, desperate to think of what I could do to make everything better.

"No. Stay." His breath was fast and gaspy. I'm not sure I was breathing, at all. I slipped my hand into the one he'd clutched over his chest, and held it as tightly as I could, as though I could hold him firmly and permanently there with me.

"You'll be okay," I said again, but my face crumpled and I started to sob. "I'm so sorry. I should have mowed the lawn. And I went out last night and didn't tell you. I'm so sorry."

"No. Kitten. I love you so much. Remember. Always. My girl."

I swallowed my sobs. Maybe if I acted like nothing bad was happening, this would all stop. "You're going to be okay. What should I do?"

He gave my hand a squeeze, but his grip relaxed and started to slip. I held on so tightly my knuckles turned white and my fingers hurt. Stubby looked past me at something that wasn't there. Then, as if a switch had flicked off, the focus left his eyes. I held my breath, waiting for him to blink, willing him to breathe.

"Stubby? Don't. I love you." My voice was weak and reedy, and I wasn't sure I'd said the words out loud.

His eyes were wide open and vacant, frightening against his greying face. Even if he'd managed to make another sound, I might not have heard him over my sobs growing into screams for help.

I must have been loud enough for Thom and Ed to hear through the open window, because they came running out the back door. They took in the scene in an instant, and Thom yelled over his shoulder for Queena. Ed hopped off the deck and ran over to push the mower out of the way, and then held on to it while he stared at Stubby. Thom had started running after him but stopped about six feet away from us, wrapping his arms tightly around himself, his eyes huge and his face pale.

Queena burst through the door and pushed past Thom, knocking me out of the way, too, so that Stubby fell out of my lap and onto the grass. She dropped next to him with a convulsive, gut-wrenching wail. Then, lifting herself on all fours, she stared into my father's lifeless eyes.

She swayed unsteadily back and forth, her face twisting from anguish to anger as she fell on him with a downpour of flailing fists.

"You LIED! You promised this wouldn't happen! You can't leave me! Come back!""

"Queena, no! Get off! Stop!" I tried to push her away, but she was an immovable wall between me and Stubby, who lay broken on the ground like Humpty Dumpty.

She peeled herself off Stubby's chest and rocked back on her heels. Her eyes were shocked and pleading, and I kept my own eyes on hers, willing her to come back into the moment so she could tell me what to do. I so desperately needed her to tell me what to do.

"I should've been here with him. I could've saved him. I wasn't here." Queena curled up like a baby next to Stubby, her head on his broad, still chest, whimpering her culpability over and over.

I pushed myself to my feet, teetering as the world went off-kilter. "I'll go get help. He'll be okay. I'll get help." I stumbled and almost fell, but Ed caught me by the elbow and steadied me.

"I think it might be too late, Kitty," he said, his voice breaking. "I think he's already—"

"No!" I pushed Ed's hand away. He couldn't say that. If no one said those words, Stubby was still alive.

I was supposed to stop this. I must have done the protection spell with the poppet wrong. Or maybe my magic wasn't strong enough. Nothing I'd done had protected him, at all.

Thom finally came over and knelt beside Queena. His eyes looked almost as empty as Stubby's. I sank down next to him, and Queena pulled us to her. Her anguish vibrated through my bones. The universe collapsed on itself, and nothing existed but us and Stubby's body and this unbearable, terrifying, sickening dread that fully inhabited every bit of me. We were in a tangle of arms, our tears mingling and hair in each other's faces. I'd never felt so intimately connected to my family, yet so frighteningly alone at the same time.

Ed cleared his throat. The universe rushed back in at me. The sun hit my eyes and the world was obscenely bright. I smelled newly mown grass (a smell that would turn my stomach from that moment on) and wondered how smells and houses and lawns could still exist. I felt like I'd stepped off the edge of the world and was in freefall.

"I'm not sure what we're supposed to do. Should I call an ambulance?" Ed asked.

Queena straightened her blouse and wiped her cheeks with the backs of her hands, staining them with her smeared makeup.

"Thank you, Ed," she croaked, her Queena-ness returning. "It's too late for an ambulance. It was the Love Heart. Donny was wrong about it. He was doomed, because of me. He had my bad luck against him."

She looked at Thom sadly, patted his face in a cosmic "Tag, you're it," and curled up again next to Stubby, burying her face in his chest and closing her eyes on the world around her.

Dead Man's Party

By the second day after my father's death, our fridge was stuffed beyond capacity with identical Pyrex dishes filled with nearly identical cheese-and-crumb-covered casseroles. Queena saw each one as a cheese-topped "I told you so"—old Cailieach thumbing her nose from beyond the grave. She took to her bed, refusing to talk or eat or greet visitors. Thom and I were left to accept the casseroles and condolences until Bunny arrived.

My body felt shaky and brittle and hollow, as if it knew on a cellular level that something terrible had happened, but my brain was revving too fast to let thoughts settle. Sometimes, when I was washing my face or walking downstairs or just waking up, I'd see Stubby's empty eyes. My body would go cold and my breath would leave and my hands would shake. But people kept telling me how calm and brave I was. The only way I could stand it was to pretend this wasn't happening: any minute now, Stubby would walk in, as alive and healthy as ever.

The wake was held at the town's only funeral parlour—an old Victorian house that smelled vaguely of cat pee, with a rabbit warren of dim rooms. The undertaker, Mr. Wickwire (or Digger, as he was more commonly called), was a round, rosy-cheeked little man who hummed and bounced when he walked and was prone to nervous giggles at inappropriate times (which is pretty much always, in his business). He reminded me of one of those creepy, homicidal clowns from a slasher film.

My family had private time with what Digger called Stubby's "earthly remains" the day before the wake. We'd finally managed to get Queena out of bed. Her eyes were puffy and glazed over, and she hadn't even bothered with makeup. I'd never seen her not care about how she looked. It made it hard to pretend nothing was wrong.

Bunny sent Thom and me out of the room with a plate of Nanaimo bars so that Queena could be alone with Stubby. We sat in a dimly lit hallway, the treats untouched on our laps, waiting to hear Queena shriek or cry or yell at Stubby again. But there was silence, and Queena emerged after only a few minutes. She dropped into a shabby velvet armchair, legs akimbo, face wraithlike. Digger appeared from the shadows and handed her a cup of tea. My mother lifted the cup halfway to her lips and left it there, suspended, as if her internal gears had wound down and she was frozen that way.

Then it was our turn, and Digger escorted Thom and me into the room Queena had exited. Bunny pulled Queena along behind us for support, murmuring soft encouragement to us and holding my mother by the elbow. The room was set up with rows of folding chairs. It reminded me of the times Stubby held readings or events at our bookstore. I tried to convince myself he'd stride in confidently any minute now to lead a discussion on funeral rituals.

His coffin was flanked at head and foot by flower arrangements. They were full of carnations, so I knew my mother hadn't chosen them. Queena despised carnations. She called them tacky grocery store flowers and said only riff-raff liked them. She didn't seem to notice these funeral carnations, though, even though she was staring straight at them.

I made myself look into Stubby's open casket, reluctant to believe this waxy, motionless thing was my father. I was grateful his eyes were closed. I used to love my father's eyes—how they'd twinkle at me when he laughed. Now I was terrified of their empty stare. I saw it in my dreams.

He looked like the poppet Tiny and I had made—small, fake, and waxy. The poppet had smelled like him, but this fake Stubby didn't. There was no aftershave, no stale coffee, no tobacco, no faint odour of musty books. The makeup Digger had put on him was obvious, and I knew Stubby would've hated it.

Thom gripped the edge of the casket.

"Why's he got reading glasses on?" he whispered to me. "He's not going to read. He's dead."

I shrank from that word. Thom used it freely, but I hadn't been able to say it—not even to myself. I ran a finger along the coolness of the satin lining the coffin. That was as close as I could get to touching my father.

"Bunny thought he looked more distinguished with glasses. Maybe she thought he'd need them to read in heaven," I said.

"Wouldn't Jesus just fix his eyes so he wouldn't need glasses?"

I shrugged. I'd zoned out a lot during Sunday school.

"They're stupid," Thom said.

He reached in and wiggled the glasses off my father's face. The tugging moved Stubby's head, and I caught my breath and turned away in alarm, knocking against Thom, who stumbled and dropped the glasses on the floor. They echoed on the tile, and he swooped to pocket them. His face was pale. I felt sick.

The clatter roused Digger from the shadows.

"Please, my darlings, do be careful not to bump into the remains. That lid would make quite a racket if it fell!"

"Yeah," Thom snorted. "Might wake the dead." We looked at each other and started to giggle. I felt like screaming or throwing up, really, but I was shaking with laughter. We had to turn away from each other as we tried to control ourselves. I was laughing so hard I wasn't even making any sound. Thom was laughing so hard I was sure he'd pee his pants. I felt like I was losing my mind.

Digger tsk-tsked and moonwalked back into the shadows. Queena didn't seem to notice our hysterics. Bunny sent us off with more Nanaimo bars and cherry balls, to sit in the shadows and compose ourselves.

———

At Queena's request, the shabby velvet curtains were pulled shut on the day of my father's wake, blocking out the glimpse of the ocean and all but a few pinpoints of sunlight. The July day was oppressive, even with the air conditioner humming, and a toxic haze of chemicals, cat pee, and drugstore perfumes hung over the room. The gloom and stink of the funeral parlour seemed fitting. The whole town exuded gloom and stink. Even in death, there was no escaping it.

I spent the wake propped against a wall behind a long chintz sofa in the reception room, with Tiny next to me. She and the wall kept me upright, and the sofa was a buffer against the grasps of the church ladies. The same bunch of them turned out for every funeral in town, to enjoy the lunch and judge the family members on how they were grieving. Each old woman leaned around Tiny to press her crepey lips to my cheek, and then she'd drag me over to the room where the coffin was, where she'd stare at my father and declare him "the handsomest corpse I've ever seen." She'd squeeze out a few tears, produce a tissue from a sleeve or her ample bosom, blow her nose like Gabriel's trumpet, and stuff the soggy tissue back in the bra. In Paradise Valley, every woman over forty kept tissues in her bra. I usually kept crystals tucked in mine. I'd put a moonstone in there that morning for protection and tucked an obsidian in my skirt pocket to ward off evil spirits.

Queena was on a chair near the front of the room, staring at nothing and speaking to no one. Her face was unearthly pale under the makeup Bunny had applied. Queena had started to put some on that morning, but her hands shook so badly as she held the mascara wand she ended up looking like Tammy Faye Bakker. Bunny persuaded Queena to let her help, but Queena wouldn't accept advice about her wardrobe. She wore a dove grey dress, and she stuck out amidst the black of the mourners, one little grey cloud in a dark and gloomy sky. She'd always had a knack for dressing for attention. I could tell Bunny was pissed that she hadn't thought of it.

I hadn't seen Queena in anything but a faded green velveteen housecoat since Stubby died. I hadn't seen much of her at all. Bunny persuaded her to come down for breakfast a couple of times, but I hadn't seen her eat anything that whole week. She ignored her tea and didn't talk. The Armageddon updates were conspicuously absent. I understood. Nothing had protected us. Not her bomb shelter, and not my magic.

Most of my wardrobe was dark and kind of goth anyway, so dressing for a funeral wasn't much different from any other day. My hair, pulled back in a neon green scrunchie (the only one I could find that morning), stuck in damp tendrils against the back of my neck. My head pounded, and it felt like every nerve in my body was on hyper-alert. Whenever I started to fade into numbness, my brain would hit me with a jolt of electricity. I was lightheaded with grief and lack of real food, but people only brought me tea and sweets.

Thom spent the day sitting in front of me on the sofa. Bunny hadn't been able to get him into a suit, but he was wearing one of Stubby's ties and he looked even more awkward than usual. He had it worse than me, in a way, because he had to endure everyone's pity—not just for the loss of his father, but for his own obviously imminent death. Stubby's death at such a young age had gotten the town talking about the Love Heart again. Each greeting, each pat on the hand, each offer of condolence, was like someone throwing a handful of dirt on Thom's coffin. I rubbed at the sweat at the back of my neck. It was getting harder to breathe. My whole family was being buried alive.

There was a silver lining in it for Thom, though, because his doomed status was like a beacon to all the girls in Paradise Valley, who thought his cursed heart and tragic backstory were romantic. They came over to console him and slip him their phone numbers. I wondered if I should point out that trying to save a Love obviously hadn't gone that well for Queena. By the end of the funeral, my brother had transformed from a basement-dwelling geek to a tragic anti-hero.

Speaking of geeks, Ed was there (as always) along with his mother, Eileen Fraser. I watched as they stopped in front of Queena and Bunny to offer condolences. Queena looked up at Mrs. Fraser and for the first time that day, her eyes seemed to focus.

"Bunny, go get tea," she ordered.

"You've got tea in your hand," Bunny pointed out.

"Get more."

Bunny stood up with a sigh. She and Mrs. Fraser exchanged wan smiles, and Bunny quickly left the room. Ed came over and sat next to Thom.

My mother stood up suddenly. All eyes turned to her, and a hush fell over the mourners. They probably expected a thank-you for coming, or some poignant words about Stubby.

They got a confession.

"It's my fault he's dead," Queena announced calmly. She paused for effect. Confused whispers filled the gap.

Queena patted her pearls. "It was my bad luck. He might've beaten the Love Heart if he hadn't married a McQuinn. I should've done more to protect him."

She smoothed her skirt, hesitated a moment, then turned and walked into a washroom just a few steps away. We heard the click of the lock, and then the air filled with her sobs. Bunny, returning with tea, smiled awkwardly at the mourners and then went to the bathroom door, tapping gently and pleading with Queena to let her in. But Queena had shut everyone out.

Digger slipped in to close the pocket doors between the reception room and the viewing room, and turned on an eight-track of Elvis singing gospel songs to muffle Queena's sobs and Bunny's pleas. A buzz went around the room. Some people left quickly. Others—including a group standing a few feet from me, helping themselves to trays of crustless egg sandwiches and asparagus spears rolled in white bread—saw the drama as permission to say what they'd really been thinking.

"Oh my lord, can you imagine?" horse-faced Rose Chapman stage-whispered. She worked at the post office and wouldn't hand over your stamps until you'd answered all her intrusive questions. Then she'd report everything you'd said to the next person. Stubby called her the Pony Express.

"Queena's always been a little unhinged," Gloria Coates said. Gloria was just back from her honeymoon with her third husband, whom she'd met at her second husband's funeral. "I guess being pretty doesn't get you everything."

"Oh, you were always jealous of her, admit it!" chided Rose.

"No!" Gloria insisted, the colour in her cheeks rising. "She might've been the prettiest girl in town, but she was so stuck up. Thought she was too good for the likes of us after she won Miss County Exhibition."

"Well, the young one there really didn't get her mother's looks, did she?" Bob Patriquin jerked his chin toward me as he smoothed his comb-over. He was the local librarian and had always been jealous that people sought book advice from Stubby and not him. He squinted at me, his eyes lingering on my chest. "Queena and Bunny were always so striking. The daughter seems a bit...dull."

I'm at my father's goddamn funeral, not a fucking pageant, I thought, tugging self-consciously at my ponytail. I knew I didn't have Queena and Bunny's technicolour glamour, although I hoped I'd wake up with it one day. Theirs was a beauty that caused jealousy. I, on the other hand, was pretty in a non-threatening way. No one had to watch their boyfriend around me.

Rose took three sandwiches, wrapped them in a cocktail napkin, and stuck them in her purse. "I think she looks a lot like Nerida did. She'd be prettier if she didn't have all that hair, though. Can't rightly see her."

"And if she wore something other than black. She always looks like an old witch." Gloria smirked.

I patted the moonstone in my bra. *A young witch. Watch out, you old cow.*

"Of course, it's the boy who'll really take after his father, hey? No sense in *him* making any long-term plans." Bob chuckled.

Tiny and I both glanced at Thom. He shook invisible dirt off his dress shoes.

"I did like Donny, though. Such a shame. A lovely man. Poor Queena. Nice to see her and Bunny together again, though. Too bad it's for another funeral," Gloria said.

"Oh, *Bunny!*" snorted Freda Landry, tugging at the elastic waistband of her black polyester slacks. Freda was best friends with Tiny's mother. She was a real estate agent and looked a lot like the houses she sold: large units that used to be grand, but now had peeling paint and sagging foundations. "Those kids have enough problems without *that.* Better that she stays in Montreal."

I felt their eyes on me as they finished off a plate of peanut butter balls.

"My daughter said the kids at school used to pay her for love spells," Rose said.

"Well, that family needs all the magic it can get, hey?" Freda said. "They really do seem cursed."

I clutched the obsidian in my pocket, rubbing it between my fingers as I stared at Freda without blinking. She stared back, shovelling a lemon bar into her gob and looking smug.

Just shut up, I thought. *You won't say another word about me.*

I grabbed Tiny's elbow and propelled both of us out from behind the sofa. "I'm going outside," I told Thom. "It stinks in here."

I elbowed my way out of the room just as Freda started choking on her lemon bar.

Spirit in the Sky

Dear Kitty,

I didn't get to go to your dad's funeral because I have to stay around here. That's the deal. You're allowed a final visit to the places that meant something to you, but after that, if you're going to stick around the Living, you pick one place and stay there. It's not like you just float anywhere you want and spook people. Well, I do try to spook Queena sometimes. I'll nudge a candy dish out of place or knock a magazine onto the floor. Then she'll look around, all freaked out, to see who did it. It's a blast. I try talking to her sometimes, too, but she's one of the Living who just can't hear. Their heads are so buzzed with their own stuff they tune out other frequencies, you know? Not that I have a lot to talk to Queena about, but still, it was pretty quiet here, all those years you were gone.

Your dad split just after his funeral. See, it's not like you die and get sucked up into the Great Beyond in a big beam of light or something. You have options. You can move on to what comes next, or you can stick around your people and keep an eye on things. But if you do stick around, you're not allowed to interfere. You just get to watch and yell, even though no one hears you. Sort of like when my dad watched hockey on TV.

There was no one for me to hang out with in the Afterlife when I died. My parents were still alive, and so were my sisters, and all my friends. The only person I knew in heaven was Jimi Hendrix. He died the week after me, but I wasn't into being some heavenly groupie. Ha. I didn't like the thought of being alone, so I stayed here. I figured I'd just wait for someone else to be ready to join me. Besides, I wanted to see what I was missing out on. I hated it when Bunny and Queena did stuff without me. Your dad, though, he knew loads of people in heaven. His parents were there, and all those other men who'd died from the Love Heart, welcoming the latest victim.

You have to understand, it's not that he didn't want to stay around to watch you grow up. It's just, staying with the Living is hard. You can't stop them from doing something that's going to hurt them. I didn't really understand what that'd be like. I think your dad did, and knew he'd hate it. He knew how hard his death would be on everyone, and he couldn't just watch and do nothing. So, he split.

If you stay here, you can leave whenever you want, but once you do, you can't come back. I'll move on once I know you're all okay. I've got an eternity to hang out with Jimi Hendrix, right? In the meantime, I have to sit here and watch the various ways you all fuck things up, like it's one of Queena's soap operas. *Another World*, truly.

It's harder than I thought it would be, though. You see the Living moving away from you bit by bit, and you know a day will come when no one thinks about you anymore. Time goes fast on this side, but it's lonely, always being on the edges of things. It's like a junior high dance that never ends.

Sometimes when I'm in my room, I look at the pictures of my friends and wonder what they're doing now. I wonder if they even remember me, or talk about me at high school reunions—"Hey, remember that girl who died senior year? What was her name?" When I first came to this side, I worried it'd be horrible to hear what people said about me. I didn't realize that the horrible thing is when they stop talking about you.

Love,
Nerida
xoxo

Cruel Summer

July 1987

Bunny helped Queena meet with the lawyer and the bank, and made sure staff were in place to take care of Fact & Fiction. She made a list of other things Queena would need to take care of in the weeks after the funeral, but Queena got dimmer and dimmer, like a cathode ray tube glowing and fading to nothing after you switch off the TV. One day, a week after the funeral, she faded to black—she went to her room, got in bed, and stopped speaking to us.

"She's a dramatic little bitch," Bunny complained. "Pardon my French."

Bunny stayed three weeks. Before she left, she sat Thom and me down at the kitchen table to talk about Stubby's will. I didn't want to listen. Wills were for dead people.

"Thom, he left you his hockey card collection," Bunny said.

Thom grunted acknowledgement.

"Kitten, he left Fact & Fiction to you."

My eyes widened.

"The fuck? Why does *she* get the store?" Thom asked.

"I'm sure he had his reasons. Did he ever talk to you about it, Kitten?"

"No." I took a cookie from one of the many plates of sweets people had dropped off after Stubby died, crumbling it but not eating it. "I mean, he knew I liked books, and working in the store and stuff. I never said I wanted it, though."

In my mind's eye, I saw Tiny and me clasping hands, manifesting a bookstore. I dropped the cookie.

"The hell is she supposed to do with a store? She's sixteen," Thom grumbled.

Bunny patted my hand. "You don't need to do anything with the store right now. We'll get a manager to take care of things, until your mother's feeling up to it. Isn't it nice, knowing it's there waiting for you?"

I got up to throw the pile of cookie crumbs in the trash. My stomach was churning. Maybe I'd manifested this. I'd wanted to save Stubby, not take his store. My magic had gone horribly wrong.

———

After Bunny left, promising to come back soon, the silence in the house hummed through me like electricity, crackling with tension. Queena had always been background noise in my life, telling me what to do, what to wear, and where I could go. Apart from reading tarot, sneaking off to beach parties that summer had been the first thing I'd done without her interference. Now, in the weeks after the funeral, I realized how much I'd relied on Queena and my tarot cards to make decisions for me. I spent my days walking around the house, room by room, looking for direction and too jumpy to stop moving, as though Stubby's loss couldn't stick to me if I was in constant motion.

Thom, on the other hand, embraced our newfound freedom. As soon as Bunny left, he went out to party nightly and meet up with an endless parade of girls.

Thom and I were born just eleven months apart, probably because Queena would rather have died than talk to a doctor about sex and contraception. He turned sixteen not long after Stubby died, so we were the same age for a few weeks. Almost everything about him changed in those weeks. He went from being mildly annoying to being angry and hell-bent on self-destruction. This made him even more attractive to Paradise Valley girls—sort of like James Dean in *Rebel Without a Cause* (but really more like Kevin Bacon in *Footloose*).

He took his driver's test on his birthday, and then he was never home. Thom had never gone to parties. He'd never had a girlfriend. He'd spent most of his time watching TV with Ed, and he still did that most evenings. But after Ed left, Thom would go into his basement lair as a dork and emerge a little while later looking like a discount Rob Lowe. He'd grab some booze from the bomb shelter and disappear until the wee hours of the morning.

One afternoon, while my brother was still sleeping off the night before, I drove twenty minutes up the coast to a beach in Elgin to be miserable in a nicer setting. I didn't even make it past the parking area, though, because of what I saw when I opened the back door to get the beach blanket. On the floor, poking out under the seat, was a box of condoms. An empty box. I dropped the blanket and wished I had a flame-thrower to fling into the backseat.

That night, I stood in front of the TV with my arms crossed, just like Queena would've. Thom craned his neck to look around me to watch a rerun of *Alf*.

"I found this in the car." I pulled the condom box from behind me.

Ed's face went red. Thom just shrugged. "So?"

"So? Listen, dickhead, I use that car, too. Stop using it as your personal shaggin' wagon. God. You're so gross."

And lo, Queena's old Pontiac station wagon was forevermore known as the shaggin' wagon, and I never, ever, sat in the backseat again.

Tiny was spending the month of August at her family's cottage. There was no phone there, and I was glad to not have to talk to her.

Everything we used to talk about seemed stupid and irrelevant. I tried writing letters to give her when she got back from the cottage, like I had in the past, but everything I wrote was so much darker than the stuff we usually talked about. I tore up the pages in frustration. Tearing them was satisfying—it was a nice release for those scary blasts of anger I'd been feeling—so I looked for other stuff to rip up. Over the next few weeks, I ripped up my collection of *Seventeen* magazines, journals I'd kept in elementary school, junior high yearbooks, and entire photo albums. I ripped up my tarot cards, and then spent a whole night crying and feeling like I'd murdered someone. I tore my past into smaller and smaller pieces until I was surrounded by confetti, like the guest of honour at some perverse party.

Bunny called long distance every week, but our conversations got shorter and shorter. Her voice was brittle, and she talked over us a lot, saying things like "So, how are things going? They're good? Good," without giving us space to say if things were good or bad. She didn't even sound like Bunny, because she wasn't being sarcastic or bitchy. Without that, her voice had a familiar but unnatural flavour, like new Coke.

It was one of the hottest summers I'd known, and I kept the attic windows opened wide to catch a breeze. One night, an owl hooted in the trees behind our house. We'd never had an owl there before.

"Whooooo?" it called. I crept over to the windowsill to look.

"I'm Kitty. Who are you?"

"Whooooooo? Whooooo?" the owl called back.

"Who?"

I'd always zoned out when Stubby talked about birds, but I knew that owls were special to witches. They were supposed to be able to travel between our world and the spirit world.

Stubby loved birds. And this bird could travel between worlds.

"Stubby?" I whispered.

"Whooo?"

I pushed my bed under the window and slept there for the rest of the summer, so that I could hear my father—who I was sure had come back as an owl—hooting his reassurance that I wasn't completely alone.

***

There was a picture of Nerida on the dining room wall that showed her sitting on a piece of driftwood, resting her chin on her hands and smiling into the camera. It looked as if she was inviting someone to come sit next to her. As I stood looking at it while I ate whatever I could find in the bomb shelter, I imagined she was inviting me. She looked like someone I might've been friends with, if we'd been seventeen at the same time. She looked like she'd understand all the stuff I was feeling.

That's when I realized I could tell Nerida everything. I could write to her instead of Tiny. I went right upstairs and started writing. I told her I was sure Stubby had come back as the owl. I wrote that I was worried Thom was going to catch herpes or AIDS or end up dead in a ditch. I told her how all day, I felt so tired that I couldn't do anything, but when I went to bed I couldn't sleep because I couldn't get the image of Stubby's eyes out of my head. I told her it was my fault he died. I told her it was so oddly quiet in our house, yet the inside of my head sounded like screaming. I told her that sometimes, I wished I could fall asleep and never wake up again, or that I could trade places with her.

***

By mid-August, there was a pile of bills on the kitchen table and the sink was overflowing with dishes. The freezer was still filled with the funeral casseroles, but we didn't eat them. I was sure they'd taste like sadness. We used the bomb shelter for its intended purpose: providing for us in a disaster. When we got tired of cereal and Spam, Thom began to teach himself how to cook, using Queena's cookbooks and PBS cooking shows for inspiration. To my surprise, he was really good at it, though no one but him really appreciated it. Queena ignored the trays we took up to her, and after a few mouthfuls, I'd push my own plate away.

"Maybe you could freeze this stuff," I suggested. "You know, for when we feel more like eating."

But we both knew the freezer was stuffed to capacity with all those Pyrex funereal casseroles. There was no room for anything else.

Never My Love

⭐

Dear Kitty,

You were right. I did understand. But there are parts of the story you're missing. Let's face it, you weren't as bad as Queena, but this whole thing was pretty heavy for you, too. Grief makes people do weird things, like staying in bed for weeks, or thinking your father's an owl, or writing letters to your dead aunt.

You thought Queena was in bed all the time, but she wasn't. Exactly a month after Donny died, it was their wedding anniversary. I don't think you and Thom even remembered. That night, Thom was out having a good time, and you were upstairs writing to me, and Queena got out of bed and went down to the bomb shelter. She took a portable record player in with her, turned the volume way down, and played the song they danced to at their wedding: "Never My Love." I watched them dance to it in 1969. It was funny to watch them dance, because your dad was so tall and Queena was tiny, but he scooped Queena up into his arms so tenderly, and you could tell they were crazy about each other. I remember watching them and hoping I'd have that, someday. Still waiting. Ha.

She went down there other nights, too, when she thought you and Thom were asleep. She'd sit on the bare cement, in the light from the one bare bulb, with a pile of Donny's clothes and boxes of photo albums. She held armfuls of his shirts to her face, breathing in his scent with big gulps of air, like she could inhale him into her. She rocked back and forth with them like she was dancing, whispering to them and smiling up into the distance, flirting with something that wasn't there.

At the back of the room, in a corner with first aid kits and jars of homemade pickles that you and Thom didn't bother with, she squirrelled away some of the photo albums and a box of your dad's clothes. Then she had everything she needed in that bomb shelter to help her survive: food, clothing, fuel, and memories. All those years, you thought she was using her bomb shelter to protect all of you. But I watched her down there. She only wanted to save herself.

Love,
Nerida
xoxo

My Girl Wants to Party all the Time

❦

Saturday, April 22, 2000

Pixie's eyes were still wide open, and I couldn't sleep either. I made sure she was fed and comfortable and warm, and then tucked her into her sling. With my Care Bears blanket wrapped around us, I headed down to the bomb shelter, took two bottles of Rockaberry cooler (since it didn't seem anyone would miss them), and went out onto the back deck.

Late at night, the only sounds in Paradise Valley were waves breaking in the distance and a sudden squeal of tires as teenagers did donuts in the parking lot of the liquor commission. I hugged Pixie against me and showed her the lights from airplanes flying over us in the inky black, wondering if any of them were going to BC.

There was an outburst of noise as a group of girls walked down the street, laughing and singing, probably heading home from the tavern a few blocks away. I looked toward the back of our yard. Just beyond those trees, a few streets over, was Tiny's old house. We used to laugh and sing like those girls.

Pixie shifted in my arms, snapping me out of my thoughts. I suddenly felt stupid for sitting alone in the dark with a skunky bottle of booze, especially when I should be focusing on my baby. I bounced to soothe her as I kicked the empty bottles under the deck and took her to bed, my Care Bears blanket trailing behind us.

September 1987

Tiny smacked her lips together as she reapplied frosted pink lipstick in the little mirror on our locker door. I leaned against the locker, checking the time on my Swatch so that I wouldn't have to look at her. We'd been arguing all week. Our birthdays—which were two days apart—were coming up on the weekend, and I'd told Tiny I was pulling out of the party we'd started planning in June. Celebrating my birthday this year seemed gross. I'd probably spend the whole time thinking about my last birthday, when Stubby had jogged up my stairs in the morning to wake me up with a pile of new books and a bag of donuts that I didn't have to share with Thom. That would never happen again. What was the point in celebrating the start of the first year I wouldn't have him around?

Tiny slammed the locker door shut.

"Okay, forget it." Her face twisted into a pout, and she looked like she might cry. "We'll just, like, forget about our fucking birthdays."

"You can still have the party. I just don't think I'm going to go."

Someone breathed in my ear. "Hey, Kitty."

It was Rodger. My heart gave a thump, which was promising. I thought it'd given up thumping for anything but dread.

He leaned up against the lockers, inserting himself between Tiny and me.

"Can't wait to see you at the party. I've got a special birthday present for you." He was as subtle as his Brut aftershave. Tiny smirked behind his back.

"Wow. Great. I don't think I'm going, actually. Family stuff. You know."

Rodger ran a hand through his dark brown hair to fluff it up. "Well, maybe we can get together some other time? It's still warm enough for the beach if you want to take a drive some night."

Tiny made a face behind him, encouraging me to say yes.

"I can't. Sorry."

Rodger peeled himself off the locker and tossed his fluffy mullet, watching a couple of tenth-grade girls walk past. "Okay then. Guess I'll see you around, Kitty."

Tiny punched me in the arm as he walked away.

"You said no to Rodger? Why?"

"I'm just really not up for it right now."

"Omigod. He might not be up for *ever*, now that you totally snubbed him!"

I watched Rodger follow the tenth-grade girls down the hall. "Rodger's always up for it, I think."

Tiny leaned against the lockers and gave me a pleading look. "So, you're sure about the party? Seriously, I can't have a birthday party without my best friend there!"

"I'd be no fun. I'm not in the mood for a party."

Tiny's face flushed. "Like, seriously, what's the point of even having a best friend if you never want to do anything? Forget it. I'll just have my own party without you."

Tiny stormed off down the hall to her next class. People drifted past in clouds of neon and pastel, happy and bright and loud. I was a black, silent storm cloud on their horizon.

Thom made me a birthday cake. Because he's an arse, he made one I hated, with peanut butter icing. He ate most of it in one sitting with a satisfied smirk, after I pushed it away.

He was doing no better at school than I was. He'd never gotten into fights before, but now, every time some jerk made a comment about him about being the next victim of the Love Heart, Thom slammed him into a locker. The principal had warned him that the next time it happened he'd be expelled. I think that's what Thom was hoping for, to be honest.

"Ed's mum said you can go over there for dinner, if you want. You know, a birthday party kind of thing," he said. We had no clean forks or plates, so he was using his hands to eat the cake, like a mullet-haired chipmunk.

"That's the lamest fucking party I've ever heard of."

"Yeah, and you've got better plans, right? Loser."

"Shut up!"

"You shut up."

I waited around the kitchen that evening in case Queena came down to wish me a happy birthday. She'd ignored me when I took her some toast that morning, but I was sure she'd remember it was my birthday. I thought mothers just knew.

Thom came in and dropped himself onto a kitchen chair. I pretended I was looking for something, opening cabinet doors and chewing on my thumb. It was getting dark, so I turned on the little light that illuminated the face of the old avocado-green stove. It made a comforting buzzing noise. I stood and listened to it for a while, staring, unseeing, into a cupboard.

The phone rang, and I jumped. It so seldom rang anymore. Thom answered it and put his hand over the receiver.

"It's Bunny."

"Tell her I'm out." I pushed past him to go up to my room. I didn't want Bunny to know what a loser I was.

I spent the rest of my seventeenth birthday alone in my attic, sitting on my beanbag chair with a bottle of bomb shelter vodka, bitching about my shitty life to the owl outside the window and writing to my dead aunt. I didn't want to go to Tiny's stupid party, but I hated that she was going to have fun without me.

I slid over to my bed and dug the Magic 8 Ball out from under the pillow. I gave it a gentle shake and asked, "Can my life get any worse?"

You may rely on it.

Our Lips Are Sealed

October 1987

There weren't any clean spoons. There wasn't clean anything. I ate handfuls of stale Lucky Charms out of the box and pushed aside our empty liquor bottles in order to find a spot to sit and write a letter to Nerida. I wondered if I should attempt to clean the kitchen, or if it'd be easier to just pitch all the dirty stuff in trash bags and get rid of it.

Someone knocked at the front door. No one ever knocked on our door. Ed was the only person who came here these days, and he never knocked. I shoved the letter into a binder with all the other letters I'd written to Nerida, and pushed away from the kitchen table so I couldn't be seen from the front door. The knocking continued, cutting through our silent house like gunfire. It hurt my head. I'd have to answer the door just to make it stop.

I opened the door just enough to see the tight, straw-coloured perm of Tiny's mother, Marjorie. Next to her was Eleanor Matthews. Eleanor taught me Sunday school the year I made my First Confession. I hadn't been able to think of what to confess, so I'd made something up based on a storyline from one of Queena's soap operas, which I figured would be more entertaining to the priest than the stuff he usually heard. I always suspected Eleanor knew of my conceit. (I guess I could've confessed that, if I'd ever bothered with confession again.)

"Oh, there you are, Kitten dear! Don't you look nice!" Marjorie gave me a thin-lipped smile. I was wearing only an oversized *Frankie Say Relax* T-shirt, and yesterday's blue mascara was smudged under my eyes. Plus, the humidity from the previous day's rain had made my hair even bigger than usual. I didn't look nice. I looked like the drummer in a hair metal band after a weekend of hookers and cocaine.

Eleanor leaned in and waved a bouquet of carnations wrapped in cellophane. The grocery store's price sticker was still on it. "For your mother. We just wanted to check in and let her know she's missed."

I knew this was bullshit. They just wanted fresh, shiny gossip to take back to their murder of crows.

I tried to steer them into the slightly cleaner living room, but they headed for the kitchen, as Paradise Valley women always do.

"I was just getting ready to clean," I explained. Eleanor looked around for a spot to leave her flowers. Finding none, she dropped the carnations rather pointedly in front of the liquor bottles.

I excused myself and ran upstairs to Queena's room. I didn't expect her to get up, but at least asking her would give me a minute to think. I couldn't come up with excuses for the state of the house, the empty vodka bottles, and Queena all at once.

"Some people are here to see you." I poked at her feet. "Get up."

"No." She rolled over and turned her back on me.

I poked at her until I couldn't bear the smell in the room anymore. It'd been weeks since she'd had a bath. My head was thick and cottony and I couldn't think. I touched Nerida's doorknob for luck, tried to smooth my hair, and headed back downstairs.

Marjorie was closing her purse. She wiped her hands against her pants as she looked at the state of the countertops.

"My mother isn't feeling up to visitors, just now." I moved to fill up the kettle, but Marjorie stopped me.

"It's all right dear. We just wanted to see how Queena's managing after your tragic loss." She said that part quietly, which I appreciated.

"She's fine. We're all fine." I tried not to let my eyes drift over to the liquor bottles or the pile of dirty dishes.

"Good, good. God doesn't give us more than we can bear."

I snorted before I could stop myself.

Eleanor was already backing out of the room toward the door.

"Do take care, Kitten," she said, clucking her tongue. "This is a terrible way for children to live."

Marjorie gave one last, disdainful look around our house before stepping outside. She and Eleanor scurried away, heads together.

I saw a flash of colour at the top of the stairs—Queena, teetering unsteadily in a blue and pink floral nightgown. She looked furious. Her bottom lip trembled, and colour rose in splotches up her neck to her hairline. I hadn't seen her look this angry in ages; not since Thom got sent to the principal's office in Grade 7 for doing a book report on some lesbian pulp fiction he'd found in the Smutty Paperback room.

I opened my mouth to say something about the mess, but Queena's plump floral rear was already in retreat. I was alone again. I went to the kitchen and started to clean up. Eleanor's carnations were the first things to go in the trash.

———

Tiny and I were going through the motions of being best friends—we still had lunch together every day and talked at our locker, but the nightly letters had stopped. I told myself I didn't care. I was writing to Nerida every night anyway. I didn't have time to write to both.

She wasn't at our locker before class on Monday. She wasn't there at lunch, either. As I grabbed the books for my afternoon classes, a small envelope fell out of my French textbook, with my name written on it in Tiny's loopy handwriting.

Dear Kitty,

Sorry I haven't written any letters lately. I guess things have been a little weird between us.

My mum told me she went to your house this weekend. She said it was filled with trash and your mother wasn't around. She said you smelled like you'd been drinking. Is that true???? I told her she must be wrong about that. I mean, it was morning, and you don't even go to parties anymore. But she said you opened the door in your underwear and smelled like a bar, and there were empty bottles all over the place.

She also found a letter on the kitchen table. It was from you and it was addressed to Nerida!?! and my mother said there was a bunch of them and you were saying all kinds of creepy stuff about Stubby coming back from the dead and how you think he's an owl and you wish you could fly away with him or trade places with Nerida.

My mother took one of the letters from your house and she showed it to me. She's a bitch and she shouldn't have taken it, but in a way I'm glad she did because I didn't know all this stuff was going on with you. I know I haven't been a very good friend lately but if you're drinking that much and you're imagining you're talking to Nerida and that your dad's an owl then I don't think you're okay. I know we used to talk about Nerida a lot when we were younger, but we didn't act like she was actually here and friends with us. I don't know what to say, but I think you need help.

But the really shitty thing is that because you talked about witchcraft and spells in the letter, my mother asked me all kinds of questions about whether I was doing it, too. I got in a lot of trouble, and she's going to talk to the priest about an exorcism or something. I'm grounded for practically forever and she says we can't be friends anymore.

She's calling the school this morning to get my locker switched. She's telling the principal about you drinking and stuff, too. I just thought I should warn you.

Anyway, I hope you're okay.

Tiny

P.S. I'm giving you back the letter that my mother stole. She shouldn't have taken it.

She hadn't signed it "Your Best Friend Forever No Matter What." Just "Tiny."

My vision clouded with tears and my breath grew into a painful bubble in my chest as I pictured Eleanor and Marjorie reading my letter and laughing about it. They loved good gossip, the sanctimonious old cows. They'd show it to everyone, and then everyone would laugh at how crazy I was.

I shoved the letter back in my book and half-ran down the hall to the bathroom, where no one would hear me crying. As I rushed around a corner, I smacked straight into Angel Dempsey. All my textbooks fell to the floor, along with her purse. Lipsticks, cigarettes, and hairbrushes spilled onto the worn tiled floor.

Angel was as much an angel as Paradise Valley was paradise. She and her friends made up the Stoners, which was the closest thing we had to a gang. Tiny and I were scared shitless of them. They'd beat up anyone who ventured into the courtyard where they smoked, and rumour had it they had dirt on the vice-principal, which is why they never seemed to get in trouble for skipping class. When we saw the Stoners heading in our direction, we went the other way.

Most of the Stoners were scruffy and rough, moving through the halls in a cloud of stale cigarette smoke and veiled threats. Angel was different. She was the most beautiful girl in school. She had long, perfectly feathered amber hair, wide blue eyes framed with blue eyeliner, and a sweet, dimpled smile that fooled people into thinking she wasn't dangerous. She floated gloriously in front of the Stoners like the figurehead on a warship, and I had just launched a volley at her.

Angel watched me scramble to pick up her stuff without bending to help. I kept glancing up to make sure she wasn't about to pound me on the head, but then I thought that making eye contact with her might provoke her, so I kept my eyes on the floor.

"I'm really sorry." I held her purse out to her and averted my eyes.

Angel made a fist and did a quick lunge toward me—just enough to make me think she was going to hit me—and then stood back and laughed at the fear on my face.

"Hey, witch. If you're so psychic, why didn't you see me coming around the corner?"

"Sorry." I stepped sideways to get past her, but she moved, too, and blocked me.

"Maybe you owe me a free magic spell for this, huh? Or I could make you pay some other way." She tucked her books under one arm and hit her fists together, her knuckles cracking.

I willed myself not to start crying in front of her.

Angel took a step toward me, and then stepped out of the way to let me pass. I was sure she'd lunge at me as soon as my back was turned. I ran for the girls' washroom, taking one look back as I reached the door. Angel was watching me, but then turned and walked down the stairs.

I checked my reflection in the cracked mirror in the bathroom. My eyes had purple half-moons under them. Had I brushed my hair that morning? I couldn't remember. I wasn't sure if I'd put my clothes on that morning, or if I'd slept in them. I gave my armpits a sniff and slumped against the wall to reread Tiny's letter.

It was gone.

I patted my pockets and searched and re-searched my books, but it wasn't there. My face burned as I realized I must have put it with Angel's stuff. She'd show all her Stoner friends, and they'd probably be waiting to make fun of me and beat me up after school. Or maybe she'd pass it around so that everyone in school saw it.

The intercom crackled and the school secretary's voice screeched through: "Kitten Love to the principal's office, please. Kitten Love to the principal's office."

I came out of the bathroom, looking both ways to make sure the Stoners weren't waiting, and dragged my hand along the row of lockers to steady myself until I reached mine. I could barely see the numbers on the lock, but it finally gave way. The door flew open, clanging against the locker next to it.

All traces of Tiny were gone. Bits of tape clung to the inside of the locker door where she'd ripped away photos. One sparkly heart-shaped sticker remained. I could see that she'd tried to peel away one corner before giving up and leaving it.

Angel was probably already sharing the letter with everyone, and Tiny's mother had probably shown it to all her church ladies. I was a joke now. The principal probably had someone from the psych ward waiting to cart me away and lock me up.

I slammed the locker door shut and ran down the stairs and out the front door, vowing to never come back.

Mad World

October 1987

The phone started ringing after the first day I skipped school. I took it off the hook and dragged it by its long cord over to the cupboard under the kitchen sink. I shoved the receiver under there, packed into a pile of dishtowels, so that I didn't have to listen to its nagging beep beep beep.

There was no one at home who cared whether I went to school or just stayed home in my T-shirt and underwear eating Marshmallow Fluff with a wooden spoon. No one noticed I was there. The house was so quiet it hurt my ears.

I spent my days getting my room in order. First, I brought out a big Barbie suitcase from the back of my wardrobe. It was so stuffed full of Tiny's letters that the zipper had busted ages ago. I dumped them into the middle of my floor. Tiny didn't want to be friends anymore? Fine. I didn't, either. She'd be nothing to me. In fact, I'd banish her.

I started making a banishing oil the day she put the letter in my textbook. As soon as I got home, I put cinnamon, black pepper, and cayenne pepper in a jar with some castor oil and let it sit a few days under a full moon to become potent. Next, I rubbed the oil onto a black candle, lit it, and wrote Tiny's name on a little piece of paper. I let it burn, chanting, "Be gone, be gone" under my breath. Then, as the candle burned down, I burned all of Tiny's letters and dropped them into my little metal Holly Hobbie wastepaper basket. It took a long time, and it wrecked the basket, but eventually I had a big pile of ashes. I dumped them out the window, into the brown autumn remains of Queena's peonies. Little flecks of burned paper and ash took off in the wind, floating toward Tiny's house. It was extremely satisfying.

Then there was the question of what to do with the letters to Nerida. I'd get rid of those, too, so they didn't fall into the wrong hands again. There was only a summer's worth of letters, so burning them didn't take as long. That was less satisfying.

I ran my hand along the rows of potted plants on my windowsills, stopping when I came to the lily of the valley. I'd grown it from a cutting from some of Stubby's funeral flowers. It was such a pretty, delicate plant. I ripped part of it out from the roots and stuck it in a plastic grocery bag, along with the poppet I'd made to protect Stubby from the Love Heart. I closed my bedroom door behind me and touched Nerida's doorknob to say goodbye, then went down to the bomb shelter. I took Stubby's old parka from the rack and grabbed a bottle of gin. Then, I left the house and walked to the old highway, where I held out my thumb until a car stopped to give me a ride up the coast to the beach.

Stubby's parka still smelled of him. I sat on the damp sand for a while with the hood up, letting the scent cover me. If I closed my eyes, I could pretend he was sitting right there with me.

I reached into one of the parka's deep pockets for the bag with the lily of the valley. The delicate, springtime scent was out of place in the biting Atlantic wind. Such a pretty plant for something so poisonous. I tore up some leaves and shoved the pieces in my mouth, forcing myself to chew even though they tasted awful, and washed the bitter taste away with long gulps of gin.

Sleet started to fall, poking at me with a thousand needle-sharp fingers. As I stood to wipe the sand off my jeans, the wind shifted and nudged me from behind. It reminded me of walking with Stubby when I was a little girl: when I'd dawdle, he'd push on the small of my back with a finger to hurry me along. A gust of wind blew the parka's hood against my face, smothering me in fake fur trim and my father's scent. It was like being caught up in one of Stubby's big bear hugs. I suddenly felt so calm.

I swear, I could hear Stubby's voice in the wind—it sounded like him, but I couldn't make out what he was saying. I closed my eyes and tried to concentrate, to listen harder, to will him to be there when I opened my eyes. When I opened them, though, no one was there but a gull, surfing a wind current offshore.

The poison and the gin were kicking in and I felt lightheaded. I staggered to keep my balance as the waves hit against my knees, biting through my jeans, and I thought of Nerida, walking out into these waves. I pulled Stubby's poppet from my pocket, took a deep breath, and threw it as far as I could. Then, like a dog playing fetch, I followed it. The wind and surf were so strong their roar drowned out the whole world, even my own thoughts. Everything was blurry and glowing, and I was suddenly so woozy that I fell backwards with the push of the next wave.

The current was strong, and I couldn't tell if I was being dragged out to sea or pushed back to shore. My feet touched bottom more than once; I knew I wasn't even in deep water, but the weight of the parka and the force of the current kept me from getting upright. I couldn't feel my legs to kick them. My arms were numb, heavy against the waves. My lungs were burning. I couldn't fight it. I stopped kicking.

Then something else—something as strong as the sea—pulled at my hair and dragged me out of the water by the hood. The parka cut into my windpipe, and I struggled against it even as I tried to gasp air into my bursting lungs. I landed on the sand, strangling and panicked.

"Kitten!" a voice shouted.

My hair was plastered against my face, filtering my view of the whole world through sodden black seaweed. I tried to move the hair away from my eyes, but I couldn't feel my hands to move them. I turned my cheek onto the sand and retched. Someone else's hands turned me on my side and pushed my hair out of the way.

"Oh God, we've got to get you warm," a woman's voice said. It was vaguely familiar. Through blurry eyes, I saw Mrs. Fraser—Ed's mother. She was soaked, and her face was as grey as the sky. Her faded blond hair looked grey, too, as the sleet coated it, giving her the appearance of an old woman. Her green eyes were young, though. Maybe she was a good witch hiding in a crone's body.

"Can you walk? If I lift you up, can you walk with me?" She spoke loudly to be heard over the wind and waves and my own thick head.

I nodded. At least, I tried to. My brain didn't seem to be in charge of my body anymore. I was gasping and coughing, and my legs hurt so badly that when I looked down, I expected to see them covered in blood with shrapnel sticking out of them. My eyes couldn't focus, and I thought I might black out. With her arm around me, Mrs. Fraser half-dragged me to the stairs leading to the row of cottages on the cliff above.

Mrs. Fraser continued a nervous stream of talk, but I didn't hear words, only noise. She finally fell quiet when we reached a little white bungalow with yellow shutters. The sea laughed and mocked me behind my back.

Mrs. Fraser shifted her weight to support me as she fumbled with the cottage door. A slight scent of mildew and cedar drifted out. It was colder inside than outside.

She sat me down on a harvest-gold corduroy sofa and threw a musty-smelling plaid blanket over me. My eyes were heavy and stinging from the salt water. They flew open when I felt someone taking off the parka.

"I need to get you out of these wet things," Mrs. Fraser was saying. "I'm running a bath. Kitten? Do you hear?"

"Okay." I couldn't be sure my voice made a sound, but I thought my lips were moving.

She shook my shoulders. "Kitten? Did you take anything?"

I stared at her dumbly.

"Did you take something? Pills?"

I shook my head.

Mrs. Fraser led me to the bathroom. My still-numb fingers fumbled with my clothes, and I couldn't undress myself. Mrs. Fraser undressed me down to my underwear while I leaned limply against the sink, feeling like I might throw up again. She held me by my arms as I lowered into the pink, chipped bathtub. Pain shot through my body as my freezing skin met the warm water, and I started to cry. I tried to draw my legs up against my chest, suddenly realizing I was practically naked in front of Ed's mother, but my legs wouldn't work.

Mrs. Fraser left for a moment, and I struggled to stay upright. I slipped lower, barely managing to keep my chin above the water. She reappeared with an armload of towels, an old velour robe, and some thin wool socks.

"There was a bottle and a bag with a plant in your jacket pocket. Did you drink all that gin?"

I blinked at her.

"What's the plant?"

"Lily of the valley." I was barely able to whisper.

"Why do you have it?"

"I ate it."

"You ate it? Why?"

I didn't answer. I leaned over the side of the tub and got sick, and she rushed to grab a garbage can.

Mrs. Fraser dragged me out of the tub. My legs flailed under me like eels.

"I'm calling an ambulance." She threw the old robe around me and led me to the sofa. I heard her yell at someone on the party line to hang up because it was an emergency. I zoned out, but then she was yelling at me to stay awake. My eyes wouldn't stay open.

I heard someone pounding on the door, and loud voices.

That's the last sound I remember for a while.

Things Can Only Get Better

I woke up in a strange room and didn't know where I was or how I got there. I smelled disinfectant—something industrial, not the lemon-scented one Queena used—and felt a flannel sheet against my cheek. It felt comforting. There was a horrible taste in my mouth, and my throat was raw. My arm was so cold. Something was digging into it, and I reached to scratch it away, but someone held my hand back. I couldn't make my eyes open. Maybe I was dead. My heart thumped erratically, hard enough that it hurt to breathe. I must not be dead if I hurt.

"Kitten?" The voice sounded far away and thin, like an old-timey record played in mono. "Eileen, go get the doctor and find Queena, she's waking up."

I managed to open my eyes, just a slit. Bunny's face loomed over me, out of focus.

"Oh, my darling girl. Thank God. How do you feel?"

I closed my eyes again. The world was too bright. "Where?"

"You're in the hospital. You've been here a couple of days now."

I opened my eyes to see what was digging in my arm. It was an IV. "Thirsty," I croaked.

"I'll get you a Popsicle just as soon as the doctor says it's okay."

"Tonsils?"

"No darling, not your tonsils. You were at the beach, remember? Eileen Fraser found you there."

I tried to remember.

"You took some poison. And then quite a lot of gin. The doctors had to feed you some charcoal or something to make you throw up."

I blinked acknowledgement, but I didn't remember any doctors.

"I got on the first flight as soon as Eileen called me. We've all been so worried."

The door opened and a tall, thin man in a white coat and tan pants came in. He sat on the edge of my bed.

"Hi Kitten. I'm Doctor Rushton. You gave everyone quite a scare. How are you feeling?" He had round John Lennon glasses and a little fringe of greying hair that reminded me of the picture of Friar Tuck in my Robin Hood storybook. I wondered if it was still safely hidden in the attic at Fact & Fiction. I wanted it.

"You'll have to stay in the hospital until we're sure there won't be any lingering effects from the poison you took. Understand?"

I tried to nod. My head hurt so much.

Dr. Rushton leaned forward and clasped his hands under his chin, looking thoughtful. It seemed rehearsed, like he was about to deliver a monologue from a very special episode of *Growing Pains* and knew exactly where the camera was.

"You're a young girl, Kitten. You've got your whole life ahead of you. After we make sure we've taken care of the effects of the poison, I'd like to transfer you over to the regional hospital. There are people there who can help you work through your problems."

My heart accelerated. He wanted to put me in the mental ward. It'd be awful, just like I'd seen in movies. They'd strap me to the bed and pump me full of drugs and make me tell them every bad thought I'd ever had, and they'd do weird experiments on my brain. It'd be even worse than when Queena interrogated me.

There was a commotion in the hallway, accompanied by the unmistakable hyper cadence of my mother's voice.

"I have done no such thing, Eileen Fraser!" Queena's voice cracked from disuse. "I haven't even left the house since the funeral!"

Other voices murmured, and then the door opened. Queena and Mrs. Fraser pushed through, looking like a couple of chickens about to have a big pecking fight over a June bug.

Queena looked as shitty as I did—maybe shittier, which was quite a feat since I smelled like a dead jellyfish and had been barfing up poison. She'd thrown on her good London Fog trench coat, but the ragged blue hem of the nightgown she'd been wearing for God knows how long peeked out from the bottom. The cafeteria tea she was carrying had splashed out of the paper cup and onto her coat, leaving a wet splotch on her chest. Her unbrushed hair made weird bumps under the pink silk scarf she'd tied over it, and it looked like she'd applied her favourite Elizabeth Arden lipstick without a mirror. She must've sprayed on some perfume, because as she moved, she left a nauseating cloud of Jean Naté and body odour. She stood next to me, grasping her handbag with both hands and swaying on her heels. She kind of looked like the queen, if the queen was down and out and sleeping in a bush outside the palace.

"Oh Kitten, you're awake! Oh, my girl!" She clasped my hands in hers and I winced as she jostled the IV.

Dr. Rushton gestured for Queena to sit on a blue leatherette chair near the bathroom door. Queena obeyed but drew herself up, her chest puffing out like a pigeon in winter. Her trench coat–wrapped rump made a rude squeak against the leatherette as she settled, but she didn't seem to notice. Her eyes were watery and confused but her attention was focused on me. The doctor was staring at me, too. I closed my eyes against the fluorescent light and wondered if this was what it was like to be captured by the KGB.

Dr. Rushton moved to the foot of my bed, farther from Queena's aroma. "Maybe we can start by chatting about how things have been going for you at home, Kitten. I'm sure you've all struggled after your father's death."

Queena's cheeks flushed at hearing that word spoken out loud. "I'm sure that has nothing to do with this, does it, Kitten? This was likely just some teenage drama. You know how they are." She gave a nervous laugh. The doctor nodded slightly and turned back to me.

"Did you go to the beach with a plan to take your life?" he asked. Queena flinched and clutched her coat tightly at her neck.

"Don't remember." Talking hurt, and I wanted him to leave so I could go back to sleep.

"Do you remember going into the water? Or Mrs. Fraser pulling you out?"

I concentrated, but it was like that whole chapter of my memory was torn out. Maybe I'd fried my brain on lily of the valley. Nancy Reagan had warned us all about this kind of thing.

"Well, maybe you'll remember more by the time we transfer you to the regional hospital," Dr. Rushton said.

"What do you mean, regional hospital? I haven't agreed to having her sent away!" Queena's voice faded in and out like an AM radio signal in bad weather. She raised herself unsteadily from the chair and attempted to look like she had her shit together. Not only did she not look like she had her shit together, but she looked like someone who'd lost her shit down the outhouse hole and dove in after it, face first.

"We can talk about that later, in private, Mrs. Love. How have you been coping with your own grief?" He folded his arms across his chest. His voice changed when he spoke to her—he sounded less like a sitcom dad and more like Phil Donahue.

"It's been a difficult time, but everything's fine." Queena stared at her folded hands and rubbed her thumbs together.

Dr. Rushton turned back to me. "Do you feel like everything's fine?"

I took a deep breath. "My mother's in bed all day. She hasn't talked to me in three months."

"Kitten! That's not true!" Queena gasped.

Dr. Rushton wrote some things on a chart. "Your aunt says you have a brother? How's he doing?"

I bit my lip. Thom might as well suffer as much as me.

"He goes out every night to drink and screw every girl in town."

"KITTEN!" Queena cried, sucking in her breath. Bunny adjusted my pillows and wiped my face with a cool cloth. Maybe I could go live in Montreal with Bunny and forget Queena and Paradise Valley existed.

"You've all been through a lot, and I'm sure you've tried your best, but we'll arrange for a social worker to come by your house and visit, and it would be good for the whole family to talk with one of our psychologists," Dr. Rushton said.

"A social worker!" Queena's face was scarlet. "We're not riff-raff! And we don't need a psychologist. There's nothing wrong with any of us, at all!"

"We just want to make sure you've all got the support you need, so that Kitten doesn't decide to take another trip to the beach. Why don't you and your sister go home and rest now? We'll let Kitten rest, too." Dr. Rushton patted my foot and was out the door before Queena could sputter any further objections.

Bunny got up to get her purse. "You heard the man, Queena. Let's go home for a bit and let Kitty rest. My arse is becoming part of that chair."

Queena dropped onto the foot of my bed, patting her bra for a tissue.

"Honestly, Kitten, how could you do this to me? After what I've already been through? Your father, and Nerida—"

"Jesus Murphy, Queena, this isn't about you," Bunny said.

"Really, Bunny? This doesn't make you think of what happened to Nerida? At the same beach? When I imagine Kitten in those waves, just like Nerida..." Queena covered her face with her hands, her shoulders shaking with sobs. "If you had to do something like this, why'd you have to go there? That just makes it so much harder for me."

"Christ on a bicycle, woman, do you hear yourself?" Bunny said. "You're the one who made things harder for Kitten. You haven't been out of bed since I left! Three months! What the hell have you been thinking?"

I kept my eyes closed and willed everyone to shut up. I wondered where the bedpan was. It might be good to throw up as a distraction.

"I wish you wouldn't use language like that, Bunny. And it hasn't been three months, don't be silly." Queena rubbed my foot. I kicked her hand away.

"Three months," Bunny repeated.

"You're exaggerating."

"It's October 27th. You've been in bed for three months."

Queena's lipstick stood out like an exclamation mark on her grey face. "Oh no. Oh no no no, that can't be! It's been a couple of weeks, maybe."

I closed my eyes again, but I'm sure Bunny gave my mother a dirty look.

"Oh no, Kitten, my God, what have I done? I left you alone. Just like with Nerida. I left her alone at the beach and she died. And now I almost did the same thing with you. Oh my God."

"Language, Queena," Bunny said softly.

Queena rooted around in her purse for another tissue and, finding none, dumped the whole thing on the floor in frustration. Bunny handed her the box of tissues on my bedside table.

"Calm yourself. You're not helping anyone like this."

Queena blew her nose loudly. "I'm the worst mother ever."

"Oh, I doubt that. Joan Crawford was pretty bad, and then there's all those wicked stepmothers in fairy tales. You'd be lucky to make the top five." Bunny said this in her usual sarcastic, jokey way, but there was an undertone of anger I didn't often hear in her voice.

Queena wiped her eyes and tossed the soggy tissue in the garbage. "I'll take care of you now, Kitten. You'll be fine, and we'll make sure no one ever knows about this. People don't forget this sort of thing, you know."

Her tone reminded me of when I got my first period, and she gave me a long lecture about Reputations and Promiscuity and Good Girls. People in Paradise Valley had long memories, she warned. You'd always be the Girl Who Got in Trouble.

I'd always be the Girl Who Talked to her Dead Aunt and Tried to Kill Herself.

The silence, once Queena and Bunny left the room, fell on my head like a cool cloth. I turned my head toward the window and realized that Mrs. Fraser was still there, sitting forgotten in the corner behind a large bouquet of flowers, pretending she saw families go batshit every day.

Little Girl Blue

Dear Kitty,

This is what I was talking about—the problem with choosing to stay with the Living. I could see what you were planning. I knew what you were up to with those plants. I wanted so much to be able to talk to you. But all I could do was watch. I won't get all heavy and lecture you. And not to say stuff that'd make Queena flip her wig, but really—what the hell? You had to do it at the beach? Shit. I guess you share Queena's flair for drama.

You kind of share some magic, too. Queena's not a witch, but when you were in the hospital for a few weeks, she did a magic trick of her own: she stopped time.

Eileen Fraser drove them home after they left you at the hospital that night. She and Bunny had been best friends in high school, but they hadn't talked in years. Not since my funeral. So, it was kind of awkward for everyone.

Queena shrugged off her trench coat and got her old green robe out of the laundry basket by the basement door. Without the coat, you could really see how much weight she'd lost since July. Eileen made tea. Bunny sat at the kitchen table, looking like she'd been dragged through the ocean, too, and started to cry, really quietly.

"I don't know how to thank you, Eileen. For everything you've done the past few days. If you hadn't been there to find her..."

Eileen sat down across from Bunny and wrapped her hands around her teacup.

"I don't usually go there at this time of year, but I had a feeling I should check on the cottage. Isn't that strange? As if someone whispered to me to go." She poured a cup of tea and slid it across the table to Queena. "I'm sorry for being sharp with you at the hospital, Queena. I know things have been difficult here. Ed's been worried. He'll be heartbroken when he hears about Kitten. He worships the ground she walks on."

"No one outside this room needs to know what happened." Queena sat up straighter and gave Mrs. Fraser her frostiest glare. "Just tell Ed that Kitty got sick. Appendicitis, maybe. Or mono."

"I feel like I'm always keeping these sorts of secrets from him." Eileen's eyes went to Bunny's, but Bunny looked away. "I've never told him what really happened to his father."

"I heard that Kenny had an accident." Bunny reached for Eileen's hand. Queena fussed with the tea cozy, weaving a loose piece of yarn back into the pink and green crochet.

"It wasn't an accident. He took his own life. Ed was just a baby. He doesn't know. I'll tell him, someday. I just hope he won't hate me for lying to him. I'm only trying to protect him."

Queena reached over and gave Eileen's other hand a squeeze. The three of them held onto each other around the table. It kind of looked like they might do a seance, and for a minute I was excited that they might want to talk to me.

Queena got up to refill the teapot, even though no one had touched their tea. "I'd like to take the same approach with Kitten. Not letting people know, I mean. I'm taking her out of school."

"She can't not go to school," Bunny objected. "There are rules."

"She can go back next year. She'll be in the same grade as Thom and Ed. I just want her where I can keep an eye on her."

"You can't keep an eye on her forever, Queena. Maybe if you gave her some freedom to find her way—"

"No. She doesn't need more freedom. Donny indulged her and let her go to the beach and look what came of it." She braced her hands on the counter, her shoulders shaking. "This is the curse. I'm the cursed one, with the bad luck. Nerida died, and Donny, and now almost Kitten."

Bunny got up and wrapped her arm around Queena. "This isn't your fault. Remember how you were after Nerida died? Things will get better again, just like they did then. Wait and see."

Queena's face crumpled. Eileen got up to find some tissue, but seeing none she ripped a piece of paper towel and handed it to Queena.

"I don't know how to go on without him. It feels like his funeral was just a few days ago. I don't know what's wrong with me." Queena cried harder and stumbled toward the living room, but she only made it to the dining room before collapsing onto a chair.

Bunny stood behind Queena's chair and took a long drag on her cigarette, blowing the smoke in Queena's direction. She reminded me of the hookah-smoking caterpillar Alice met in Wonderland.

Eileen took a humbug from the candy dish on the sideboard and rubbed it between her fingers. "Some families seem to have more than their share of sadness. Maybe there were things you did after Nerida that could help you now, do you think?"

"I suppose there were a few things. We kept Nerida's room just as it was, for one thing. It would've felt terrible to pack everything up or give it away. And we put up lots of photos, so it'd be like she was still part of things here." Queena stared into the distance, somewhere beyond the cloud of Bunny's cigarette smoke. "Yes, I think I might have some ideas."

———

Time's different on my side. What's five years for you is like five seconds to me. I think that's what happened to Queena. It was like time stopped for her, or she was in between my world and yours for a while, I don't know. It's kind of trippy.

You were kind of in between worlds too, though. I think that's what happens to the Living when they lose someone they love. A little part of them gets pulled over to this side, and sometimes it's not so easy to pull it back.

I sat with you every night after you came home. Right over here, by your beanbag chair. You slept a lot, but I talked to you the whole time, just dumb stuff about school and parties. I figured we were the same age, so we probably had stuff in common.

Maybe you knew I was there, maybe you didn't. I didn't care. I just didn't want you to be alone. I know how it feels.

Love,
Nerida
xoxo

Always Something There to Remind Me

Sunday, April 23, 2000

The early morning air was chilly, but I'd opened the window just a crack in case I could hear an owl. Pixie was wrapped up warmly in my arms. All this change had been so disruptive for her, and she was probably wondering where Matt was. I wondered where he was, too. It'd been almost a week since I'd left, and he still hadn't called.

I wished I'd brought some of Pixie's books, but I hadn't dared to go back into her room after the fight with Matt. Singing to her might be good. It'd fill the silence and elbow out my unwanted thoughts, but I was too tired to remember the words to any lullabies. I scooted over to the milk crates and sorted through mixtapes until I found one that Tiny had called "Make Out Tunes." I put it in my boombox and closed my eyes, swaying back and forth with Pixie in my arms as Bonnie Tyler sang "Total Eclipse of the Heart."

My peace was interrupted by a pounding on my door.

"Pussy! Queena wants you!" Thom yelled.

"For fuck's sake," I muttered, before I remembered that Pixie was listening.

I pulled open my door a crack. "What do you want?"

"Queena called. She forgot her lunch and needs you to take it to the store."

"Wait a minute, it's Sunday. The store's not even open."

"She and Bunny are doing inventory or something. I dunno. Anyway. she needs you to go take her lunch. Ed and I are watching a ball game so I'm not going." Thom turned and walked away.

"For fuck's sake," I said again, before remembering Pixie.

———

I took my first shower in a week and stood in front of my suitcase, trying to decide what to wear. I'd been in such a hurry when I packed that I'd thrown in random things. Having a wardrobe that was mostly black made it easier, at least. I put on jeans, a t-shirt and an oversized sweater that I could wrap around Pixie's carrier, and headed downstairs.

Thom and Ed were on the sofa, as usual, with a table full of snacks in front of them.

"Hi, Kitty. You look nice," Ed said, holding out a bowl of Cheezies. I ignored him and waved Queena's lunch bag at Thom.

"I'm going, you lazy fucker. You owe me one."

He flipped me off with one hand and turned up the TV volume with the other.

I was grateful it was Sunday, because there weren't many people around. The air smelled exactly how I remembered springtime in Paradise Valley smelling—like wet earth and salt water, with the ever-present fart smell from the mill when the breeze blew downwind. I patted Pixie's back. It probably hadn't been fair for me to keep her inside so long, but she was so little and delicate, it worried me to take her out.

I walked four blocks west, toward Paradise Valley's downtown—really just one long street with some stores, a park with a bandstand, a Baptist church at one end, and a Catholic church at the other. Fact & Fiction was on my right. I hurried past, turning my head slightly so I wouldn't have to see the quaint yellow building with its white gate out front. I continued five buildings down and stood in front of Queena's store. I thought about leaving her lunch bag on the step, knocking, and running away, but it was too late—she'd already seen me through the plate glass window.

"Prepare to be glittered," I whispered to Pixie, and walked through the door.

1988

Queena kept me home for the next ten months so she could watch me constantly and make sure I was safe. I was confined to my attic like a discarded Victorian wife, forbidden to have plants in my room or to go beyond the borders of our yard without her or Bunny escorting me. I sat in front of the attic window, watching people live their lives and wondering if Tiny was at her house, just visible through the evergreens out back. I had no one to talk to. I missed writing to Nerida, but I didn't want anyone to make me go back to the hospital. It'd been awful. They'd put me in a room with just a mattress and asked me if I worshipped the devil because I'd read tarot cards, or if I was hearing messages in the music I listened to. I told them that Prince had told me to go crazy.

Now that Queena was finally out of bed, every bit of our house reminded her that Stubby was no longer there. Bunny offered to help her go through his clothes to give things away, but Queena didn't want to let anything go. When she wasn't checking on me, she spent most of her time in the bomb shelter, looking through piles of old photos.

It only got worse when Bunny showed her an article in the *Ladies' Home Journal* about making scrapbooks—she thought it might be a way for Queena to organize her photos and keep herself occupied. Next to her bomb shelter, scrapbooks became Queena's mission. She didn't stop at sticking photos in a book—she made her whole world a scrapbook. She preserved our entire house like a snapshot of how it'd been the day Stubby died. When I re-emerged from my attic house arrest, time outside our house had moved on. Time inside our house never would.

That's why my brother slept for decades on a waterbed in a room covered in Muppet wallpaper. It's why the house's only bathroom kept the brown shag rug that crept partway up the walls and up the sides of the bathtub. My mother, herself, stayed exactly as she appeared the day my father died: same hairstyle, same clothes. Her only personal concession to post-1987 material goods was underwear, and if she could've found a way to keep her 1987 underwear from wearing out, she would've.

Queena's scrapbook pages told the story of our family exactly the way she wanted—which was as much a fairy tale as those I'd read as a child. She cut pictures of Stubby out of duplicate photos and pasted him into the post-1987 photos, so it looked like he'd been there when Thom and I graduated high school or for birthdays and Christmases. Her scrapbooks let her create the world she wished was real. The universe might have screwed her over by taking Stubby from her, but Queena wouldn't let it have the final word.

Bunny moved back to Paradise Valley after I got out of the hospital, and she took over managing Fact & Fiction. She kept an eye on Queena while Queena was keeping an eye on me. She jokingly called Queena "Scrapzilla," but was relieved that Queena was out of bed, and she was pretty supportive, for Bunny. So supportive, in fact, that a few months after moving back, she told Queena she'd keep an eye on me while Queena went on an overnight road trip to New Brunswick for a scrapbooking retreat.

When she returned, Queena had a fervent zeal in her eyes, and the shaggin' wagon was crammed full of scrapbooking supplies.

"I've found my purpose." She stood in our driveway, clutching a bag of scrapbook paper to her chest, her eyes bright. "God has shown me how to use scrapbooking for a greater good."

"What now? You're saving us from nuclear annihilation through scrapbooking?" Bunny asked.

"No, Bunny. It's called faithbooking. The Lord will reveal clues through my scrapbooking, so that I can keep everyone safe and none of these tragedies will happen to us again."

"Sweet baby Jesus weeping with the angels. You're not serious?"

"Is this like the time people thought they could see Jesus's head on the bathroom wall of the Lick-A-Chick?" Thom asked. I elbowed him in the ribs.

"No. It's nothing like that." Queena spoke slowly, as though to simpletons. "I had a vision when I was driving home. It was the mother Mary, telling me my faithbooks will show us the way forward."

"Is it like Pussy's Magic 8 Ball?" Thom asked. I elbowed him again, and he shoved me back.

"It's probably not safe to have visions while you're driving," Bunny said, flicking her ashes into a rose bush.

Queena ignored her. She put her arm around my shoulders and piloted me toward the house. "A faithbook can remind us how much joy there's been in our lives. And when we see the lessons and gifts our family has received, we can find clues about what God has in store for us. So, I can find ways to keep us all safe!"

"Wait! I think I get it now!" Thom said. "When life hands you crap, scrap!"

Bunny punched his arm. "Now, Thom, you're not taking this seriously. The Virgin Mary told Queena she'll be Our Lady of Scrapbooking, which is a big step up from Miss Cunty Exhibitionist."

"Bunny! Language! People can hear you!"

Bunny crushed her cigarette butt under her heel on the front step. "The Bible's too wordy. But now, my sister will bring religion to the illiterate by revealing God's word through Polaroid snapshots of Stubby passed out under the Christmas tree. Praise Jesus! Praise Queena!"

And so, just as I'd pored over fairy tales and spell books in search of the answer to my family's curses, Queena now spent endless hours creating scrapbook layouts and staring at them with the scrutiny of a biblical scholar deciphering a newly discovered Dead Sea Scroll.

———

A few months later, Queena sat smiling at us all through dinner one Sunday night. Ed was there too, of course. We hardly noticed him, really. He was like a piece of furniture, or Thom's Emotional Support Geek.

Queena shushed us all just before dessert.

"I have an announcement. So. Donny left me a little money when he...you know."

(None of us could yet manage to say "died." It was still always "you know" or "went away," as if he was on a hockey road trip and would be home in time for supper.)

Queena mistook our silence for rapt interest and charged on. "There's an empty store just down from Fact & Fiction. It's tiny, but it's just what I need. I'm going to set up a little store of my own and sell scrapbooking supplies!"

No one said anything.

Queena beamed at us. "I'm calling it 'The Memory Garden.'"

"Sounds like a pet cemetery," Thom said, as he cut himself another piece of Deep'n Delicious cake.

Bunny scowled. "I've got my hands full running Fact & Fiction, and I thought you were going to help me out there when you're feeling up to it."

"I can do both." Queena placed her napkin across her plate and folded her hands in her lap. "I know all about running a store, and we can send customers to each other! The Memory Garden will be mine. Fact & Fiction is Donny's."

"It's Kitten's, actually."

"Yes, of course, but not until she's done school. Until then, we'll manage both."

Bunny pushed back from the table and started cleaning up. She patted me on the head as she passed behind me. "Well, Kitten, you'd better hurry up and finish school and take over your store so I can get a day off now and then."

I hadn't set foot in Fact & Fiction since Stubby died. He was in every part of that store—in the books he'd put on the shelves, the armchairs in the attic, and the taxidermized birds on the bookcases. I'd wished for it to be mine, and then Stubby died. It felt like a crime scene. I never wanted to run that store. I had to find a way to get out of it.

I stared at the calendar on the wall and tried to mentally calculate the days until I could finish school and get away from Paradise Valley, but that was one of those practical applications of math I'd never been very good at. Fuck that.

PART IV
That Which Has Passed

High School Confidential

Monday, April 24, 2000

"Pussy! Get Up! Queena wants you!"

I held the pillow over my head, but it didn't drown out Thom pounding on the door.

"Puss!"

He'd wake Pixie if he kept on like that. I dashed down the steps and pushed open the door, coming close to thumping Thom in the nose.

"Watch it! Jesus."

"Shut up, doofus. People are sleeping, you know."

"You sleep all fucking day. Anyway, Queena called. Wants you to go to The Memory Garden. Like, now. She's got some kind of message for you or something. I dunno. She sounded excited."

I caught my breath. It must be a message from Matt. Maybe he was even there, if Queena was in such a hurry for me to go to The Memory Garden. I shut the door on Thom and ran back upstairs to get dressed.

Pixie smiled up at me from the bed, her eyes sleepy and half-open. I bit my thumb, a bubble of anxiety growing in my throat. I shouldn't leave her. But I shouldn't take her with me. Not if Matt was there. It was best I see him alone. Well, he'd just have to wait. He'd been making me wait, after all.

I held Pixie against me to feed her, and then made my Care Bear dance for her to make her giggle. Her laughter gave way to yawns—she always settled in for a nap quickly in the morning. I could be back before she woke up again. I leaned over to kiss her cheek, smelling the sweet baby scent of her hair. It always calmed me. Which was good, because I didn't want to look out of control in front of Matt.

On the way out, I popped my head into the living room. "Could you turn the TV down a bit? You can't hear anything over that racket," I said to Thom.

Thom wrinkled his nose at me. He reached for the remote and turned the volume up.

"Thom!"

"Weirdo," Thom muttered, turning the volume back down.

———

I burst through the door of The Memory Garden and scanned the small store for Matt. Queena came over and, with her best beauty pageant smile, took my arm and led me over to a man standing near a display of decorative papers. It took me a second to register who it was.

It wasn't Matt. It was Rodger, the guy I messed around with at a beach party the night before Stubby died. I felt a confusing combination of disappointment and relief.

"I'll just leave you two to catch up, then." Queena winked and walked to the other side of the store. I glared at her, furious she'd trick me like this.

For the first time that week, I was aware of how I looked. Rodger had been a lifetime ago, when I was a whole different person, and I didn't care if he thought I looked like crap. But somewhere inside me, sixteen-year-old Kitty cared. I tried to pat my curls into something that didn't look like I'd just gotten out of bed, and hoped my fading rash wasn't too noticeable.

Rodger leaned in closer. "So. You're back in town, eh?

I leaned away. "Apparently."

"Yeah, I just came in to deliver some office supplies for your mother, and she told me you're back." He flashed the seductive smile that had once made my knees weak. He didn't look all that different, although the mullet was gone and the hair that had been so fluffy was starting to thin.

"Your mother says you're not married," he said, when I made no move to speak.

"She's right."

"Yeah, marriage is rough. I used to be married. You remember Tina? You guys were pretty close at one point."

"Tina? You mean Tiny?" I felt lightheaded. "Wait, you're married to Tiny?"

"Yeah. Tiny." He laughed at the name. "We *were* married. We had a kid a few years ago. Nicholas. Tina was a real bitch after he was born. Tired all the time. Never wanted to do anything. I couldn't take it anymore. So I moved on. Life's too short, you know?"

Even all these years later, hearing Tiny's name was a gut-punch. We'd never spoken again after she wrote me the letter, but I still thought about her all the time. I'd smile when I heard a song we'd liked or remembered one of our private jokes, and then I'd feel the sting of the loss of our friendship all over again. I still cared enough to bristle at Rodger's criticisms of her, but I couldn't process the idea of the two of them together.

"Anyway, maybe we can get together sometime. You know, catch up." He winked at me.

"I'm pretty busy while I'm here. Short visit. Family stuff. You know." I gave him a feeble wave and headed for the door, shooting Queena the stink eye as I walked past.

I made it two blocks before I needed to sit down. This was the most I'd walked since February, and I felt weak from the combination of activity, seeing Rodger, and hearing about Tiny. I sat on a bench outside the public library to catch my breath.

"You okay?" a woman's voice asked.

It was Angel Dempsey. I shifted to the end of the bench, gripping the seat and with one leg ready to run, in case she was going to give me the beating she'd threatened in high school.

Angel's face looked as young and perfect as it had back then. The feathered bangs were gone, replaced by a long bob. The blue eyeliner was gone too, but her blue eyes were just as piercing as I remembered. She looked like any other woman walking past, but I was sure she must still beat up girls behind the hockey rink, just for the hell of it.

She parked the stroller she was pushing and sat down at the other end of the bench.

"Kitty Love, right? I remember you." She sounded curious but not threatening, and I tried to look less terrified. "So, are you okay? I saw you walking just now, and you looked like you were going to keel over."

"I haven't been feeling great lately. Just getting over something."

Angel leaned companionably back against the bench. I leaned to peek into the stroller. "How old's the baby?"

"Six months."

Pixie was only two months.

"Is she your first?"

Angel laughed. "Oh no, she's not mine. This is my granddaughter. Her name's Hannah."

"Granddaughter?"

Angel laughed a deep, throaty laugh. "Yeah, I'm a grandmother. My daughter's fifteen. Little idiot." She turned to me and shrugged. "Apple doesn't fall far from the tree, I guess. I had to leave school when I had her and missed a year, remember?"

I shook my head. I didn't really know anything about Angel, apart from the rumours and scary stories I'd heard about her. "I missed a lot. I left school for a while, too. I graduated a year late."

She nodded. "Anyway, she's at school now, and I help her out as much as I can. I can't do it much because I have my own business to worry about."

"What do you do?" My mind flipped through the possibilities of what a grown-up Stoner might become. Maybe she was something exotic, like a stripper at the "gentlemen's club" down the coast. I wondered if you could still do that when you were a thirty-two-year-old grandmother.

"I make stained glass." I thought I saw her blush, but she turned her head and her hair fell to block her face. "I have a little studio at my house. My husband built it for me. Doesn't make me rich, but the tourists buy it."

I couldn't reconcile the idea of the tough girl I'd run from in high school with that of an artist. Unless, of course, all her stained glass featured skulls or AC/DC logos.

"What about you?" Angel asked. "What do you do?"

The baby woke with a wail before I could answer, and Angel stood to scoop her up.

"Can you hold her for a sec? I need to get her bottle." She held the baby out to me and I took the crying bundle, holding her against my shoulder and rubbing her back. She was so much bigger than Pixie. She had a similar baby soap smell, though. I closed my eyes and breathed it in.

Angel set a bottle on the bench and reached to take Hannah from me. My anxiety bubbled up. I needed to get back home to Pixie. I needed to feed her. I needed to cuddle her and keep her safe. I shouldn't have left her, even if she was sound asleep. My stomach twisted—I was a horrible mother.

With the baby quieter in her arms, Angel turned her attention back to me.

"So, how long you here for?" It sounded like a question one inmate would ask another.

"I'm not sure. It wasn't really planned. Spur of the moment vacation kind of thing."

She looked at me sceptically. "Why don't you come by for drinks tonight. I make a mean margarita. You look like you could use one."

I sat up straighter, ready to leave. "Maybe another time."

"Should I threaten to beat you up if you don't come?"

I looked over to see if she was kidding. If she decided to pummel me now, I was too tired to run.

She put Hannah over her shoulder to burp her. "I've always felt like shit about that day outside the library. You know what I'm talking about. After you ran into me? I got that letter from Tiny in with my stuff. And the letter you wrote to your aunt, too. I read them, but I didn't show them to anyone. Honest."

"Why not? I'm sure the other Stoners would've loved it."

Angel rubbed Hannah's back and rubbed her cheek against the baby's head. "When I came back after having a baby, people talked about me. Even my friends. Your letters sounded like you were in a bad place. I guess I knew how it felt."

"I guess I just assumed you'd show it to everyone, because you were..."

"An asshole? Yeah, I was an asshole. But people change, right? Or maybe you're the same person you were in high school?"

"God no." I pulled my shirt sleeves over my hands and sat on them to keep them still.

"You know, when I broke up with my ex, I went to a therapist because I felt pretty shitty. And you know what she told me to do?"

Hannah pushed her bottle away and babbled. The sound made me woozy. I really needed to get home to Pixie.

"She told me to write in a journal every day about what was going on and how I felt. It felt dumb just writing to myself though. Then I remembered you writing to your aunt, so I started addressing mine to Céline Dion."

I relaxed enough to laugh. "What the hell? Why Céline?"

"It was a bad divorce, and I figured Céline could relate to over-the-top drama, you know? Maybe I should try it again. Maybe you should too."

"I don't think Céline's really my thing."

Angel stood to tuck Hannah into the stroller. "So, are you coming over tonight? Or do you have a hot date? Is your husband with you?"

"I'm not married. My boyfriend's in BC."

"Then I think you're just scared of me. I promise, I haven't beat anyone up in a really long time." She reached under the stroller and pulled a brochure out of the diaper bag. "There you go, then. That's my studio, but the address is the same as my house. Come any time after eight. The drinks will be waiting."

I watched as she walked away, already wondering how I could get out of this. What if Matt called while I was out? But if I didn't go, maybe Angel would show up at Queena's and beat me up. I chewed my thumb, remembering how terrifying she'd been in high school.

Rodger walked past, touching my shoulder before moving on. "See you 'round, Pussy," he said, too loudly. Some girls walking nearby started to giggle.

I'd go for drinks. If I became friends with a Stoner, she could protect me from Rodger and other Paradise Valley horrors. Besides, Angel seemed to have turned her life around. Maybe she could tell me how to do it.

Ladies Night

I didn't know what to wear for drinks with a Stoner. Angel had been more pulled together than I'd been that day, but I still pictured her in her boyfriend's hockey jacket with a studded black collar around her neck. My closet was filled with lots of lacey black shirts and dresses from my Love Witch era, and a couple pairs of acid-washed jeans. I tried on a oversized thrifted jacket, but the shoulder pads I'd sewn in made me look like David Byrne. I settled on a loose black turtleneck sweater and a long black ribbed skirt and turned to look at myself in the full-length mirror. I was basically Ally Sheedy's character in *The Breakfast Club*.

Pixie was tucked up in her bed, asleep for the night. After leaving her that morning, I was torn about leaving again. I made sure she was fed and happy, and I cuddled her well after she'd fallen asleep before I worked up my resolve to set her in her bed. Nothing bad could happen to her here. Everyone was home, and Bunny's room was directly below the attic if there was a problem. Still, I didn't like being away from her. I bent over to give her a kiss, but the tarot cards on the floor behind her stopped me in my tracks.

A new card was on top of the three that had been there earlier. This one was The Tower, with its image of a stone tower being struck by lightning and pummelled by waves, while people either fell or jumped from the top. It was placed in the position of the recent past, and meant collapse of an old way of life, crisis, a moment of truth, hospitalization, separation. That did sum up my recent past, but I had no clue how the card had gotten there. I hadn't been near the cards all day, and the rest of the deck was still in a neat pile. I couldn't have done it and forgotten about it, unless I was reading tarot cards in my sleep.

I stood up and wound my hair around my fingers, my heartbeat pulsing against my temples, and wondered what was worse: the fact that Nerida's tarot cards might be moving of their own accord, or that I might be seeing things that weren't real. I grabbed my bag and ran down the stairs, hoping Angel's margaritas would clear my mind.

I hesitated in front of a tidy white house with perennial gardens lining the walk and a large piece of beautiful stained glass hanging in the front window. I double-checked the address before I rang the doorbell.

The door was opened by a friendly looking man of about forty, wearing a golf shirt and khakis.

"Hello there! You must be Kitty." He held out his hand for me to shake.

"Yeah. Yes. Kit. Kitten."

"I'm Terry, Angel's husband. Come on in, the girls are just out back."

Girls. Oh God, she'd invited the whole gang of Stoners. It was an ambush.

Terry pushed open the French doors to the deck. "Angel, Kitty is here!"

The conversation stopped, and two women with drinks in their hands stared at me.

One was Angel.

The other was Tiny.

The enormous bangs were gone, and her blond hair was cut in a Jennifer Aniston shag, but her brown eyes were the same ones I'd always known. I felt a rush of happiness that was crushed seconds later under a pile of hurt and anger, and I took a step backwards.

"Hey Kitty. Glad you came." Angel's expression gave nothing away. "You remember Tiny?"

Tiny set her drink on the table, her hand unsteady, and looked at Angel without acknowledging me. "You didn't tell me she was coming."

I took another step back. "I didn't know you'd be here. I'll go."

Angel put her drink down and looked from Tiny to me. "Come on. High school's over. Sit down, Kitty." She gave me the same menacing look she had the day I'd run into her in the hall. Maybe this was how grown-up Stoners tortured people—by putting them in socially awkward situations.

I sat on the edge of the chair across from Tiny, ready to escape. "I didn't know you two were friends."

"Tiny and I started talking at one of your mother's scrapbooking workshops a few years ago and we hit it off."

"She sat next to me and I was scared shitless she'd beat me up," Tiny said. "She asked me over for drinks, and I thought she might be recruiting new members for her gang."

"It's a very small gang now. Just Tiny and me. So, okay you two, let's just get this out in the open. I read the letters. Tiny, I know what you said to Kitty, and I know about Kitty writing to her dead aunt and talking to owls. Okay? You guys were really good friends before that. It's time to move on."

"What the hell, Angel. Are you Judge Judy now? You can't decide when it's time to move on," Tiny said.

I took a cocktail napkin off the table and twisted it in my lap. "I'm not sure I want to move on, anyway. I mean, you were always the one telling me to make my own decisions and to stop doing everything my mother wanted me to do. And then your mother tells you not to talk to me anymore, and you just do what she says."

Tiny let out a deep breath and leaned forward, staring me straight in the eyes and crossing her fingers, the way she used to when she wanted me to know she was telling the truth.

"My mother spent a whole night questioning me about whether we were witches. She thought I was worshipping the devil and went through all my tapes and threw out anything she thought might be sending me 'satanic' messages. She threatened not to let me go to university. She said she'd send me to a nunnery. She said if I promised not to be friends with you anymore, she'd reconsider." Tiny tucked her hair behind her ear. It was weird to see her without the enormous, teased bangs. "She found the money we'd made from tarot readings, too. She thought I must be selling drugs or something, and when I told her where it came from, she called me a 'magical whore' and took it all."

Terry reappeared with a pitcher of drinks and a huge bowl of chips, and topped off all our glasses while we sat in a tense silence. I took a long drink while we waited for Terry to close the door behind him.

"So, did she get over it?" I asked.

"She didn't send me to a nunnery. But she wouldn't give me the money back, and she wouldn't help me pay for school, so I ended up staying in Paradise Valley. I think that was her plan all along. She thought if I went away to school I'd do too much sinning."

Angel laughed. "As if we're so pure in Paradise Valley."

"That's how I ended up with Rodger. My mother wouldn't let me live on my own, so marrying him was a way out, I guess. It was just an exit to another pile of shit, though."

I sat back in my chair, pushing my shoulders down from around my ears. "Rodger was never your type."

Tiny tipped her glass from side to side so that the drink came dangerously close to spilling on her white jeans. "And also...well, my aunt used to volunteer with the library cart at the hospital in Elgin, and she told my mother that she saw you there, wearing a johnny shirt, in the psych ward. And then you dropped out of school and no one saw you for ages, and you know how people talk. My mother said she was glad we weren't friends because you were 'unhinged.'"

"Unhinged."

"Those were her words, not mine."

I ran a lime wedge around the rim of my glass and dipped it in the little dish of margarita salt before I poured myself another drink. Witches use circles of salt to protect themselves and to keep unwanted energy out. Maybe if I kept drinking these salt-rimmed margaritas, they'd protect me from imagining my tarot cards were moving. Maybe they'd drive all the bad stuff away from me.

Tiny reached across the table for my hand. "I'm really sorry."

"Me too." It was all I could manage to say, but I felt it to my core. I had to hold my breath for a minute as joy and regret and love cracked open something inside of me. There was too much to say, but I couldn't say any of it.

Angel shifted in her chair to face me.

"So, Kitty. Let's hear your shit. Why are you back in town, anyway?"

"You look kind of crappy," Tiny said. "No offense. Are you sick?"

"No. Sort of. I was a few months ago, I guess."

Angel wrapped her sweater around her as the fogbank moved in for the evening. "You said you had a boyfriend in BC."

"Yeah. We've been living together almost six years."

"And you said this was a spur-of-the-moment trip. Did you break up?"

I laughed as if the idea was absurd. "Why would you think that? He's just super busy and couldn't take the time off to come here."

"You haven't been home in years. I know, because your mother tells me every time I go into The Memory Garden. And then you show up looking like you're sick or you've been through something."

Tiny leaned forward and sniffed at me. "What are you wearing, anyway? You smell like high school. How is that even possible?"

"It was in my closet." I picked at fuzz on the sleeve of my sweater and watched the breeze carry off the little pieces of black lint as I dropped them.

"So...?" Angel prompted.

I could make something up. They'd never know the difference. But the margaritas had ripped off my filter.

"I left him," I heard myself blurt. "We had a big fight and I think we're over. I didn't know where else to go, so I came back here."

"Shit. That sucks." Angel pushed the bowl of chips toward me. "Is it for good?"

"I don't know. I didn't really think it through. I left everything there, so I guess I have to go back at some point."

"What's he like?" Tiny asked. "Is he worth going back to?"

I dug through my bag for a photo I kept in my wallet—Matt and me on a beach in Costa Rica. That trip had been such fun. We'd dived into waterfalls and hiked in the jungle, and a couple of times we'd just stayed in bed together all day. It'd been wonderful, until it wasn't.

I pushed the photo across the table to Tiny.

"Oh wow. He's hot," she said. "He looks just like that poster of Sting you used to have over your bed."

Angel leaned over to take a look and raised an eyebrow. "I'd go back, if I were you."

Tiny pushed the photo toward me. "Maybe she doesn't want to go back. Maybe he's a dick." She glanced at the photo again. "Is he a dick?"

I frowned, trying to grasp solid thoughts through my margarita-haze. Was he a dick? I felt like maybe I was the dick. What exactly had happened? Why was I here? I was stabbed by a sudden longing for Pixie. I should get back to her. I couldn't explain all this, anyway. I couldn't ever talk about any of this.

"You need to get your mind off him," Angel suggested. "You know, rebound a little. Although you're not going to find much better than that around here, that's for damn sure."

"Speaking of which, I see Ed's car at your house all the time," Tiny noted. "Isn't he a prof or something now?"

I drained my glass and reached for the pitcher. "Yeah. Something sciencey." My words came out slurred, like "schlilenshy."

"He's not as geeky as he used to be," Tiny said. "I saw him at Zellers last week and I thought, you know, he's filled out. He looks smart or something. A bit moody. Maybe we underrated him. You know, like Keanu Reeves."

"Ew. But then, you thought Thom was hot once, too."

"How is Thom, anyway? I know he's back, but no one ever sees him."

I stood up to shake the chip crumbs off my sweater. "Kim left him last year, so he just watches *Oprah* and eats Cheezies and waits for the Love Heart to kill him."

"Your family's kind of messed up," Angel said.

"Yeah."

Tiny took a handful of chips and tucked her legs under her. "So, tell us about this guy. Maybe we can help you figure out what to do."

"I doubt it."

"C'mon. How'd you meet?"

"You really want to hear?"

Angel got up and opened the French door. "Honey, could you bring us some blankets? It's getting chilly out here but we're just getting to the good stuff."

She and Tiny settled in to listen. I took a deep breath and a big gulp of margarita and went back to the beginning.

Here Comes Your Man

January 1994

I woke up in a strange room and had no idea where I was or how I'd gotten there. My hair smelled of cigarette smoke. My head throbbed, and there was an aftertaste of beer in my mouth. Daylight poured through a large window and burned my eyes, so I buried my face in the sheets. These weren't my sheets, though. They felt softer.

This wasn't the apartment I shared with Thom and his girlfriend. It wasn't my friend Tammy's place where I sometimes stayed after a night downtown. God knows, it wasn't outdated or bleached enough to be Queena's house.

I stretched one leg out across the bed and rolled over. There was a man sleeping next to me. A very good-looking man, with blond hair flopped over his eyes. A very good-looking man who was (I remembered now) naked.

And so was I.

I nestled back into the pillow, smiling at the memory of the night before. His eyes fluttered as he woke, smiling slowly at me.

"Morning," he said.

"Good morning."

His eyes traced a line from my collarbone down my body.

"I'm going to get some water. Do you want anything?"

I didn't want anything, at all. For the first time ever, I felt like I had everything.

I answered by reaching under the sheets to pull him to me again.

The Night Before

Thom cut me a piece of the devil's food birthday cake he'd made, and we sat down at the little chrome kitchen table. We still had a cake for Stubby every year, because it seemed weird not to acknowledge the day.

It would've been Stubby's forty-eighth birthday—the year few Love men made it past. I didn't point that part out to Thom, though. He worried about the Love Heart enough as it was.

There weren't many days when I didn't think about Stubby, but that morning, I'd woken with a sense that he was near, somehow—like if I moved my head suddenly, I might catch him in my periphery. I'd felt jittery all day.

"Do you ever wonder if Stubby can see us? You know, if he can watch us, and if he's proud of us?" I asked.

Thom licked icing off his fork. "Nah. How the hell could he see us? Like a ghost? You into that witch stuff again?"

"No. I just wondered what he'd think of us, or what he'd say to us."

"He'd tell you to get off your lazy ass because it's your turn to clean the apartment."

"Shut up."

"You shut up."

I'd been sharing an apartment with Thom and Kim since the summer before, when I moved to Halifax for school.

When we'd graduated high school, Queena refused to let Thom and I both out of her sight at the same time, so Thom went off to the culinary institute in Prince Edward Island, and I waitressed at a hotel in Elgin for two years and took a few classes at the university there. It took another year of cajoling to convince Queena to let me move to Halifax for university. In the end, she only allowed it if I moved in with Thom, who was working as a sous chef there. We had to call Queena four times a week and go home at least two weekends each month.

I put my plate in the sink and looked around for my keys. "I'll probably stay at Tammy's tonight. Have you seen my keys?"

"If you'd clean the apartment, you might find them."

"Shut up."

"You shut up."

As I went through my closet, checking each pocket for my keys, I knocked over an old shoebox, and a collection of junk and mementos spilled out. The Magic 8 Ball that Thom gave me years earlier rolled across the floor and under the bed. I fished it out and sat with it on the floor, rolling it from one hand to the other. I started to give the ball a gentle shake and closed my eyes.

"Are my keys in this room?"

As I see it, yes.

My eyes rested on a framed photo of Stubby and I at the beach, the first summer I was allowed to go there. I started to shake the ball again.

"Is my father here, too?"

It is certain.

"Prove it," I whispered.

And that was the night I met Matt.

———

I first saw him at the Seahorse, playing pool with his friends, back at the beginning of January. I was sure I knew him from somewhere. He was tall and blond, with dimples that left deep laugh lines even when he wasn't smiling, and an endearingly boyish habit of pushing a floppy bit of hair off his face. After watching him from across the room for an evening, I realized why he looked familiar—he looked an awful lot like the picture of Robin Hood I'd fallen in love with when I was a little girl. Back then, I'd sent an intention into the universe that one day I would meet this Robin Hood, and here he was—except hotter, and without the tights.

For once in my life, without Queena or tarot cards telling me what to do, I knew exactly what I wanted. Unfortunately, getting what I wanted required a kind of magic I hadn't practised since my night with Rodger at a beach party.

———

Late on this cold winter night, downtown Halifax smelled like beer, donairs, and bad decisions. Tammy, Lisa, and I walked down the stairs to the Seahorse and were hit with a blast of cigarette smoke and Sloan's "Underwhelmed" coming from the sound system. My eyes adjusted to the dim light and scanned the bar, even as I told myself he wouldn't be there.

He was there.

Tammy followed my gaze. "You go get some drinks. Lisa and I will find a place to sit."

Tammy played guard for Dalhousie's basketball team—she loomed over most people, and I could usually see her long black ponytail from anywhere in the room. And Lisa—well, you couldn't miss Lisa. She was stunning. She had long, wavy blond hair, she surfed, and she had the nerve to look good hungover. She attracted men like mosquitoes to a bug light. Despite how noticeable my friends were, I couldn't find them when I turned away from the bar with our drinks. I finally spotted them by the pool table, waving at me from the wall right behind my Robin Hood. Lisa was already chatting up one of his friends. She came over to get her beer, whispering in my ear as she stood next to me.

"He's twenty-eight. Med student. Just finishing his residency. From BC. Going back there in June."

"You got all that while I was getting beer?"

Lisa flashed her dazzling smile. "It's not rocket science, Kit."

As he turned to walk to the other side of the pool table, my Robin Hood's eyes met mine and he smiled. I smiled back, imagining that I looked as awkward as I had in my Grade 7 school photos.

And then he was next to me, holding out his cue.

"Are you waiting for the table? We're just leaving."

"Oh, no, I don't—"

Tammy stomped on my Doc Marten. "Thanks! Maybe you could stay and have a game with us?" She took the cue and shoved it at me.

He looked from her to me, and then at his friends.

"Yeah? Well, yeah, sure. If it's okay?" He glanced at me. I smiled again, hoping I looked like Maid Marian and not seventh-grade Kitty.

He went to tell his friends. I grabbed Tammy's arm.

"I don't even know how to play pool!"

"Do you want to talk to him or not?"

"Yeah, but—"

"Then you're going to learn to play pool. Just do what I do."

I was still holding the pool cue in front of me like it was Excalibur when he walked back over.

"I'm Matt, by the way. Matt Gordon." He leaned in close so I could hear him over the music. God, he smelled good. A comfortable, earthy scent like warm cedar and sweet apples that made me imagine us in front of a warm fire on a cool night.

"I'm Kit. Kit Love."

"Are we playing?" Tammy asked, expertly making the break shot.

I took the cue and leaned over the table, twisting my hair with one hand to keep it out of the way, and tried to do what I'd seen people do in movies. I was supposed to do something with my hand on the table, I thought, but I couldn't remember what. I bit my lip and aimed, although I didn't even know which ball I was trying to hit. The tip of the cue dug into the felt.

Tammy and Lisa looked like they wanted to laugh, but they smiled encouragement.

Matt stepped in beside me. "Here, let me help."

He leaned in next to me, almost behind me, with one hand covering mine on the table, and the other on my back. His hand rested just a bit above the gap between my black mock-turtleneck baby tee and the top of my jeans. I was convinced that not only he, but the entire bar, could hear my heart racing. My skin tingled. I knew my stupid face must be flaming red, and my throat was dry. I wished I could reach for my beer, but I didn't want to move.

"Which one am I aiming for?" My voice sounded too loud in my head. I started to straighten up, but as he was leaning into me, our bodies pressed even closer together.

"This one over here. Like this."

He slid his hand up my arm to show me how I should aim the cue. My arm wobbled. His left hand held mine, and I drew my right arm back and hit a ball into a pocket.

"I did it!" I exclaimed, standing back up.

"Good shot."

"I don't actually play pool," I admitted.

He laughed. "Really? You did great for your first time."

"I had a good teacher."

"Another beer?"

Lisa and Tammy exchanged a look. "I think we're ready to head out," Lisa said.

I picked at the label on my empty beer bottle. Tammy and Lisa never wanted to go home early, but they were already putting on their coats.

"You don't have to come with us," Lisa said.

Matt leaned close to my ear. "Do you want to go for a walk?"

I hoped my relief wasn't too obvious. Tammy winked at me. She and Lisa were already walking away, blowing me kisses as they headed up the stairs.

In Your Eyes

t was quiet at this time of night, except for the occasional blast of Rawlins Cross from the Lower Deck as groups of drunks stumbled outside, singing. We walked in the opposite direction, toward the light on Georges Island, while we asked each other awkward getting-to-know-you questions. He told me his father and grandfather had been doctors, too.

"It's like our family business," he said.

"We sort of have one too, I guess. We have a bookstore," I said. "Well, it's mine, actually. My aunt's running it right now."

"Wait, you own a bookstore? At age, what, twenty-...?"

"Twenty-four. It was my dad's. He died when I was sixteen, and he left the store to me." I turned my face away to look up at the moon disappearing behind some clouds.

Matt stopped walking and faced me. "I'm so sorry."

"It's okay."

I felt a pressure rising in my throat. I concentrated on keeping it down, but it threatened to escape as a sob. I took a deep, slow breath and gulped hard.

Matt squeezed my hand. "So, what kind of books do you sell?"

"Antiquarian and used books. Some rare editions. There's a whole room that's floor-to-ceiling Penguins. And another that's basically smutty paperbacks, so we can pay our bills. That was my brother's favourite."

"Not yours?"

I smiled. "Mine was the legends and fairy tales. I spent a lot of time reading about magic, too. I thought I was a witch, for a while."

"A witch? You mean, like hocus-pocus stuff, with spells?"

"It was a long time ago." My words were sharp and poked a hole in any intimacy that had started to grow between us. We walked in silence for a minute before Matt spoke again.

"Well, the store sounds great. I'd love to see it someday."

I took a deep breath before answering, so that my voice wouldn't shake. "It's great, but...it reminds me of my father, so I...hate it."

The bubble in my throat burst, and tears began to fall.

"I'm so sorry! It's just, today is his birthday. Would've been. Sometimes the feelings just sneak up on me." I laughed awkwardly and fanned my face with my hand to try to distract from the fact I was falling apart twenty minutes into our first conversation.

Matt led me over to a bench and sat close to me, not letting go of my hand.

"What was he like?"

No one had ever asked me that. Everyone in Paradise Valley knew what Stubby was like. And outside of Paradise Valley, no one asked, because I shut down any conversation about him. But Matt was looking at me with genuine interest, waiting for me to talk.

"He was...I don't know..."

"What's your favourite memory of him?"

I stared at the psychiatric hospital across the harbour as I tried to crack open the door to my memories, just a little, without letting them all rush in and bowl me over.

"He always ordered the weirdest item on a menu. He'd get fried clams at a gas station because he said he had a sense of adventure." I laughed, thinking of that time he'd eaten a shrimp cocktail from a truck stop on one of our family trips. We thought for sure he'd get food poisoning but he had a stomach of steel. "But my favourite memories are of him at the bookstore. He was so good at suggesting books for people—it was like he knew what someone should read at any point in their life."

I pictured Stubby behind the counter, his eyes twinkling at me as he handed me a book he thought I'd like, or a bag of donuts. Even when he'd caught me doing something I shouldn't, I knew everything would be okay when I saw that twinkle in his eye.

Matt squeezed my hand again, and I lifted my eyes to his.

His eyes twinkled at me, just like Stubby's used to. My breath left my body. I was sure it was a sign.

A foghorn sounded in the distance and I jumped, my lungs functioning once more. Matt pulled me to my feet, unaware that some cosmic force was dancing around us.

"Do you feel better?" He pulled my coat collar higher around my neck.

I nodded. "I'm usually much more entertaining, I swear. Well, no, maybe I'm not." I laughed. I wondered if I was becoming hysterical.

"Meeting a real-life witch with her own bookstore is pretty entertaining." He took my hand again. "Do you want to walk up to Pizza Corner? Maybe get a donair?"

I nodded, and we turned to walk in silence back up toward Salter Street. Up by the Maritime Museum of the Atlantic, a busker played Blue Rodeo's "Lost Together" on guitar and sang while a girl accompanied on fiddle. Matt threw a loonie into the guy's guitar case and pulled me close. The guy was hideously off-key, but it was the most beautiful thing I'd ever heard. I relaxed against Matt, tingling with happiness.

Matt lifted my chin to look in his eyes. I was about to apologize again for saying so much, but he brushed my hair back gently and kissed me. I lost myself in that kiss. I was vaguely aware of people walking by, of loud, drunken bursts of conversation and the spray of slush against my legs from passing taxis. None of that mattered. The world was perfect. This moment was perfect.

The cops were breaking up a fight near Pizza Corner, so we skirted around the crowd and up to the library on Spring Garden Road. It was quieter there, and by the time we slowed to a stop by the statue of Winston Churchill, it had started to snow.

"It's getting late." Matt looked over my head to Spring Garden Road. I was sure he was getting ready to say goodbye, and I tried to arrange my face to hide my disappointment and the anger I felt at myself for crying and ruining my chances with him.

Winston Churchill sported a little hat of snow, and I stared at him for inspiration as I searched for something to say that'd make it sound like it was no big deal. The only quote of his I could remember was *Fear is a reaction. Courage is a decision.*

Matt shoved his hands into his pockets and shivered. "I live just up Spring Garden a bit. We could go there so you can get warmed up. I can drive you home later, if you want."

He took my hand, and I smiled my answer. I wondered if I should call Tammy and tell her what I was doing. She and Lisa and I had a system worked out to phone and let each other know we were safe. I couldn't remember what I was supposed to do, though, because I'd never had to use it.

When we got to Matt's sixteenth-floor condo in a building across from the Public Gardens, I excused myself and slipped into the bathroom. My reflection in the mirror showed cheeks that were a hectic pink from cold and excitement, and hair that had grown like a Chia Pet in the damp wind. I gave myself a pep talk as I tried to smooth it down.

"Don't mess this up. Don't look desperate. Try to act older. Stop talking about witchcraft. For the love of God, do not tell him Stubby's ghost sent him. Don't scare him away. Don't get scared away. Think of Winston: *Courage!*

I tossed my hair back, adjusted my boobs, and walked out to the living room. Matt was shuffling through a pile of CDs and cassettes next to his stereo.

"What kind of music do you like?"

"Anything, really," I lied. I picked through the cassettes he'd moved to the side. They were mixtapes. I peered at the covers, trying to decipher his handwriting. "Did you make these?"

"Yeah, I needed eight days' worth of mixtapes for the drive from BC."

I smiled and started to relax, pushing his CDs aside to make a pile of the mixtapes I liked. "I have milk cartons of them back at home."

"Romantic songs from your admirers, I bet."

I blushed. "No. My friend made most of them. I never got one from a guy." A little dart of pain pierced my joy as I thought of Tiny. It still hurt.

"Maybe I'll make you one sometime." His eyes twinkled at me, and his dimples stirred butterflies inside of me.

"I'd like that."

"It's a deal, then."

I pushed a mixtape toward him. He reached for it, his hand touching mine and lingering there, just for a second, before he opened the cassette case and turned on the stereo.

I went over to the small leather sofa, tucked my legs under me, and waited for Matt to join me. The radio came on when he switched the stereo receiver, and my stomach dropped. It was "Livin' on a Prayer" by Bon Jovi—the song that'd been on the radio when Stubby died. I swallowed back nausea and fought to push the images of that day out of my head.

Then Matt pressed play, and the room filled with the hiss of an often-played tape before the first notes of Peter Gabriel's "In Your Eyes" drifted out. I exhaled.

Matt sat down next to me and leaned an arm on the back of the sofa. "Is everything okay? You look sad again."

I kept my eyes down and picked at the frayed threads around a rip in my jeans. "To be honest, I'm just really embarrassed about getting so upset and telling you all that stuff. I'm sure the other girls you bring here don't cry or talk about books and they know how to play pool already. Not that you bring them here to play pool." I glanced around as though expecting to see a pool table I'd overlooked before. My face was burning, and I wished there was a trap door in the sofa I could fall through.

Matt reached over to touch my flushed cheek. "I'm glad you told me. And really, it's not like I bring a lot of girls here."

"Ha. I bet you say that to all the girls you bring here. Women," I corrected myself.

He shook his head. His dimples deepened, but his eyes weren't smiling. "No, really. I broke up with someone before I moved out here. Well, she broke up with me. And after that I didn't want to meet anyone for a long time. Sometimes I think I forgot how to talk or something."

"I know what that's like. The awkward part, not the broken heart part. Not that you're awkward. You aren't. I am, obviously."

"You've never had your heart broken?"

"I've never let anyone close enough to break my heart." I really didn't want to explain my years of social isolation, stuck in Queena's attic, so I rushed to shift the questioning away from me. "So, who broke yours?"

Matt's eyes stopped twinkling, and I cursed myself for saying the wrong thing. Again.

"I'm sorry. It's none of my business."

"It's okay. We were together a few years, and I was coming here for my residency, and she was going to come for graduate school. And then she told me she'd changed her mind. She'd reconnected with an old boyfriend, and she'd decided to stay with him. I came out here anyway. I couldn't wait to get away, really."

"I'm sorry. I really know how to kill the mood, don't I?"

"Look, I've already made you cry tonight. We're off to a great start." He reached over to play with my hair. "I've seen you at the Seahorse before, and I thought you were beautiful. But when we talked tonight... anyone who feels things so deeply is someone I want to get to know."

"You're beautiful, too." I laughed at my own awkwardness. I was so glad Tammy and Lisa couldn't hear me.

His hand travelled down from my cheek to trace my collarbone. "If you want me to drive you home, I will. I guess it was kind of a rough day for you, so maybe you just want to call it a night?"

"Do you want me to go home?"

"No. No, Kit Love, I really want you to stay." He ran his thumb along my lip, and my heart thumped in my throat. I wished I could call Tammy and ask her what to do. Even Bunny. But I knew what they'd say. They'd tell me to do what I wanted. And for once, I knew.

Courage is a decision. Churchill was a dick, but turns out he gave decent love advice.

"I want to stay," I whispered. He kissed me, and I melted into him. Soon, we were a tangle of limbs and discarded pieces of clothing, and we'd made our way to his bedroom.

I hesitated as he pulled me onto the bed with him. "Matt—I've never actually...done this before."

He pulled back slightly. "We don't have to. We can stop."

"I don't want to stop. I just wanted you to know that I might be as bad at this as I was at pool."

He laughed and started kissing his way down my body. Thank God, I finally had a practical use for everything I'd learned in the Smutty Paperback room.

Eternal Flame

Saturday, April 23, 1994

Thom and Kim wanted a spring wedding, which would be lovely if they were having it anywhere but Nova Scotia. Spring in other places is about daffodils and baby birds and warm afternoons. Spring in Nova Scotia is impatience and dirty snow and thawing dog poop. You might get a few warm days. You might also get a snowstorm and weeks of slush and rain. I thought it was extraordinarily optimistic for Thom and Kim to plan a wedding in April, not knowing what they'd end up with.

"Well, marriage is all about being extraordinarily optimistic when you don't know what you'll end up with, isn't it?" Bunny pointed out.

I used my upcoming exams as an excuse to avoid spending more than a weekend in Paradise Valley. I'd also managed to avoid telling anyone that I was bringing Matt as my date. In fact, I'd managed to avoid telling my family about Matt altogether.

Thom's wedding meant the end of my freedom. He'd gotten a job at a resort in Elgin, and he and Kim were moving there when they got back from their honeymoon. I'd be out of a place to live. Tammy wanted me to move in with her, but Queena wouldn't hear of it. She insisted I move back to Paradise Valley. Without her help to pay for school and living expenses, I had no choice but to move back home.

"You can take some classes at the university in Elgin, love. Then I'll have you both back where I can keep an eye on you." She had the same flushed, eager look she'd get on Christmas morning.

Of course, Queena didn't know I had a bigger reason for wanting to stay in Halifax: Matt. Everything had changed for me since that night in January. Like when Dorothy arrived in Oz, everything inside and out turned to thrilling and dazzling technicolour. I was completely in love and had never felt so happy, but I hadn't shared that happiness with Queena. She'd see Matt as a threat—an intruder who might keep me away from Paradise Valley and life under her thumb.

Matt and I had our first real disagreement over Thom's wedding. He assumed he'd be coming with me, as my date. He was eager to meet my family, visit the bookstore, and see where I'd grown up, but I didn't want him around any of that. He loved me for the person I was in Halifax. If he experienced Queena's time-capsule decor, the bomb shelter, and Paradise Valley's stink, he might change his mind about me.

I was too nervous to tell him I didn't want him there until a week before the wedding, over Sunday breakfast at our favourite diner.

"I don't understand. What's wrong? Why don't you want me there?" Matt pushed his cup away, sloshing coffee onto the paper placemat. Queena would hate that. And she'd hate that he didn't drink tea.

I tried to keep my voice light, but I couldn't meet his eyes. "I want you to meet them," I lied. I watched the diner door, hoping someone I knew would come in and interrupt us. "I just don't think it's the right time. Everyone will be so busy and stressed out. You know how weddings are. Maybe some other time."

I finally raised my eyes to Matt's face. He was studying mine, his eyes confused and hurt.

"There's something you're not telling me. You're hiding something."

I reached for his hand. "I'd never hide something from you."

Matt moved his hand away and reached for the bill, sliding out of the booth without waiting for me.

Later, I sobbed on my bed until Tammy told me I had a choice: I could go to Thom's wedding alone, hurt Matt, and have Queena cluck about my lack of a boyfriend, or I could take him and smooth things over, and listen to Queena crow about my handsome, successful boyfriend.

"If you show up with Matt, you'd probably steal all the attention from Thom," Tammy added.

The promise of annoying Thom sealed the deal.

I didn't tell my family he was coming until the morning of the wedding, hoping Queena would be too busy to interrogate me.

I was wrong. Wedding preparations came to a screeching halt as she grabbed some tea cups and sat down at the kitchen table. Her face was glowing.

"Is he a real doctor? Or is he one of those phoney ones who call themselves doctors but only know history?"

"He's a medical doctor."

She nodded in approval. "That's useful, isn't it? Does he know anything about hearts?"

"Well yeah, I guess. But no—he's not going to fix the Love Heart, Queena. Geesh."

"He must be a fair bit older than you, if he's a doctor," Bunny mused.

"He's twenty-eight."

Queena's eyebrows shot up. "Twenty-eight! Oh my. He's likely been around, Kitten. He might expect things."

Bunny rolled her eyes behind Queena's back.

"So, where's he from?" Queena continued. "What did you say his last name is? Gordon? I don't know any Gordons. Who are his people?"

"He's not from around here." I ran a spoon around the edges of my tea, collecting bubbles. "He's from BC."

Queena leaned in close. Thom burst through the front door, saving me. Bunny had sent him out to occupy himself with tying teal and pink streamers to the shaggin' wagon, so that he and Queena wouldn't feed off each other's nerves.

"That boyfriend thing of yours is here," he yelled in my direction. "Driving some goddamn yuppie car."

"Thom! Language!" Queena warned.

"Could everyone just try to act like a normal family, please?" I begged.

Bunny tucked her pack of cigarettes into her robe pocket and laughed. "We've got no experience with that, my darling girl." She butted Queena out of the way to be first out the front door to ambush Matt.

I felt the eyes of Paradise Valley boring into the back of my head at the wedding. I saw the heads leaning together to share whispers about who I was with. As soon as Matt and I arrived at the Legion for the reception, the questioning began. Freda Landry's severe helmet of hair cut through the guests like a shark's fin before the rest of her appeared in front of us, ready to pounce.

"Kitten! Don't you look nice! And who is your friend?"

I faked a smile and pulled up one of the spaghetti straps of my short black slip dress. "Freda, this is my boyfriend, Matt Gordon."

"Gordon, is it? Any relation to the Gordons in Pictou?"

"No, I'm afraid not. I'm from BC."

Freda made a face as though she'd smelled something bad. "Oh dear. Well. What is it you do, Matt?"

"I'm a doctor."

Freda's eyes widened. "Oh! That's good, Kitten, hey? This place is desperate for more doctors. When are you setting up shop?"

I stared at my feet as Matt answered. "Actually, I'm headed back to BC in a few months."

Freda stuck out her lower lip and looked at me with fake sympathy. "Oh no. Well, don't despair, Kitten. I'm sure the local boys will be delighted to have their Pussy home." I cringed, and Matt shot me an incredulous look.

Freda tugged at her waistband and looked over at Thom and Kim. "What a shame your father isn't here to see this, Kitten. Kim's a brave woman, to take on someone with the Love Heart. Hope it works out better for her than it did for your mother." She smirked and slipped back into the crowd before I could respond.

Matt leaned forward and whispered, "Can I call you Pussy?"

"Don't you friggin' dare."

I looked over at Freda, who was filling in a group of women about my love life. They all glanced over, looking approvingly at Matt and looking sorry for me.

"Want something from the bar?" Matt asked.

Bunny appeared at my elbow. Bunny always seemed to know when someone was getting drinks. "Yes! Gin! Gin all around! There's a good boy," she said, shooing Matt toward the bar.

Mrs. Fraser came towards us and wrapped me in a hug.

"How are you, Kitten? You look so lovely." She pulled back and gave Bunny an awkward smile. "Bunny. Hello."

"Hello, Eileen." Bunny turned her head to see if Matt was coming with the drinks. She'd had a lot to drink already, but Bunny didn't go out much, so I figured she was calming her nerves or something.

Mrs. Fraser gave my arm a squeeze. "I'm so glad to see you looking so happy, Kitten. Take good care. Bye, Bunny."

Matt returned with the drinks just as Mrs. Fraser walked away, and Bunny took her gin from Matt and tossed back half of it straight away.

"Between here and the bar three different people asked who I am, who my parents are, and when I'm moving to Paradise Valley," Matt told me. "And that guy asked me to look at the growth on his neck." He nodded toward a large bald man by the bar.

Bunny set her empty glass on a table. "Oh, that's Oscar. He didn't ask because you're a doctor. He just likes everyone to look at that thing on his neck."

The lights dimmed and Whitney Houston's "I Will Always Love You" started to play as Thom and Kim took to the dance floor.

I wrinkled my nose. "Don't they know this song is about breaking up?"

"Well, no one listens to the lyrics," Bunny said, watching Thom and Kim and looking sentimental.

"I listen to the lyrics. It's probably bad luck to have a breakup song for your first dance."

"Some people might say it's bad luck to wear black to your brother's wedding." Bunny looked pointedly at my dress.

Matt slipped his arm around my waist and leaned close to be heard over Whitney. "Why don't you show me that beach you're always talking about?"

"What, now? It's dark. It's not exactly beach weather."

"I want to see it. It's not far, right? We'll be back before anyone even notices we're gone."

I saw my mother watching as we headed off the dance floor to grab our coats. Queena would notice if I was gone. She always did.

———

There was no moon that night, and the inky sky and flat sea blended into each other. We sat in silence, watching stars get blotted out by clouds and listening to the waves roll gently into shore.

Matt pulled the blanket tighter around us and leaned his head against mine. "Kit, we never talk about the fact that I'm leaving soon."

My stomach sank and I tried to keep my voice neutral, but it shook a bit. "No. We don't."

"Is that why you didn't want me to come to the wedding? Because I won't be around much longer?"

"Yeah," I exhaled.

He shifted to face me. "I didn't ask to come here just to see the beach. I wanted to get you alone so we could talk about what happens next."

"Oh."

"I know we've only known each other a few months, but I feel like I wasn't completely alive until I met you." He laughed awkwardly. "God, that sounds corny. I'm no good with words."

"It's not corny. I feel like that, too."

"The thing is, at this wedding, thinking about you coming back to Paradise Valley and me leaving, I just..." His voice faltered, and I heard him trying to steady his breathing. He found my hand under the blanket and turned to face me. "Kit, I love you more than anything. I can't leave here without you. I want to be with you forever. Come back to Kelowna with me. Will you marry me?"

It was so dark on the beach that I couldn't see his face clearly. In the darkness, it felt like we were part of the stars and the sea. Everything fit together and made sense. This was the happiest I'd ever felt in my life, but it was also the most terrified I'd ever been. How would I know I was making the right decision? I wondered if I could tell him I needed to think about it, so that I could talk it over with Bunny. She'd know what I should do.

"But what if I go there with you and we realize we only worked in Halifax? Maybe I'm just a Maritime souvenir. Like a lobster trap."

"Is that how you see us? A short-term thing?"

"Of course not. I just…I didn't think this was going to happen tonight. I'm a little dazed. And what'll your parents say, when you show up with some random girl you met at the Seahorse?"

"I've told them all about you. I left out the Seahorse part. Look, Kit, the only thing that matters is that we're together. We'll have such a wonderful life. You'll love Kelowna. The mountains and the lake… There are beaches, too. We'll travel, and get a house up in the hills, and we'll have babies, if you want. With curly hair and beautiful eyes, just like yours." He stroked my cheek. "And we'll wake up next to each other for the rest of our lives."

I looked out into the darkness, matching my breath to the rhythm of the waves. Happiness flowed through me, intoxicating me, and I realized I was shaking a little with the giddiness of it. I thrilled at the idea of waking up with Matt every day and growing old with him. A little tingle went up my spine as I pictured having babies with him. I'd never thought much about having a baby, but I'd started to daydream about it since I'd met Matt. I wanted everything with him. I could be a whole new person. Happier. Free from Queena. Not cursed.

Going to Kelowna would mean leaving school, though, and everything I knew. I'd wanted to leave Paradise Valley behind for so long, but now, I felt a tug of doubt.

"It's just such a big decision…"

Matt took both my hands and looked into my eyes. "Let me make it for you, then. Come with me. I'd move heaven and earth to be together forever with you."

I squinted through the darkness at him. "Did you just propose to me with Rick Astley lyrics?"

"I told you, I'm no good with words. I thought you'd appreciate the music reference." He swiped the floppy bit of hair from his forehead. "So, what do you say?"

I closed my eyes and took a deep breath, picturing us, and mountains, and babies, and forever.

"Yes," I said. "I'm saying yes."

The dish of salt was empty, the pitcher of margaritas was drained, and my head was fuzzy.

"That was exactly six years ago, yesterday. I guess Thom and I share an anniversary." Remembering that date made my heart break all over again. I glanced at my watch and pushed back from the table.

"Wait, you can't go. Matt sounds great, so why isn't he here? We need the whole story," Tiny said.

I teetered to my feet. "Another time. This was fun. Sort of."

Angel laughed. "I kind of threw you two at each other. Consider it an initiation for our little gang, Kitty. You got off easy. Twenty years ago, our initiations were pretty scary shit."

"This was scary enough." I braced one hand on the French door handle for support and turned to look at Tiny. "It was good to see you again."

"It was. Really good."

There was an awkward silence as we looked at each other. It was wonderful to talk to Tiny again, but the old hurt was still there, the wound not quite scabbed over.

Tiny stood up, clutching the ends of her blanket across her chest. "Listen, my cousin runs a spa downtown. Maybe we could go there, sometime, for a little bonding or something? Get some massages or manicures or whatever."

"She'll take care of your bikini line, too," Angel added.

I stumbled home, certain that no one would ever care about the state of my bikini line again.

We Run

Tuesday, April 25, 2000

The buzz in my head was as much due to seeing Tiny again as it was the margaritas. There was an undercurrent of regret, too. I couldn't spend another evening like that. Tiny and Angel would want the rest of the story about me and Matt, and I'd told them as much as I could before things got hard to explain. Besides, there were parts of the story that weren't my secrets to tell.

I sank down next to Pixie, a sob rising in my throat as I watched her sweet, sleeping face. I felt sick from the tequila and guilt—I shouldn't have left her. Not when I'd promised myself I'd keep her safe. I picked her up gently, careful not to disturb her, and cuddled her in the crook of my arm. With my free hand, I picked up the Tower card.

It'd been such a strange day—Tiny, and Rodger, and Angel. All these years, I thought she would've shown my letter to the whole school, but it seems she thought the letters weren't a bad idea. Maybe I should try it again. Maybe if I told Nerida the next part of the story it would help me understand it, myself, and then I'd know how to fix things with Matt.

I found an old notebook in my desk and started writing. Drunk ghost writing at 1:00 a.m. seemed like the least crazy thing I'd done lately.

———

<u>April 1994</u>

When Thom and I were little and played so roughly that one of us would get hurt (a daily occurrence), Queena would throw her hands up in exasperation and sputter a phrase that became as ingrained and prophetic as the rest of our family's curses: "First comes the laughter, then come the tears."

She hadn't said it to us in years, but I heard it on repeat in my brain as Matt and I drove back from the beach after he proposed. Nothing was allowed to change in Queena's house. Nothing new could enter, nothing old could leave. That didn't just mean the July 1987 *TV Guide*. That meant me, too.

I'd had my happiness. Now I must suffer. All was as Queena had foretold.

———

Queena lowered herself into her favourite chair in the kitchen and kicked off her shoes.

"Ah, that's better."

"Your feet are fat little sausages," Bunny noted as she dropped tea bags into a pot. "You should've taken those shoes off hours ago."

Queena looked horrified. "I couldn't just take off my shoes in public! People would think I was riff-raff! Matt and Kitten, sit down and we'll have cake for bed lunch. Bunny, get some plates." The wedding cake had been enormous, and Queena had brought half a layer home with her.

Every nerve in my body was dancing for joy and my face had been in a permanent smile since Matt proposed. Even Queena's kitchen looked beautiful. I'd been bursting to tell the whole world the news, but now that we were back home, I couldn't think of the right words to soften the blow for Queena. I wanted her to be happy for me. I gazed at Matt as he helped Bunny get some plates, and I couldn't imagine Queena not being happy. Matt was as handsome and charming as the Robin Hood I'd imagined when I was little, and he was going to sweep me away to a much better, less stinky kingdom.

Queena wiggled her toes and sighed contentedly. I braced myself against the kitchen wall, a safe distance from her. I fought to quiet the excited buzz in my head so I could speak.

"So, um, there's something Matt and I want to talk to you about."

Queena looked up expectantly, and Bunny, catching the nervous tone of my voice, turned around, licking frosting from her fingers. Matt came over and slipped his arm around me, and I felt braver. I sensed he was about to ask Queena for my hand, like this was one of her soap operas. But this was reality, and I wanted to protect Matt from Queena's reaction.

"Listen, Queena, I know you've always thought I'd come home and run Fact & Fiction, but the fact is, ha ha, no pun intended...well, the thing is, I'm not sure I want to. Well, I don't want to. And the thing is, Matt and I took a drive to the beach after the reception, and, well, he proposed! And I said yes! I mean...yeah, we're in love and I'm going to move to BC with him. We're getting married."

Bunny bounced on her toes in excitement. Queena sat with her hands folded on her lap, rubbing her thumbs together. She looked from Matt's face to mine.

"You're getting married?"

"Mrs. Love, Kit means the world to me. We'll—"

Queena pushed herself up to stand. Matt stopped talking.

"You can't just up and move to the other side of the country. How will I take care of you?" She ignored Matt completely and stood close to me.

"Seriously, do you think I'm going to live in your attic my whole life?"

Queena's eyes burned through me. She got up and started to head downstairs, but stopped and came back to grab the cake. Then she and the cake disappeared through the curtain of orange beads, and in a minute, we heard the heavy door of the bomb shelter clanking shut. My happiness fizzled out like the bubbles in a glass of flat champagne.

Matt looked shell-shocked, which is a pretty normal response to being around Queena. I wasn't surprised, though. Not at all. This was her bomb shelter's finest hour. She'd been preparing for attack for decades now. She just hadn't expected it to come from inside the house.

———

Bunny sent Matt to gather my things and load up the car while she and I had a chat on the deck.

I shivered in the damp chair. "Jesus Christ. This is the best thing that ever happened to me and she acts like it's the end of the world. I have to get out of here before Matt sees just how off her nut she really is."

"He's seen the shag carpet in the bathroom. Trust me, he knows she's off her nut."

"She can't lock me up again like she did when I was seventeen."

"Does Matt know about what happened to you back then?"

"It's kind of hard to work into conversation."

"It's kind of important, isn't it?"

"It's kind of embarrassing and I don't want him to know. It's not important anymore, anyway." I waved my hand to dismiss my past.

"You have no idea how much you sound like Queena."

"I don't sound like Queena. She's stuck in the past, and this is about my future."

"Matt seems like a lovely boy, but are you sure you're not just trying to get away from Queena? Not to sound like her, but British Columbia's awfully far away."

"Look, I adore Matt, and I'm marrying him, and I'm getting the hell out of Paradise Valley, forever."

Bunny shook her head and sank back in her chair.

"Nowhere's far enough to run, darling girl. You've got to face the hard things sometime. Trust me, it'll catch up to you: your sadness or Queena or thinking you're cursed."

"But you went to Montreal after Nerida died. You did the exact same thing to forget about the curse."

Bunny laughed, but not her usual throaty guffaw. This laugh was quiet, and a bit remorseful.

"It wasn't the curse. You know I think that whole thing is a crock of shit." Her words slurred because of all the gin. "I might as well tell you. You should know that I'm not the person Queena's made me out to be in her scrapbooks."

"No one is."

"I left because I was in love. It was...an affair, I guess you'd call it."

"You were having an affair? Who was he?"

Bunny snorted. "She."

I blinked. She stared at me.

"I was in love with a woman, dumbass. Christ on a bicycle, this family!"

I stared at her while I tried to reorganize my understanding of the world.

"You're shocked," she said.

I shook my head. "I'm shocked at myself. Why didn't I know?"

Bunny shrugged. "You grew up reading fairy tales in a small town. It didn't occur to you that not every girl was after a prince."

"It's just, I always imagined you had this exotic life in Montreal, going out with a bunch of gorgeous men and having wild times."

"I tried one or two men. Wasn't for me." Bunny flicked her ashes on the deck. Queena would be pissed when she saw them in the morning. "I had some good times, but I wouldn't really call my life in Montreal 'exotic.'"

"More exotic than here, I bet."

"I've always been too exotic for Paradise Valley. I'm a great gaudy bird that got blown off course."

"Does Queena know?"

"Of course, Queena knows. I might've stayed around here if she'd stuck up for me a bit, but she was more concerned with whether people would talk and how it would look. Didn't matter. Freda Landry will always talk about it, stupid old cow tit. I saw her staring and whispering tonight."

I had a dim memory of Freda Landry gossiping about Bunny while she ate all the asparagus sandwiches at Stubby's wake. "What's Freda got to do with it?"

"She found us together. In the church hall. At Nerida's funeral."

"At the funeral? Jesus, Bunny."

Bunny pulled pins out of her updo, shaking her curls free and sending pins skittering through the darkness. "It was after the funeral, not the middle of Mass or anything. I'd gone down to the bathroom in the church basement to pull myself together, and she was comforting me. Anyway, Freda came downstairs to use the bathroom and caught us. I'd never had someone look at me that way." She stared ahead with unfocused eyes, watching it play out again in her mind. "She told everyone. She walked around the reception and whispered about it, so people were coming over and offering condolences to Queena and our parents and shooting me dirty looks. Queena didn't clue in until weeks later, of course, because she wasn't doing so well, herself. But oh, she was furious. She said I'd made us all look like riff-raff. My parents wouldn't talk to me. It felt like the whole town was against me. I don't go in for all that curse business, but it felt like I'd brought on the bad luck."

I reached for Bunny's hand. "You're not bad luck."

"People said some awful things, let me tell you." Bunny closed her eyes. "It felt impossible for us to be together after that, with a whole town of small-minded Fredas watching us. So, I lied. I told her I wanted something different. I found an accounting course in Montreal, and I moved there a couple of months after you were born. I ran. I've always wondered what might've happened if I hadn't."

"Oh, Bunny! Jesus. You must've been heartbroken. How can you stand being back here after that?"

"You needed me. And then I saw that Queena needed me, too." She fumbled in her pocket for her pack of cigarettes and lit the last one.

"Yeah, but I don't know why you'd help her. It doesn't sound like she was really there for you."

"Queena was preoccupied after Nerida died. But, yeah, she didn't seem to mind that I was leaving and she was losing me, too. She never stood up for me, that's for sure."

My anger at my mother rekindled. "Wait, what about your girlfriend? Is she still here? Who is it?"

"Never mind, Nosy Parker. It's ancient history. The people we were don't exist anymore." She took a long drag on her cigarette and looked up at the sky. "You know, it always amazes me that people just go on with life after they've had their heart broken. I guess I'm a bit like Queena. Time kind of stopped for me, too."

"You must be miserable."

"Yeah, it's miserable. But it's not a red-hot misery anymore. It's just a dull, weekday pain." Bunny teetered to her feet and drew me in for a hug. Her hair was a cloud of Chanel No.5 and Craven A cigarettes.

"You know you can always come back if you need to, right? I'll always be here for you," she whispered.

I wrapped my arm around her waist and propelled her inside. "I know. But I won't need to. I've found my prince, and I'm getting free from Queena and the whole idea of bad luck and curses. It'll be a whole new life."

Bunny sighed and locked the sliding door behind us. "The old life has a way of leaking into the new one. Pretending a problem isn't there doesn't mean it's gone. That's Queena's way of thinking—magical thinking."

"I don't need magic anymore," I said.

And just then, I think I believed it.

Undun

✦

Dear Kitty,

I'm so happy that you're writing to me again. It's the closest I've come to a conversation since you left thirteen years ago. When you first wrote to me you were the same age I was when I died, so when I read your letters now it's sort of like hearing about the things that might've happened to me (the sexy bits, especially. Ha.).

I don't know what happened for you after you left with Matt. But I can tell you what you missed here.

Queena didn't completely fall apart when you left—not like she did with me or your dad. But then, you weren't dead like we were, and she could still hope you'd all be back together really soon. That doesn't mean she wasn't obsessing about you.

She made a bunch of scrapbooks about you with old snapshots, but she used the pictures you sent her from BC, too. Just like with your dad, she'd cut your photo out and stick it on one of her photos, so it'd look like you were still part of things. That helped her get through all the Christmases you didn't come home, and I guess it made it feel like she was keeping an eye on you, somehow. She made a little shelf dedicated to you in the bomb shelter, too. It's next to the one for your dad and above the one for me. So, I guess we'll all get to spend a nuclear winter together. Lucky.

For the first year you were gone, she tried coming up with schemes to get you home. She and Bunny were watching *General Hospital* one time while they made supper, and there was a character who was in a car crash and fell into a coma.

"Do you think Kitten might come home if we told her there was an emergency?" Queena asked, as she put some pork chops in the oven.

"What's the emergency?"

Queena nodded her head at the TV screen. "Well, like that. If we told her Thom had been in a car accident, for instance. Or that you were in a coma."

"I'm sure Kitty would come back right away if something awful happened."

Queena folded her arms and looked at the TV without really seeing it. "Yes. Yes, I think if I told her there's an emergency, that'd get her home."

Bunny stopped chopping carrots and faced Queena. "You want to tell her something awful's happened just to get her here? Queena, for chrissakes."

Queena turned away from the TV and went back to peeling potatoes. "Of course not. No. But if there was an emergency, she'd come home."

She didn't say anything like that again until a couple of years later, when she came home from The Memory Garden with news for Bunny.

"Did you hear about Eileen Fraser?"

Bunny didn't look up from doing Fact & Fiction's accounts at the kitchen table. "What about Eileen?"

"She's got breast cancer."

Bunny set down her pencil. Her face had gone white as a ghost (although for the record, that saying isn't accurate. I'm transparent, not white.)

"She's at the regional hospital for treatment, but I hear it should go well. Thom heard it from Ed," Queena said.

"Is Ed home with her? Is she alone?"

"He's coming home soon." Queena leaned forward on the table. "Do you suppose if I told Kitten that I was sick like that, she'd come home? She hasn't been home in such a long time."

Bunny blinked. "Jesus Murphy. You're not thinking of lying about having cancer to get her home? That's really effed up. Pardon my French."

"Of course not!" Queena picked up her magazine and flipped through it without looking at the pages.

Bunny reached over to put her hand on Queena's. "I know it's been a long time. I miss her, too. She'll come back when she's ready."

After a couple of years, Queena kind of gave up trying so hard. It hurt her too much to think of you, living your life somewhere she couldn't see you, so she just used the scrapbooks to pretend you were still around. I was sad you weren't around, too, but I hoped it meant you were having fun (your boyfriend was really a fox—I might be dead but I'm not *dead*, if you know what I mean).

Love,
Nerida
xoxo

1999

July 1999

It was such an awkward silence.

I hadn't really thought of him in years, but then he called out of the blue to say he was passing through and wanted to stop by to say hello. And now we sat, with nothing to say after that hello. I pulled the flimsy cover-up I'd thrown over my bikini a bit tighter and reached for my glass of wine.

"So how was Vancouver? Did you finish your PhD?"

"Last year," Ed said, squinting into the sun and looking toward Okanagan Lake.

"What was it you studied again? I know Thom told me—something science-y?"

"Conservation biology."

I didn't know what that was, but I tried to look suitably impressed. It was weird seeing something from Paradise Valley in my house. Weirder still that it should be Ed. A silence dragged on.

"I'm sure it means a lot to your mother that you're moving back," I said, searching for things to talk about. "How's she doing?"

"Not great. She didn't tell me the cancer was back, at first, because she didn't want me to worry. But I don't want her to go through it alone."

We fell into another awkward silence.

"That's quite a ring." Ed nodded at the diamond sparkling in the bright sunlight. "Thom told me you were engaged. That was a while ago, though."

"We just haven't decided on a date. It's hard for Matt to take time off." I tugged at the hem of my cover-up, wishing it would cover a bit more of my thighs. "Anyway, what about you? I thought Thom mentioned a while back that you were getting married?"

Ed moved his chair so the sun wasn't directly in his eyes. "He must've been talking about someone else."

"Oh." I distinctly remembered Thom telling me he was supposed to go to Vancouver to be best man in Ed's wedding, but he'd been too depressed about Kim.

"I didn't know if I'd find you home in the middle of the day. I thought you might be at work," he said.

"I don't really have a job right now. Still not sure what I want to do when I grow up, I guess."

"I remember you and Tiny saying you'd do your witch stuff and have a bookstore, like Stubby's."

"Most people don't end up doing the thing they talked about when they were sixteen." I looked away and pretended to be very interested in the bird feeder. A peculiar feeling was growing in the pit of my stomach.

Maybe the silences were too much for Ed, too, because he pushed his chair back to leave. I walked him to the front door, where we stood awkwardly, each of us waiting for the other to speak.

"It was great to see you again," he said. He sounded like he meant it. "You look great. You look happy."

"I am. Tell your mother I'm thinking of her."

"I will. Thanks. Well. Goodbye, Kitty."

"Goodbye, Ed."

He opened the door and looked back at me. I took a step forward so that I could close the door behind him, and he stepped toward me and pulled me into a hug. I tried not to noticeably shrink away from him.

"Take care of yourself." He was slow to let me go.

"You too."

I shook off the hug as I walked back out to the deck. The sky over the lake was still bright blue, but the air felt heavier. That peculiar feeling in my stomach was still there, and I felt anxious but didn't know why—just like when I'd wake up from dreaming about Stubby and couldn't remember the dream, but the anxious feeling of loss stayed with me all day.

I was still sitting on the deck when Matt came home. He kissed the top of my head and slid into the chair next to me.

"Did you drink all this wine yourself?"

"I had a visitor. My brother's friend, Ed. You met him at Thom's wedding. Anyway, he was doing his PhD or something in Vancouver, and he's driving back to Paradise Valley because his mother is sick."

"Hmmm." Matt looked over at me with one eye closed. "Thom's friend? What'd you talk about?"

"How much he's accomplished, and how I haven't accomplished anything." I picked up my wineglass, but it was empty.

Matt opened both eyes. "You've accomplished a lot. You moved here with me. We've got a great house. We travel."

"Yeah. I guess."

"Probably more than you would've done if you'd stayed in Paradise Valley, right?"

"I should have a career by now, or at least a job. Tammy's been a nurse for four years already, and she's married with a baby."

"Kit, you just need to settle on something. Whether that's a job, or a baby, or whatever. Honestly, why are you so bad at making decisions?"

"I make decisions."

He tweaked my nose. "You only manage to get dressed each morning because your entire wardrobe is shades of black and it all looks the same."

"Thanks. You make me feel so glamourous."

"Even your bikini's black."

"I look good in black, okay? Geesh."

Matt adjusted the sun umbrella to keep himself in the shade. "Okay, let's work on decision making. Your birthday's in a few months. Let's get married that day. You can pick where. Anywhere you want. You decide."

We'd been down this road before, so many times. The first year we were together, we thought we'd elope to Vegas at Christmas. But I couldn't figure out what I'd wear or which chapel we should use, and then Matt was too busy to take time off work, so the moment passed. The next year, we were going to get married during our trip to Costa Rica. The first week of our vacation was perfect. Then, the day before we were going to get married, I heard a lawn mower while I was sitting on the balcony, and all I could see was Stubby's body on the lawn, and the poppet, and Tiny and me holding hands and manifesting our own bookstore. Matt came out of the shower and found me in bed, sobbing. He cancelled the wedding ceremony because I was too upset to get out of bed. He was as shaken by it as I was, but he never mentioned it again.

In the five years we'd been together, there'd been five different plans for us to get married. It'd become a joke. Matt teased me that this had become my career, this eternal wedding planning, but I knew his patience was wearing thin, and his family and our friends saw me as a flake. I'd wanted to become a different person by moving to BC, but not this person.

Matt pushed the floppy bit of hair off his face, still waiting for me to answer. I bit the side of my thumb and stared at the bird feeder.

"I know you think this sounds bonkers, but it's just...I remember my mother saying that the smallest decision can have horrible impacts. What if I pick the wrong wedding date, and it leads to disaster?"

Matt squeezed my hand and held it against his chest. "Kit, I won't let anything bad happen to you. You can't be so scared of things that it keeps you from living your life."

"My father said almost those exact words to me once."

"There you go, then. The two smartest men in your life agree." His eyes sparkled at me. "I just want us to move on, Kit. I know decisions are hard for you. I can make them for both of us." He pushed back from the table and nodded toward the patio door. "I'm melting out here. And I'm starving. Come on. I'm sure we'll talk about this again. And again."

I followed him inside and set the wine bottle and glasses on the counter while he checked out the freezer.

"We've got steaks we could barbecue, or I could just make some pasta. What would you like?" He closed the freezer and turned to look at me.

I stood by the sink, winding my hair around my fingers and weighing the pros and cons of steak vs. pasta. People made hundreds of little decisions like this every day, without giving it much thought. That wasn't a magic I possessed.

"Either is fine."

Matt sighed. He grabbed a beer from the fridge and went back outside. I bit my lip to keep from crying and headed upstairs to change out of my bikini.

At the back of the walk-in closet was a shelf with shoe boxes of things from Paradise Valley—mostly letters from Queena, pleading for me to go home so she could keep me safe, and photos from Bunny. A copy of my father's obituary. And my Magic 8 Ball.

I hadn't touched the ball since I'd put the box in the shelf five years earlier. The last time I'd given it a shake was the night I met Matt. I reached for it and turned it in my hands. It wouldn't provide the guidance my tarot cards would've, but it was the best I had.

I bit my thumb and shook the ball in my other hand.

"Steak or pasta? Wait, no, let me rephrase—should we have steak for dinner?"

My sources say no.

Okay, good start. Pasta. I'd show Matt I could make decisions.

"Should I plan this wedding for my birthday?"

Concentrate and ask again.

I shook harder.

"Should we try to have a baby?"

It is decidedly so.

Oh God. What the hell was I doing, asking a Magic 8 Ball to decide something like this? Still, I wasn't upset by the answer. Maybe the Ball was just clarifying things, telling me things I already knew to be true.

Fear is a reaction. Courage is a decision.

I'd take my courage from the 8 Ball.

I walked downstairs to tell Matt that we should have pasta for dinner, and we should try to make a baby.

This Woman's Work

February 2000

We told Matt's parents a couple of weeks after I got the positive pregnancy test. I told Tammy just a week later because she'd called to tell me she was expecting their second baby, and we squealed with delight that we were pregnant at the same time. Matt wanted to tell my family when we called on Christmas morning. I imagined how that call would go. Queena would demand I come home. She'd sob about Stubby not being around to meet his first grandchild. She'd obsess about the curse. She'd want to keep both me and the baby locked in her attic. I didn't want her anxiety to make me doubt myself.

"Maybe after New Year's," I told him. "Now's not a good time. Queena's busy worrying about Y2K. She'll be terrified the world will end before she gets to see her grandchild."

But now it was February, Y2K had been a bust, and I was thirteen weeks pregnant—but I still hadn't told Queena. When we had an ultrasound the week before, we saw the strong little heartbeat, and the baby even looked like it was waving a hand at us. In that moment, I felt the biggest surge of love I'd ever known, and the rare (for me) satisfaction of knowing I'd made the right decision.

Matt kissed me softly as he left for his shift at the hospital that night. I settled into my pillow and opened my groggy eyes. Pregnancy made me so tired, I'd been going to bed just after supper every night.

"What time is it?"

"Just after eleven. Go back to sleep. Can I get you anything before I go?"

"No," I yawned. "Have a good shift."

He kissed me again. "Goodnight. I love you."

I woke just after four in the morning. My head was pounding, and the T-shirt I'd worn to bed was clammy with sweat. I kicked off the blankets and started to roll over, but a jolt of pain shot down my leg from my hip, freezing me mid-motion. I waited, not moving, to see if it was just some weird pregnancy thing—a tendon stretching, maybe. Matt and my doctor had assured me some aches and cramps were normal.

A hot wave of pain spread from the back of my hips around to my belly before shooting down my legs, and I reached for my barely perceptible bump. I hadn't felt the baby move yet. It was too soon. I had no way of knowing what was going on in there.

I switched on the lamp on my nightstand and choked back nausea and a sob. I wasn't just damp with sweat. There was blood.

A mile stretched between me and the phone on Matt's nightstand. Inch by painful inch, I slid myself across, hoping even this slight movement wasn't making things worse. I called Matt's pager and left a message with the answering service, saying I was on my way to the hospital and to meet me in the ER. Then I phoned his mother, Marilyn.

"It's Kit. I'm sorry to call so late. Or so early." My voice was calm and benign, like the recorded voice that tells you that your call is important. "I need you to come over right away. Use your key to open the door and come upstairs. I need you to take me to the hospital."

"The hospital? George, get up, something's wrong! Kit needs to go to the hospital. Kit, are you—"

"Just come quickly. Please," Another wave of pain seized me as I hung up.

It seemed like I'd only just managed to take a few breaths when I heard Marilyn throwing open the front door and bounding up the stairs. She was tall and blond, like Matt, and I'd always seen her hair in a perfect, sleek bob, but now it was rumpled from sleep, and her alarmed face, without any makeup, looked like that of a little girl who'd just awoken from a bad dream. Her eyes moved from my face to my stained t-shirt to a pair of sweatpants tossed on a chair in the corner. She grabbed them, and without a word, gently lifted my legs over the edge of the bed, one then the other, to wiggle the pants as far as my rear end. They were Matt's, and were much too long for me, and I wished they were tighter—so tight they'd keep everything that was still inside me where it was.

Matt's father, George, walked in behind her. He was an athletic-looking man with grey hair and Matt's broad smile, but tonight his face was tight and serious. I felt a flicker of hope now that he was here. He was a doctor, too. Maybe he could fix this.

"I'm going to carry you down the stairs to the car, okay?" George spoke in soothing tones as he handed Marilyn a towel he'd taken from the ensuite. I started to protest that it was a new towel and it'd be ruined, but I swallowed the words because it hardly seemed important. Marilyn folded the towel and tucked it between my legs, then helped me wiggle the pants the rest of the way up. Her eyes were shining and didn't meet mine.

George bent over me. "Shh, Kitten. Try to stay calm. We'll take care of you. Now, it'll be uncomfortable when I pick you up."

"I'll walk. I'm too heavy."

"Not at all." George carried me to the stairs. "You're as light as a feather, and you're going to be just fine."

I leaned my head against his shoulder, knowing that neither of those things was true.

The nurse who came in to draw blood took a johnny shirt off a cart and placed it next to me. She told me to get into it and then hurried away. I clutched the thin blue hospital gown to my chest, not knowing how to get it on. I was so scared to move.

"Let me help." Marilyn lifted my T-shirt over my head and helped me into the johnny shirt. Then, moving carefully, she helped me out of the sweatpants. She left the towel where it was.

George picked up the T-shirt and held it in a crumpled ball. I noticed he turned the bloodstains away from me. "We'll take this home and wash it for you, Kit."

"No. Throw it out." I never wanted to see it again.

A doctor introduced himself as Dr. Whitcomb, the obstetrician on call. I thought I remembered meeting him once, at a Christmas party.

"Why does it hurt so much?" I whispered. "Where's Matt?"

The doctor leaned over me and spoke slowly. His breath smelled of stale coffee. "We're going to do an ultrasound. Matt's on his way." The nurse came back in. Dr. Whitcomb turned away to talk to her, and then disappeared out the door.

The ultrasound room was dim. I kept my eyes screwed shut and tried to hold my legs together as tightly as possible to stop any more bleeding as the technician adjusted the table to raise my legs. She inserted the ultrasound wand, turned the screen toward her so I couldn't see it, and quickly removed the wand.

"I'll just be a minute," she said. She disappeared through the door before I could say anything, just like the doctor had. I remembered Alice's complaint when she arrived in Wonderland: people came and went so quickly here.

The door opened and Dr. Whitcomb entered in a flood of bright light from the hallway. Without saying hello, he reinserted the transvaginal wand and had a long look at the screen. The silence made me want to throw up.

Matt burst through the door and came straight over to sit on my bed. He grasped my hand hard, his hand warm against my clammy skin.

Dr. Whitcomb removed the wand. "When did the bleeding start, Kitten?"

"I woke up. I don't know when. Two hours ago, maybe three? There was already a lot of blood when I woke up, and it hurt."

He sighed deeply. Only a few seconds ticked past before he spoke, but I crammed a whole world of hope into that pause. "I'm sorry to have to tell you both this. There's no longer a heartbeat. You're having a miscarriage." He shifted the screen a bit so I could see it, but I turned my head away. If I didn't see it, it wouldn't be real.

"No. Check again. We just saw the heartbeat a few days ago." I looked up at Matt. "We just saw it a few days ago."

Matt stared at the screen. "Kit, there's nothing we can do."

Dr. Whitcomb sat down on a little stool next to me. "Kitten, you're bleeding heavily but the products of conception are still in the uterus. You should go home, where you can be more comfortable. There's nothing to do but wait and see if nature takes care of things in the next few hours. But you're just past thirteen weeks, so we don't want to wait too long. Come back at noon so we can do another scan, and I'll go ahead and book you in for a D&C this afternoon."

"What do you mean, 'products'? What's a D&C?" I asked. In my head, the words ran into each other, panicky and desperate, like passengers leaving a sinking ship. But spoken out loud, they were cool and flat, matching Dr. Whitcomb's tone. I wanted to sound like nothing was happening. If I could just keep Matt and Dr. Whitcomb focused on explaining medical terminology, if I could keep them from paying any attention to the ultrasound screen, then maybe they'd forget about this whole miscarriage. If I acted like nothing bad was happening, this would all stop.

Matt sounded infuriatingly calm and doctor-like, as though I was just another patient. "Kit, it means a procedure to remove everything and make sure the bleeding stops. So that you're okay. You're just into the second trimester, and it can be dangerous if the...if anything stays inside. You risk infection."

Another wave of pain gripped my belly, but I grimaced it away and focused on a rising swell of anger. "But wait, no, you can't just send me home! Can't you do something to make this stop?"

Dr. Whitcomb put a hand on my shoulder. "It's over, Kit. I'm sorry. It's already over."

I looked at the screen. Everything went dark.

The sun was coming up as Matt helped me into our house. He got me settled on a sofa and brought me Popsicles and held me close, and we sat for hours without speaking, both of us tense and waiting. I didn't cry, because it made the pain worse. I wanted the morning to be over. But at the same time, I didn't want it to end. The pain was all I had left.

By the time we were back at the hospital at noon, I was exhausted, body and soul. The deep, desperate sorrow I'd felt when George and Marilyn had brought me in was replaced with a stoical numbness. I knew the desperation would be back, but for now, I just had to get through this.

Another doctor—I didn't pay attention to her name—did another ultrasound. She didn't turn the screen toward me.

"It doesn't look like anything's changed. I think we should go ahead and do the D&C." She gave my hand a squeeze. "There's no sense in prolonging this."

I closed my eyes and turned my face away from her as she described the procedure. I didn't want to listen.

Two hours later, I was strapped down to an operating table. I couldn't really see anything happening below my chest. I felt like the assistant in a magic act—the one who gets into the box with only her head and feet poking out so she can be sawed in half. There was no magic here.

I woke up in a bright room and didn't know where I was. There was a strong smell of disinfectant, and loud sounds of beeping and hissing and moaning. It took a minute to realize the moaning was coming from me. A blood pressure cuff hissed as it squeezed my arm, over and over. I wanted to rip it off, but I had no strength to lift my hand. As I turned my head, my vision swam and I thought I might throw up. I saw a nurse nearby.

"Is it over?" I whispered. My throat was raw, and my tongue was thick, and it reminded me of that other time I'd woken up in a hospital. The effort of speaking made me cough. I braced for the coughing to bring the fierce, hot pain in my abdomen, but there was nothing. I was a cracked eggshell, with everything inside me scooped out.

The nurse placed a hand on my shoulder and held out a plastic cup filled with ice chips. "You're in the recovery room now. Everything went well."

I remembered the sound of my mother wailing in the backyard the day my father died. I remembered how it had echoed through the silence of the neighbourhood.

And then I realized it wasn't a memory. It was me.

Sweet Child o' Mine

February 2000

We only had three television stations in Paradise Valley when I was little: two English, one French. Sometimes, Thom and I would sit in front of the TV and turn the dial to channels we didn't get. Through the static and fuzz, we could just make out shadows of people and garbled voices. I'd stare at those in-between worlds, hoping that if I squinted long enough, the pictures would become clear.

For the next couple of weeks, I lived in between channels. My thoughts were muffled by mental static and fuzz and everything around me was garbled white noise. At first, I slept a lot. But then the nightmares started, and I didn't like sleeping anymore. I'd dream I'd left a baby in the apartment I'd shared with Thom, and it had been there for years, but I only just now remembered and I was trying to go back to get it, but I couldn't remember where the apartment was. Sometimes I dreamed I was holding a baby girl—blond, like Matt—but then she'd be gone, and Matt would be mad that I couldn't remember where I'd put her. Every time I woke up, I felt the dread and fear of that night. The night I'd lost my baby.

Matt held me when I'd wake up crying or was scared to go back to sleep. Then he'd go to work in the morning to be a normal, functioning human. His parents came over to check on me while he was gone. Marilyn sat on my bed and read magazines to me. She didn't seem to mind that I didn't acknowledge her, even though she read increasingly smutty things from *Cosmopolitan* to try to get a reaction from me. When it was George's turn, he often didn't say anything at all. We sat silently, or he'd turn on the radio and we'd listen to music while he sat on the edge of the bed, holding my hand.

When Matt came home from work, he'd lie in bed with me and tell me what he'd done all day. He didn't ever tell me how he felt. We didn't talk about what we'd lost. At first, he didn't seem to mind that I was in bed all the time. After a month, though, he thought I should get up.

He sat on the edge of the bed, but I couldn't see him because I'd wrapped the blankets around me like a cocoon. "I called your family. They want to come help," he said.

I poked my head out. "Oh sweet Jesus, no. Why'd you do that?"

"I didn't know what else to do. You won't get out of bed. You're hardly eating, and you never come downstairs. I just want to help you—"

"Move on?" I suggested. "Get over it? Forget it ever happened?"

"That's not what I mean."

I stuck my head out a little further. "This is all my fault. She was right here with me for thirteen weeks and then she was gone, and I didn't even know anything was wrong. What kind of shit mother am I, to not even know?"

Matt reached under the blankets for my hand. "You couldn't have known. Everything seemed fine."

"You said nothing bad would happen."

Matt dropped my hand and rubbed his hands against his legs. "Kit, maybe you should talk to someone. A psychologist or something. I'm worried about you."

I remembered the weeks I'd spent in the psychiatric ward at seventeen. I didn't want to be stuck in a room with nothing but a mattress. I didn't want to answer endless questions that left me feeling weak and shamed.

"I'm just sad. I lost a baby. That doesn't make me crazy."

"I didn't say you were crazy. I just don't think it's healthy that you're in bed feeling miserable all day. Are you sure you don't want Bunny to come here? Or Queena?"

"God no. Promise me you won't ask them."

"If you come downstairs for something to eat, I'll promise." He got up and reached out his hand, backing toward the door.

"You promise?"

"Anything if it'll make you feel better."

I swung my legs slowly out of bed. By the time I reached Matt, I was exhausted by the effort of walking across the room, or quite possibly just from the effort of existing.

The next morning, after Matt went to work, I wandered restlessly around the house. I hated my house for looking the same. Colours should have been muted. The sunlight should have dimmed. I understood why mourning Victorians draped themselves and everything around them in black crepe.

I made tea because I couldn't think of anything else to do. Neither of us had turned on the dishwasher the night before, so there were no clean spoons. I was flooded with an irrational rage and threw my mug of tea at the dishwasher, swearing with satisfaction as the mug smashed and splintered onto the floor. Then the rage passed as quickly as it'd come, leaving me scared and shaky, like something outside me was taking over.

Cleaning up my mess drained me, and I went back upstairs to rest. I paused in front of my bedroom, drawn to the closed door right next to it. It would've been the baby's room. I hadn't gone in there since I'd come back from the hospital.

My heart pounded and I hesitated, my hand shaking on the doorknob the way it used to when I'd sneak into Nerida's room when I was little. I pushed open the door.

It didn't look like a baby's room. It would've taken months to decide what I wanted it to look like, so there was no furniture except for a dresser and a rocking chair Matt's parents had given us. There was nothing here that spoke to the life that could have been. Angry tears filled my eyes. It wasn't fair that no one would even know this baby had existed. I knew. She was real. She'd been real to me, and I'd loved her.

My eyes fell on an opened package on the dresser. It hadn't been there the last time I was in the room. There was a card, too, sticking out of a little envelope addressed to Matt and me in Tammy's handwriting.

I wanted to be one of the first to give your beautiful baby a gift, she'd written on the card. *Who would've guessed that Kit's awkward flirting at the Seahorse would lead to this?*

My tears fell on the box as I opened it. Tammy had sent three little board books, some soft receiving blankets, a package of baby soaps, and a little cloth doll. I felt sick at the thought of telling Tammy what had happened. I felt guilty for feeling angry that she was still pregnant.

One of the ultrasound photos peeked out from under the wrapping paper. I touched it like it might break apart in my hands and carried it back to the rocking chair.

If I squinted at the baby in the grainy photo long enough, like when I'd watched those in-between TV channels as a child, I could make her look real. The baby was a girl. I'd felt that all along. She'd have blue eyes, like both me and Matt. Her hair would be fair, like Matt's, but curly like mine. In my mind's eye, I saw her perfect little pink mouth, her tiny little fingers. See? There they were, waving at me.

She'd look a lot like the doll Tammy had sent. It had straight, yellow, yarn hair, but I could pretend it was curly. It had big blue eyes that never closed. It was tiny and soft.

I went back to the dresser to get one of the receiving blankets and gently wrapped the little doll in it. There. She looked so cozy, like a real baby.

We'd only just started to talk about names. And of course, since she was a girl, her name was important. It had to be just right, so that she could fend off the curse. Nothing ugly though. It needed to be unusual, but as sweet as she was.

I went to the window and looked at the forest outside, hoping for inspiration. Something like a magical creature in the forest. Elf. Fae.

Pixie.

"Your name is Pixie," I whispered to the doll. But she wasn't a doll. She was Pixie.

We didn't have a crib yet, so I made Pixie a little nest in a dresser drawer in her room. As soon as I heard Matt come home, I'd tuck Pixie in, give her a kiss, and put my finger to my lips to remind her to be quiet and go to sleep. Then I'd slip out before Matt came upstairs, closing the door behind me.

Pixie and I spent most of our days in the rocking chair in her room. She'd be wrapped up snug in her blanket, and I'd read her the books Tammy had sent. I'd close my eyes and rock and imagine how different life could have been.

It was hard to keep track of what day it was, let alone what month, but judging from the daffodils and birds outside Pixie's window, I figured it must be sometime in April. It felt like such a long time since that horrible night in February. Then again, it felt like it had just happened. I still had nightmares about it, and sometimes, during the day, images would push into my head and I'd have to squeeze my eyes shut and refuse to see them. Sometimes, it was memories of that ultrasound screen and memories of Stubby's eyes when he died, all jumbled up in one. Those days were the worst. I couldn't even read to Pixie on those days. We just rocked.

A new street was being built, pushing further into the woods at the top of our street. I could see the machines from Pixie's window as we rocked, and I was annoyed at the noise. It would keep Pixie from her nap.

I decided I'd read a book to drown out the noise and lull her to sleep. I picked up *Goodnight Moon*. That was Pixie's favourite. I turned the chair to catch the late morning sun and started to rock and read, pointing out all the little details in the book as I read. I knew Pixie would like that.

"Do you see the little mouse? And there's the bowl of mush by the little bunny's bed."

"What are you doing?"

My head snapped toward the doorway, where Matt stood watching me. The sunlight shone through the hall window behind him so that he was just a dark presence at the door, looming over me like an ogre.

Everything was suddenly very quiet. The construction crew must have stopped for lunch, because all I heard was birdsong and my heart pounding in my ears. The oxygen seemed to have been sucked out of the room.

"Why are you home? It's early," I asked, my voice shaking.

Matt walked closer and his features came into focus. His brow was furrowed. Even his laugh lines didn't look very laughy. His gaze fell on the top of the dresser, where I'd put the ultrasound photos in frames and lined up the books to start a little library for Pixie. He looked down at the dresser drawer and its cozy nest of blankets. And then he looked over at me, in the rocking chair, with Pixie nestled against me as I held *Goodnight Moon.*

"What are you doing?" he asked again. I recognized the tone in his voice. It was the tone I'd used the day Stubby died, when I was trying to convince myself this wasn't happening.

I tucked Pixie beneath my arm, out of his sight. I was angry with myself for not listening for him. I could've kept everything the way I wanted if only I'd been paying attention.

Matt crouched next to the chair. "Kit. Are you talking to a doll?"

I stared at *Goodnight Moon.* Goodnight nobody. Goodnight mush.

"Are you pretending this is a baby?"

Goodnight mittens. Goodnight Kitten.

"Are you pretending this is our baby?" His voice was shaking, and he spoke slowly.

I stared out the window and tried not to hear him.

"Kit, look at me. Why have you got this doll all wrapped up like this?" He reached out to touch Pixie, but I moved her away.

"It's okay. I can keep her safe." My voice was barely a whisper, and I hoped Matt would lower his voice, too. We weren't used to so much noise. "Nothing's going to happen."

Matt's face went pale. There was no sparkle in his blue eyes now. "Kit, give me the doll. Let's just stop this." Matt stood up, knocking the chair and making me drop *Goodnight Moon.*

"I warned you. About my bad luck. But it's okay. I'll be more careful now."

"Oh Kit, for fuck's sake!" He hit his hand against the top of the dresser, and the framed ultrasound photos clattered over, making me jump. "You didn't cause this! There is no bad luck. It's not real. No wishful thinking or talking to a doll is going to change anything."

I'd never seen him look like this—so angry, and so broken at the same time—but he should be happy; I was taking such good care of

Pixie. I stood up and held her tighter. "I just wanted to be able to keep her safe." My voice was barely a whisper. I looked down at Pixie and adjusted her blanket around her little face.

"Oh come on, Kit! You really think playing pretend will fix things? Why can't you just let me take care of you so we can move on?"

Anger broke through the fog in my brain. "I don't want to move on. I want what we had before my bad luck ruined everything."

"Kit, you're not bad luck." He folded his arms and took a deep breath. "Actually, you know what, maybe you *are*. Because you're making us both miserable. I lost the baby, too, Kit, and I still have to get up and try to function every day. You know what? I can't do this anymore. If you'd rather have your make-believe world than us, fine. Have it. I'm done."

The shock of his words made me stop crying.

"You're leaving?"

Matt gripped the dresser as if it was the only thing keeping him connected to the earth.

"Just put the doll down. Please."

I shook my head and worked my way around the perimeter of the room. I backed out the door quickly, hoping he wouldn't try to take Pixie from me. But he didn't come after me. He slammed the door to the room behind him and ran down the stairs. I heard the front door close and his car pulling out of the driveway.

The room swam. He'd said I was bad luck.

He'd probably gone to get some of his medical people to take my baby away. What if he tried to get me locked up again? I needed to get Pixie somewhere safe.

I went into my closet, pulled a suitcase off the shelf, and threw things in it as fast as I could. I was crying too hard to see what I was packing. I found a scarf and fashioned a little baby sling so I could hold Pixie under my shirt. Skin to skin contact is very important, I remembered.

The airport wasn't busy when the taxi dropped me off.

"I need a ticket. One way," I said to the man behind the counter.

"Where to?"

I had to go where Pixie and I would be safe. I booked a ticket east.

Both Sides Now

Dear Kitty,

I'm really sorry.

I didn't understand the deal with Pixie, but it's not like I can ask for clarifications. Now I get it, kind of.

Queena and Bunny were older than me, so they were always ahead of me in things. And I can't see what my friends are doing these days. I only know them like they were, in the pictures in my room from thirty years ago, but I'm sure they're doing things I never even thought of. Stuff I'll never get to do.

You've had all this life happen to you. Love. Sex. Babies. I didn't have a chance to have any of that. It's like watching your best friend get a boyfriend. You get left behind. It's such a bummer.

I know what happened to you was really shitty, and I'm not trying to be like Queena and make everything about me. But reading your letter—this is the first time I've really understood what I lost, too. Isn't that wild? All this time on this side, I really didn't get it. I didn't just lose the life I knew. I lost all the things I didn't know yet.

Even with everything you lost, you get to keep on living. You get to keep trying. You'll get more love. You'll get second chances. You get to keep moving forward, but I'll always be here in my

1970 bedroom, in Queena's 1987 house. I'm as useless and out of date as her girdles.

You get to keep on, Kitty. You think everything's over. From where I sit, you're life itself.

Love,
Nerida
xoxo

PART V
That Which Helps
or Hinders

I Wanna Be Sedated

Thursday, April 27, 2000

It would've been a lot easier to write to Nerida if I didn't keep getting interrupted by Rockaberry coolers.

I'd thought that putting everything down on paper would help, but it shone too bright a light on things I didn't want to look at. I needed to take the edge off, so when everyone was asleep, I got coolers out of the bomb shelter and sat outside, watching satellites blink past in the night sky while I rubbed Pixie's back and drank until the wee hours of the morning. I'd never really sobered up after the margaritas at Angel's house, to be honest.

My late-night Rockaberry habit meant that I spent most of the day sleeping. I managed to avoid seeing my family for three days, despite Queena knocking on my door to try to entice me with sausage or meatloaf.

When I woke up on the third day, I rolled over and saw another new tarot card added to the spread behind Pixie. I felt a chill, like a breeze kissing my cheek, and was too scared to move. How were cards just showing up like this? My first thought was Thom, but he'd never manage to get up my squeaky stairs without waking me. Besides, whoever or whatever was pulling these cards knew exactly how to place them in a Celtic Cross pattern.

I slid out of bed and onto the floor to look. It was The Star, in the position of things that are possible. It could mean finding a path to hope and healing. Or it could mean I needed to look at the stars while I drank coolers.

The door squeaked open, and footsteps came up the stairs.

"Bunny, go away!"

"It's not Bunny." Tiny appeared at the top of the stairs, and she looked around my room in amazement. "Ohmigod, Kitty. It's like one of those nightmares where you're back in high school."

I shifted slightly to be in front of Pixie and reached behind my back to pull her blanket over her.

Tiny came over to sit on the beanbag chair. It'd been her favourite place to sit when we read tarot cards. "Bunny said you haven't come downstairs in days and I should come over. Angel and I thought you might want to get together again."

I closed my eyes. Maybe if I played dead, she'd go away.

She spotted the tarot cards and leaned over to look. "You're reading cards again?"

"They're not mine. I found them in Nerida's room."

Tiny bounced a little, the way she always did when she was excited. "Nerida had tarot cards? Wow. I had no idea."

"Me neither."

"These are some intense cards." She laughed. "You should've seen the spreads I got after Rodger left me. The cards were pretty much screaming, 'Get away from that asshole.'"

"You still read cards?"

Tiny settled back in the beanbag, her foot pushing against Pixie's bed. I sat on my hands to keep from pulling it away. "I got a deck after he left. I missed it all so much. Tarot. Magic."

"Yeah. Me too."

"I missed you, too, you know. Even more than I missed magic. Kitty, I'm really, really sorry about what happened. I wish I'd been able to stand up to my mother. I was a shitty friend. I hope you can forgive me."

"Of course, I do. Our mothers aren't easy to stand up to." I moved so that my back was supported by the wall, stretching my legs between Pixie's bed and Tiny's feet. "Besides, I'm sorry too. You wouldn't have gone through all that with your mother if not for me. I mean, maybe you wouldn't even have ended up with Rodger."

Tiny narrowed her eyes. "You're right. I should be really mad at you." She laughed and kicked at my leg. "Can we be friends again, do you think?"

Something inside me came to life. "That'd be the best thing that's happened to me in ages."

Tiny reached into her pocket and pulled out a little bracelet made of slender silver and blue cord braided tightly around a crow's feather. It was knotted nine times and strung with agate and quartz beads – a witch's ladder. I held out my wrist as she tied it on.

"I made it with a spell to keep our friendship strong forever. I've got one, too." She pushed up her sleeve to show me. "And I made one for Angel. She's pretty interested in our magic. She might want to learn some things."

"Would that make us a coven?"

"A coven, or a gang. The Stoners have evolved."

I spun the little beads and rubbed the soft feather. "Cool. Gang jewellery."

Tiny sniffed. "It smells like the '80s up here. Baby Soft and cassette tapes and...why does it smell like the beach?"

"I noticed it too. So weird."

Tiny sniffed again, and I remembered that I hadn't showered in five days.

"I smell booze."

"I found a few Rockaberry coolers in the bomb shelter."

"Do they even make those anymore? They must be ancient. Bunny brings in stuff from the bomb shelter sometimes, so we can use it up before it goes bad."

"She brings it where?"

Tiny looked at me blankly. "The store. Fact & Fiction."

I looked at her blankly.

"Didn't Bunny tell you I work there?"

I shook my head.

"She caught me crying in the fairy tale section one day after Rodger left and insisted I have tea with her, and that led to her offering me a part-time job. She said we could make the store an asshole-free zone."

"That sounds like Bunny. Well, at least you get to work in the store. Just like we always planned."

Tiny rubbed my foot. "It's your store. You should come in."

"It'll always be Stubby's store. It shouldn't be mine." I picked up the Star card and fanned myself with it. "Did you ever think that it was all our fault? I mean, we tried to manifest our own store, and then a few weeks later, Stubby died and the store was mine. I just...I can't go in there. I feel like I murdered him."

Tiny's face went white. "Kitty! No! That's not what we meant at all. And we did the protection spell for him, with the poppet!"

"Yeah, but we'd already put other magic in motion, trying to manifest the store. Maybe it cancelled out the poppet." I pulled up my legs and rested my chin on my knees. "It wasn't your fault. It was my idea in the first place. Sometimes I think I'm the bad luck."

Tiny was looking at Pixie's little bed under the window.

"I don't know everything that went on with Matt, but Bunny told me about your miscarriage."

I stared across the room at a poster of Kate Bush. She'd know what to say in this kind of situation. I didn't.

"I had one too, before Nicholas. I thought everything was okay and then we had the first ultrasound and there wasn't a heartbeat. I felt like I was a horrible person because I didn't know anything was wrong."

"I'm sorry. That's how I felt, too."

"When we got home from the hospital, Rodger never mentioned it again. Like it hadn't happened. Things already weren't great between us, honestly, but it was so much worse after that. I thought maybe Nicholas would make things better. Stupid."

I scooted over to the milk crates and rummaged through the cassettes until I found the one Tiny needed: *Boys Suck, Part 5*.

"I think we must be up to Part 20 by now." Tiny flipped the tape over and scanned the songs. "So, is that what happened? Was Matt shitty about the miscarriage?"

"We were both shitty, I guess." I tried so hard not to look at Pixie that it felt obvious, like I'd put a big blinking arrow over her.

"Maybe you should do a love spell. Or maybe make some of your love tea." Tiny suggested.

"The love tea never worked for me. It just made me gassy."

Tiny pushed herself out of the beanbag chair. "I should let you rest, or whatever it is you're doing up here. Weird '80s things." She looked around, shaking her head. "Seriously, come hang out with me and Angel again. It doesn't have to be drinks. We can just talk."

"I don't know. I think I'm better off alone."

"Don't be so dramatic. Come for drinks." She started walking down the steps. "Maybe take a shower, first."

I was halfway through my second cooler on the deck that night when the light switched on and Thom stepped outside, lugging his old hockey bag. He dropped it at my feet with a crash of tinkling glass.

"What's this?" I asked.

He waved his hand with a flourish and gave the bag a kick. My empty cooler bottles spilled out. "Look, Puss, I don't know what happened between you and Matt, but you need to get your shit together."

"You're a fine one to talk."

The sliding door opened again, and Queena and Bunny came out, holding their robes against their chests.

"What the fuck is this? An intervention? Look, everyone just frig off." I pushed back my chair, knocking over the four cooler bottles I'd put there. The one I'd been drinking spilled out, spreading from my feet across the deck in a big, purplish-red stain. We all watched, like it was a slo-mo scene in an old murder mystery: *Murder on the Going-Nowhere-Fast Express.*

"Just look at you!" Queena flapped her arms in frustration. "You're a drunk! You look like riff-raff!"

"I'm not a drunk. I'm just working through some stuff. This helps me think."

Bunny pulled me back to my chair and sat next to me. "Drinking does not help one think, Kitten Love. Tiny told me she came to see you and that you smelled like you'd been bathing in Rockaberry coolers."

"Oh, great. Did you tell her to pretend to be my friend so she could snitch on me?"

"She wasn't snitching. She loves you. She was worried."

"Why don't you just tell us what's happened, so that we can fix it?" Queena fussed with my hair. I slapped her hand away.

"You can't fix it. I was pregnant. And now I'm not. And Matt and I are over." I reached for a new cooler and started to cry. "He doesn't want me anymore. He told me to get out. He says I'm bad luck."

Queena's hand flew to her throat. "How dare he!"

Bunny leaned over and grabbed my hands. "I'm so desperately sorry, sweetheart."

I could feel Pixie under my sweatshirt. She was okay. We were fine. We'd both be just fine if everyone would leave us alone.

Thom was standing next to me, and he started to rub my shoulder. I think it was probably the first time he'd ever touched my shoulder without punching it. I hated it. He cleared his throat and glanced at

Queena and Bunny for encouragement. "Listen, Puss. Why don't you show us what you've got there under your shirt?"

"Ew, don't be such a perv!"

"No, you eejit. The thing you're holding under your shirt. The doll. We've seen you with it. Tiny saw it, too."

I grasped my sweatshirt.

"You should talk to someone. Help sort things out. You know." Thom looked at Bunny again. They'd obviously rehearsed this whole scene.

"Oh God, not you, too. You think I'm crazy, just like Matt."

"Oh, sweetheart, you're not crazy," Bunny said.

"That's debatable," Thom muttered. Queena smacked him on the arm.

"You're not. You had a terrible loss, and you're very sad. I'm sure if Matt said that he's just upset, too." Bunny patted my hand. "Can I see the doll?"

I shook my head.

"We just want you to feel better," Thom said.

I wiped my eyes on my sweater and looked up at him. "I must be seriously fucked up if you're being nice to me."

"Oh yeah. You're totally fucked up."

Bunny swatted him on the head. "She's no more fucked up than the rest of us. Kitten's problems are just more obvious right now."

"Could everybody PLEASE mind their language!" Queena pleaded.

I closed my eyes and let Bunny rock me, the way I rocked Pixie. But Pixie wasn't a real baby. I knew that. Of course, I did. But hadn't I done a better job at keeping her safe? I didn't want to give her up. She was all I had left of the baby.

Thom picked up all the bottles and took them inside. Queena fussed over me, promising she'd take care of me, but I swatted her away and Bunny sent her in to bed. The two of us stayed out in the dark.

"Matt should be here with you," Bunny said. "Whatever passed between the two of you, I can't see how it would be enough to keep him away. He must know how much you're hurting."

"He knows where I am. He hasn't called. He doesn't care."

I stared out into the dark, at the last spot I'd seen my father. Right on cue, the image of him looking at me for the last time flashed into my consciousness, blotting out everything else. Maybe I really had inherited all the bad luck that had missed other generations, and the universe would keep piling crap on me until I broke. Maybe I already had.

Big Girls Don't Cry

Dear Kitty,

I've been watching talk shows with Thom and Ed. I like *Oprah* the best. It's wild, some of the stuff people spill on that show to total strangers. We never did that when I was with the Living. God, I sound like an old person, don't I? I guess I am. The oldest seventeen-year-old you'll ever meet. Ha.

When I used to fall off my bike and scrape my knee, my mother would kiss it and say, "There. All better," which basically meant I was supposed to stop crying and get over it. We didn't talk about stuff. We just moved on. Well, most people moved on. Our family's not so great at that, obviously.

When my date for the spring formal flaked out on me at the last minute, I was so bummed out. I stayed in my room the whole afternoon and cried. All my friends were going to that dance, and I had this beautiful silver dress I was going to wear. My mother came in with her hands on her hips and told me to get up and get over it, because big girls don't cry.

That was the way we did it, back then. I don't know if I'd want to talk to Oprah, but I wish I'd been allowed to feel sad, at least.

I'm still really bummed I didn't get to wear the silver dress.

Love,
Nerida
xoxo

What's on Your Mind

May 2000

The family doctor I'd gone to as a child, who'd been approximately one hundred and forty years old at the time, had long since retired. Queena had gone through five other doctors in ten years as they cycled in and out of Paradise Valley for greener pastures. Bunny made me an appointment with the latest doctor—Dr. Davies—and she came with me because she considered me a flight risk. Dr. Davies looked like someone Matt would work with. Matt thought I was crazy. This doctor probably would, too.

I reacted to questions about my mental health the same way I'd done at seventeen. I gave one-word answers. I sat with my arms folded and stared petulantly at an old yellow water stain on the dropped ceiling while Dr. Davies asked way too many questions about the miscarriage. I'd rather not have thought about that let alone talked about it, especially in front of Bunny. Bunny was more than happy to fill in the blanks, expounding on Pixie, Matt, my drinking, past suicide attempt, hysterical mother, curses, father's death, witchcraft, and general family fucked-upedness. Really, Bunny had a pretty good time at my doctor's appointment.

Dr. Davies referred me to a psychologist at the university in Elgin and wrote a prescription for Fluoextine for depression.

"It'll take a few weeks for you to notice a difference. It sounds like you've been dealing with these feelings for a long time, so it won't change overnight."

"But she can get better, can't she?" Bunny watched a lot of *ER* and was very comfortable in medical settings.

"It's not terminal, Bunny," I muttered.

Dr. Davies looked at me seriously. "It was almost terminal for you once, though, wasn't it? Mental illness is no different from your body being sick."

"Oh, so I'm mentally ill now? Just because I'm sad about having a miscarriage?"

"No, grief isn't mental illness, but this seems like more than just the miscarriage. Depression isn't just about feeling sad. It can affect your thinking, and your ability to make decisions. It can make you avoid things. If you don't treat it, things can get a lot worse. You can hurt yourself, and your relationships, and develop some unhealthy ways of coping."

She'd pretty much summed up my whole adult life in that last sentence.

———

Angel set a vegetable tray in front of me and sat down. "Was it awful?"

"The therapist is really nice. Honestly, it was just like talking to you guys, but with less swearing and more crying. I'm going twice a week, plus she wants me to go to a weekly grief group."

"Oh Jesus. Aren't we your grief group?" Tiny started pouring drinks, but I put my hand over my glass.

"It's okay," Angel said. "They're mocktails."

"That sounds awful. You guys don't need to skip the margaritas on my account."

Angel kicked off her sandals and put her feet on an empty chair. "We could stand to skip a few margaritas."

"So, how does it work? Do you get homework?" Tiny swatted a bug away from her drink. It was the first warm day in May, and the mosquitos were waking up.

"I have to face things I've been avoiding. Like going to the store."

Tiny reached for my hand. "I'll be right there with you. Just say when."

"What about Matt?" Angel asked. She held a baby carrot between her fingers like a cigarette.

I shrugged and twisted my hair around a finger until it turned purple.

"What if you just went back? You know, showed up on his doorstep?"

"It's her doorstep, too," Tiny pointed out.

I watched a fly dive into my mocktail and pushed the glass away. "I doubt he wants to see me."

Tiny shaded her eyes with one hand and squinted at me. "Do you even want him back, if he can't be bothered to call you when you obviously weren't in a good place? You deserve better than that."

"I don't know what I want. I really don't." I looked up hopefully, thinking that either Angel or Tiny would have the answer, but Angel had closed her eyes and lifted her face to the sun, and Tiny was sorting through the vegetable tray in search of celery that wasn't limp. I slumped in my chair and traced circles in the margarita salt with a used-up wedge of lime, hoping salt for fake margaritas didn't offer fake protection.

PART VI
That Which is Before You

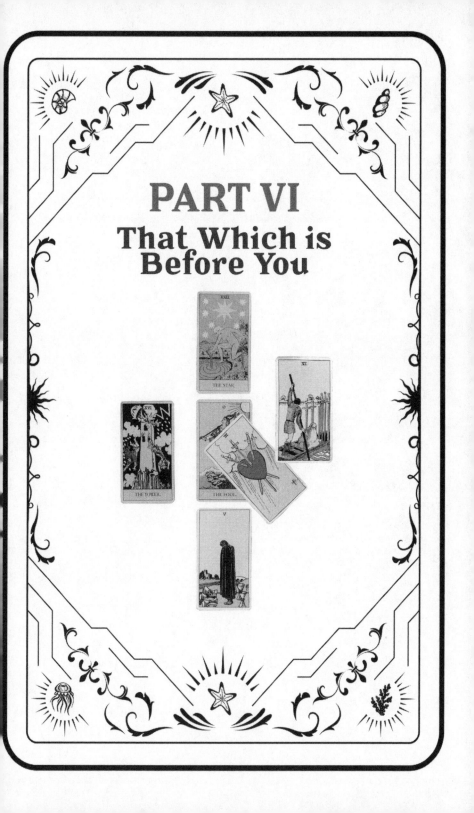

The Ghost in You

June 2000

Tiny and I had been walking up and down the sidewalk in front of Fact & Fiction for at least fifteen minutes while I gathered the nerve to go in. I wanted to take deep breaths to calm myself, like my therapist had taught me, but Paradise Valley smelled particularly farty that day. Deep breaths would result in deep nausea.

"Maybe I should wait. I might need stronger medication before I can handle this." I looked up at Fact & Fiction's yellow facade. A tree branch knocked against the attic window. It hadn't reached that window, last time I'd been in.

Tiny took me by the elbow and steered me toward the little walkway leading to the front steps. "You've got this. Even your tarot card said so this morning."

I'd found the Six of Swords that morning, in the Near-Future position. It meant leaving troubles behind or severing ties. I was pretty sure my ties were already severed. It'd been approximately twelve hundred hours since I'd talked to Matt. If there'd been word problems about depression and relationship issues on my high school math exams, I probably would've gotten better grades.

Tiny glanced at her watch. "Bunny's in there waiting for you. I wish I could stay but I've had this doctor's appointment for weeks." She gave me a gentle push. "Go. Face your ghosts."

I nodded and bit my lip. Tiny gave me a quick hug and started to back away. I turned and walked up the path, taking a deep breath of farty air before I pushed open the front door of Fact & Fiction.

The smell hit immediately—a comforting perfume of musty paper and pine shelves mixed with my best childhood memories. The same threadbare red carpet covered the warped oak floors, and the stained-glass window on the landing was still cracked. The only real difference was Bunny behind the front counter, and the absence of Stubby. I'd never been in Fact & Fiction when he wasn't there.

Bunny slipped out from behind the counter and caught me in her arms. "I'm so glad you're here. The store is so glad you're here. I can feel it."

"Don't let Queena hear you talking like that. She'll call you a hippie."

Bunny put her hands on my shoulders and beamed at me. "Now, should I come with you?"

"I'm okay, I think. Can I have the key to the attic?"

She went behind the counter to take her key chain from her purse. "It's probably a mess. I only go up there to get the Christmas decorations."

She gave me the key and an encouraging smile, and I headed up the two flights of stairs to reach the attic door. The narrow, unpainted stairs were more intimidating than I remembered—the stairwell was dark, and the steps groaned like an old pirate ship as I climbed them, emerging at the top into a constellation of dust in sunbeams.

It looked like my younger self had just walked away. I flipped through the pile of books next to my favourite armchair—*Celtic Lore, Evil and Shadow in Fairy Tales, Witchcraft for Healing*—and felt pangs of nostalgia for the girl I'd been.

I slipped my hand under the seat cushion, bracing myself for dead spiders or mice, and pulled my vintage copy of *Robin Hood* from its hiding place. The mustiness of the old pages was even stronger now, but the illustration on the cover made my stomach twist. Matt hadn't looked exactly like the Robin Hood in the picture, but he'd seemed close enough. It wasn't Robin Hood that caught my eye now, though. Maid Marian, with her long black hair and silver dress falling over her horse, looked a lot more badass than I remembered. She wasn't looking at Robin Hood adoringly, like a damsel in distress. She was looking down on him from her horse as though he was blocking her way.

As I went to tuck the book in my bag, two envelopes fluttered to the floor and I jumped back, still thinking of mice and spiders. I hadn't left any envelopes in the book. I bent to pick them up, remembering Tiny's letter falling from my French textbook all those years ago.

One envelope was addressed to me, and one to Thom, in Stubby's spikey printing. I touched where he'd written my name and lifted the envelope to my nose in case any of his scent lingered. With shaking hands, I opened the one addressed to me. The glue on the envelope was as dried out and crisp as the corsage in Nerida's night table, and it gave way easily. I pulled out the small sheets of paper and unfolded them just enough to see the top.

July 1987
My darling Kitten,

I had a dream last night telling me that I should write you this letter. I hope I'm just being silly. If you find this in your book and I'm still downstairs, talking about birds with Howard Barker, just put the letter back in the envelope and tuck it away until I'm gone. I hope that won't be for a long time, but death comes when it wants. Nothing anyone does or doesn't do can stop that.

I'd been holding my breath as I read, and I exhaled as I stuffed the envelopes back inside *Robin Hood*. I wasn't ready to read the rest of the letter now. I shoved the book to the bottom of my bag and glanced around the attic one last time in case it was hiding other secrets, before I headed downstairs.

I stopped in front of the full-length mirror on the second floor to check my cheeks for smeared mascara. A voice boomed behind me.

"Kitten! Is it really you?"

I turned and saw my father's birding friend, Mr. Barker, coming up the stairs.

He grasped both my hands in his. "It's so wonderful to see you, Kitten. I don't think I've seen you since your father's funeral."

I braced myself for a flood of emotion but felt only a gentle wave that retreated as quickly as it had washed over me.

"I used to love when you'd come in here. You and my father would laugh so much, I could hear it all over the store."

Mr. Barker smiled. He had a way of smiling so hard that his eyes almost disappeared.

"Oh, I do miss your father, Kitten. I always hoped I'd see you here, running things like he did."

"The store's in good hands with Bunny."

He waved a hand scornfully. "Oh, Bunny. She doesn't have your father's knack for finding things. Nor for making conversation, for that matter." He looked down the steps toward the counter and shot Bunny a look. "Sometimes she just scowls and hands a book to me, *without discussing it!*"

I laughed. "I think discussing books cuts into the time she can sneak out for a cigarette."

"Smoking! Like some ghastly book dragon." Mr. Barker shuddered. "She does care about you an awful lot, though, so I suppose she's not all bad. She told me you've been having a bit of a sad time. I know what that's like. Your father helped me through some rough times. He had such kindness and wisdom."

I smiled at my feet, blinking back tears.

"I was in earlier and Bunny said you might be here today, so I popped out to get something for you."

He handed me a brown paper bag that he'd balanced on top of his armload of books. I peeked inside.

"Sugared donuts!" I laughed. "My favourite!"

Mr. Barker smiled his enormous smile. "I know. I remember your father always making sure there were some here for you. It's not much, but I wanted you to know that you're not alone."

I held the bag up to my face. The sugar and fried dough mingled with the used books and pine shelves, wrapping me in a warm hug.

"You're all grown up. I can still picture you downstairs reading fairy tales, all tucked up in the corner," Mr. Barker said.

I held out the bag of donuts to offer him one. "I don't much believe in fairy tales these days."

He plucked a donut from the bag and cocked his head. "I don't pretend to know what's made you sad, Kitten, but don't forget, fairy tales often have a dragon or two in the middle." He reached for my hand and gave it a squeeze. "I do hope we'll see you here behind that counter someday. You belong here every bit as much as your father did."

Mr. Barker disappeared into the Military History shelves, and I stood in the hall composing myself, letting my new sense of peace fill me up. Stubby hadn't left. He was in every book on every shelf of this store and every speck of dust in the air. There were memories, but they were sweet and poignant; a little painful, but also a relief. The store felt like a hug from my father, a hand on the small of my back hurrying me back to myself, and I felt welcomed home.

Bunny and Queena were waiting for me at the front counter.

"I can't stay long," Queena said, glancing out the window. "I just popped over on a break."

"I was chatting with Mr. Barker upstairs. It was so nice to see him."

"Pompous old windbag." Bunny dropped a pile of magazines on the counter with a satisfied look, as though she was squashing Mr. Barker under them.

Queena smirked. "Bunny's still mad because Howard Barker told her she looked like an ornamental cabbage in her prom dress."

"He was rude in high school and he's rude now. Queena, I'm croaking for some tea, and I think Kitten could use some, too. Go. Fetch."

"Speaking of rude!" Queena rolled her eyes and headed to the kitchen. Bunny and I leaned over the counter next to each other, knocking into each other with our hips. I took one of Mr. Barker's donuts and slid the bag toward Bunny.

"Did you ever leave anything up in the attic for me? Like, any letters?" I asked.

Bunny looked confused. "Like I told you, I only go up there for the Christmas decorations. The place gives me the creeps. I swear it's haunted. I never could see why you liked it."

"What about Queena? Or Tiny? Have they been up there?"

"God no. Queena's terrified of mice. And Tiny doesn't have a key. What's this about?"

"Nothing. I just found something I wasn't expecting, in a place I wasn't expecting it."

"Well, that's mysterious."

Queena placed a teapot and a package of cookies on the counter. "What's mysterious?"

I inspected the package. "These cookies. Are they from this decade? Will we get food poisoning? It's a mystery."

"They're still perfectly good, Kitten. 'Best Before' doesn't mean 'Poisonous After.'"

I shoved the cookies toward Bunny. "So, would it be okay if I started coming here to help out, sometimes?"

"It's your store. I should be asking you if I can help out. You come here whenever you want, sweet thing. That's what your father wanted."

The little bell on the door chimed and Rodger walked in with a little boy who had Tiny's big brown eyes. Rodger took him into the children's section, and then came back over and leaned on the counter in front of me.

"Hey, Kitty. Haven't seen you around." His attempt at looking seductive might've worked when I was sixteen, but now it just made me wonder what I'd even seen in him.

Queena pulled an old Instamatic camera from behind the counter. "Don't mind me!" she called as she walked around the room, snapping pictures of shelves and books.

Bunny and I rolled our eyes at each other. Queena had a vast collection of random bookstore photos she used for scrapbooking.

Rodger was still at the counter, leering at me. "Thought you might want to go for a drink sometime."

I leaned over the counter to get closer to him. He leaned in too, thinking he was getting somewhere. I looked him straight in the eye.

"You broke my best friend's heart. Go fuck yourself."

Queena was suddenly next to us, snapping another photo. "Language, Kitten! Goodness."

Rodger shrugged. "Your loss," he said, retreating into the children's room.

I punched Bunny in the arm. "I thought you'd made this an asshole-free zone."

"Well, I can't just bar him from the store. He does buy a lot of books for the little one. And he only comes in when he knows Tiny isn't here."

"I remember you being quite taken with him when you were younger." Queena came back around the counter to get her purse. "Maybe the two of you could get together some time and catch up."

"He's an asshole and he dresses like a Muppet. Just, ew. Fuck."

Queena didn't even reproach me for my language. She put the camera in her purse and didn't meet my eyes.

"Fine then, dear. I just thought it's time you start trying to move on, since you're not hearing from Matt." She patted her purse and looked distracted. "I'm off to The Memory Garden, then."

Bunny elbowed me in the ribs as Queena shut the door behind her. "Dollars to donuts she's making a whole scrapbook about you and some imaginary boyfriend. You and Rodger, together again." She reached into the bag of donuts and speared one with a finger.

"For fuck's sake," I shuddered. "She's the best fiction writer in this whole bookstore."

"Ah well, she enjoys her little fantasies. It's all harmless, and it keeps her happy. And when Queena's happy, we're all happy."

A Little Bit Me, A Little Bit You

Dear Kitty,

I hope I'm not freaking you out too much with the tarot cards. It's not like I'm *really* interfering. It's up to you what you read into it. Still, I hope I don't get in trouble for it. Getting grounded on this side means something way worse than it does on yours.

I didn't exactly pick the Six of Swords for you. It fell out of the deck, so I'm not sure if it was really meant for you or for me. I figured it was you, because I don't have a lot of change or troubles to leave behind on this side. But then I looked at it for a while, and I realized that maybe the message was for both of us?

I know I've got to move on at some point. Donny and my parents (and Jim Morrison!) are there now, so it's not like I'd be on my own. It'd be weird not to be around Bunny and Queena, though. And you, too. I always thought I'd stay until I was sure you'd all be okay. I'm not sure you're there yet.

I really wish I could take my silver dress with me for when I meet Jim Morrison, because you know I'm checking him out first when I get to the Afterlife. Ha.

Love,
Nerida
xoxo

Trouble Me

June 2000

I left most therapy sessions with my tear ducts burning, feeling like my brain had been power washed. I needed time to decompress and get my energy back before driving home from my therapist's office on the university campus in Elgin, so I'd started dropping by a nearby coffee shop. I'd just settled at a table on the deck overlooking the water when I heard a voice behind me.

"Can I join you?"

It was Ed. I almost didn't recognize him out of the context of Queena's living room—he was wearing proper clothes instead of sweats and was carrying a briefcase instead of the usual bowl of Cheezies.

"Sorry, didn't mean to startle you. I was just getting some coffee."

"A coffee shop's a good place for that." I mentally willed him to go away. It didn't work. He pulled out a chair and sat down.

"What are you doing in Elgin?" he asked.

"I had an appointment. What are you doing here?"

"Teaching a summer class."

"Oh, right," I said. "That explains why you're not in sweatpants."

I tried to calculate how quickly I could drink a coffee and get out of there. I didn't want another painful conversation like the one we'd had in Kelowna.

The waitress came by to take our orders, and she and Ed started chatting. He seemed to be a regular, and the waitress was clearly flirting with him. I remembered Tiny telling Angel and me that Ed really wasn't that bad. Clearly the waitress agreed, unless she was just sucking up for tips.

Ed had always been a gangly kid, and even as an adult was still a bit lanky. His dark hair, which already had a few threads of grey in it, was always a bit messy from his habit of running a hand through it, and his nose had a bump from the time Thom had accidentally broken it with a Pogo Stick when they were ten. If you'd asked me before to tell you what colour Ed's eyes were, I'd have pulled a blank even though I saw him (and ignored him) almost every day for years. Now I saw that his eyes were a mossy green—a colour that reminded me of the forest floor. They were just like his mother's eyes, I realized, because I remembered noticing them on the day she rescued me. There was a broadness in his shoulders that I'd never noticed before, and a certain maturity and ease about the way he held himself. Away from the couch and the talk shows and the Cheezies, he didn't look quite as pathetic as I remembered. In fact, out here in the real world, he looked surprisingly good. Maybe Tiny hadn't been so wrong. I wondered why I'd never noticed it before.

I whipped my eyes back to the menu as my stomach lurched.

Jesus Murphy, Kitten, I lectured myself, *it's Ed, for chrissakes. You need to get your meds adjusted.*

The waitress took my order (and didn't spend as much time chatting to me, I noted), and then too efficiently cleared away the menus, leaving me nothing to hide behind.

Sitting with him, at a loss for conversation, reminded me of that day in Kelowna—the same day I'd decided Matt and I should have a baby. Well, the Magic 8 Ball decided, I guess. That hadn't even been a year ago. Matt and I might not have made that decision that day if Ed's visit hadn't provoked us to talk about my lack of direction. And if we hadn't made that decision that day, I might not be in the situation I was in now. I looked at Ed out of the corner of my eye. Maybe he was bad luck.

"You must've missed the ocean when you were in the Okanagan," Ed said, thanking the waitress as she placed our coffees in front of us.

"I did. The ocean's calming. I went to the lake sometimes when I felt crappy. It wasn't the same though."

"Were things crappy in Kelowna?"

"Oh, no!" I backpedalled. "There's just stuff, you know? Some days it catches up to me. For some reason, staring at the water helps calm me down. It's good for heartache. And stuff."

Ed was quiet for a moment and fiddled with the handle on his coffee cup.

"I know exactly how that is." He pushed his cup away but kept his eyes on it. "After things ended with Sara, I spent a lot of time walking on the beach."

"Who's Sara?"

He shifted uncomfortably in his chair.

"I'm sorry. You don't need to tell me," I said.

"It's okay." He cleared his throat and forced an unconvincing smile. "I was engaged to Sara in Vancouver. But we called it off. I called it off, actually. The week before."

"The week before? Jesus. What happened?"

"I guess I just clued in that it wasn't just about a wedding," Ed said. "It was about spending my life with this person. I thought I loved her. I did love her. But then I realized I didn't love her enough. I couldn't go through with it."

"Shit. That must've been awful."

"She was pretty upset. You can imagine. Her brothers wanted to beat me up. I still feel guilty. I really didn't want to hurt her."

"But it was probably for the best, right? I mean, you shouldn't get married if you're not sure it's the right person."

Ed turned a sugar packet over and over between his fingers. Instinctively, I reached for his hand and gave it a quick squeeze. "It must've been really hard to do that."

Ed looked up at me. "So why didn't you and Matt get married? You were together what, six years?"

I jerked my hand back and stared at the finger where the ring had been. I'd taken it off after the first week in Paradise Valley.

"I guess I was scared to commit. I was sure my bad luck would just mess everything up." I took a deep breath. If Ed could share stuff, so could I. "And it did. I got pregnant, not long after you visited. But then I lost the baby—"

"Oh Kitty, I'm—"

"—and then I really wasn't doing okay. You know how we Loves react to things." I gave him a meaningful look, and he nodded. "Matt was...horrified? Angry? He said he was done with me."

"That's pretty shitty of him."

"You don't know the whole story. I made things difficult. Anyway, he left, and then I left, and now here I am." I sat straighter and looked out at the water again. "Since I'm just blurting things out now, I'm in Elgin today because I'm seeing a therapist. I have to come three times a week, in fact. So now you know. I'm alone. Back at Queena's house. I might be even more fucked up than Thom. I can't make decisions, and then when I do, they turn out to be shitty decisions. I do shitty things. I'm bad luck."

Ed reached over and put his hand on my knee, retracting it so quickly I barely had time to register he'd touched me.

"You're not bad luck."

I wiped my eyes on my sleeve. "Matt said I was crazy. And you, of all people, know he was right."

"You're not crazy. Can't you just go back and talk things over with him?"

I grabbed a sugar packet and started playing with it like he had, but mine ripped open and made a mess. I threw the torn paper onto the table and sat back in my chair. "He's just cut me off. It's not like him. I don't think what I did was unforgivable."

Ed grabbed another sugar packet. His broke, too. "You haven't actually told me what you did, so I can't say whether it's unforgivable. You don't need to tell me if you don't want. But I'm happy to listen anytime."

"Yeah?"

"Yeah."

"Well, if you ever want to talk about Sara, I'll listen, too. We can have a nightly pity party on Queena's sofa." I frowned. "I mean, I guess we already do."

The waitress glared at the pile of sugar on the table and slapped down my bill. Her attitude softened a bit when she gave Ed his. He reached over and took mine. I started to object, but he waved me off.

"It's just a coffee."

"One coffee and an hour of therapy," I countered. "I owe you, like, a gazillion dollars."

Ed smiled at me and cocked his head. "This is weird. Is this weird?"

"It is a bit, isn't it?" I glanced at my watch. "I have to get going. I promised Bunny I'd do the bank deposit today." I reached over and gave his hand a quick squeeze. "Thank you. That helped."

He returned the squeeze. "Listen, would it help if we met for coffee after your appointments? You could relax a bit before you go back to face Queena. We could talk some more."

"Well...yeah. I've been coming here afterwards for coffee, anyway. It might be nice to have some company." I hadn't hated talking to him, but I didn't want him to think I wanted to see him on a regular basis. He was still Ed.

As we walked out to the parking lot, I stopped and grabbed him by the elbow. "Hey—maybe we shouldn't tell Thom about this.

I mean, you know how he is. He might think I'm stealing his friend like Dickhead stole Kim."

Ed gave me a wry smile and nodded. "Sure. You can go on ignoring me and insulting me, like usual."

I laughed. "If I was suddenly nice to you after all these years, Queena would probably think it was a sign of the coming apocalypse and she'd lock us all in the bomb shelter."

We stood awkwardly again until finally Ed took a step backwards.

"See you on the sofa tonight, I guess?"

"It's *Survivor* night."

PART VII
That Which Gives You Power

Message in a Bottle

A sliver of light from the bomb shelter's one bare bulb streamed out of the partly open door and across the concrete basement floor. Thom's door was open, too, and a brighter light from his Montreal Canadiens lamp made a line that met the shelter's light in the middle of the basement. I stood in the crosshairs, steeling my nerve. I patted the pocket of my long black cardigan and rapped on the bomb shelter door.

"Are you decent in there?"

I heard a scuffle and a sniffle, and then Thom pulled the door open.

"I was hungry. Couldn't sleep." His cot was littered with empty boxes of Pop-Tarts, a tube of squeeze cheese, and a half-eaten box of Sociables crackers.

"God. You're going to do yourself in, eating all that crap."

"It's gonna happen anyway. Might as well be well fed."

I kicked at an empty bag of chips. "How the hell were you a chef when you eat this shit?"

"Shut up!"

"You shut up."

We sat staring at the floor, each waiting for the other to break the silence. I pulled out the envelope and leaned over to put it next to Thom. He picked it up and stared at Stubby's writing, looking like he'd seen a ghost.

"What is it?"

"A letter. I've got one too, but I haven't read it yet. I found them in an old book of mine in the attic at Fact & Fiction." I reached over and took a handful of crackers. "Go on. Read it."

Thom was touching the writing, just like I had. "You read yours, first."

"Not yet. It feels like once I do, that's the end. That's the last I'll hear from him." I folded my arms for warmth. The bomb shelter was always cooler than the rest of the house.

"Then I don't want to read mine, either." Thom set it next to him on the army blanket but kept watching it, like he expected it to move. "What do you think it says?"

"No idea. I don't know why they were hidden like that. I guess he didn't think it would take me thirteen years to find it." I got up and walked to the door. "Let me know when you're going to read yours."

Thom shook his head. "I'm not reading it. Maybe he's telling me something awful, like a message from beyond the grave telling me what day the Love Heart's going to get me. Or maybe he's telling me he's not my real dad or something."

"For fuck's sake, Thom! You look exactly like him. You need to stop watching *Jerry Springer*. Jesus."

"Shut up!"

"You shut up."

He threw a cracker at me as I pulled the door shut.

———

Pixie had been sitting on top of my wardrobe, next to the Cabbage Patch doll, since three weeks after I started therapy. I'd started by not carrying her in her sling and instead leaving her in her blankets. Then I stopped reading to her, and gradually, I stopped talking to her, until finally, I was ready to put her away. I still instinctively reached to pat her against me, and the floor under the window seemed empty without her little nest of blankets, but letting go of her wasn't as hard as I'd expected. In fact, I realized that having her close made me feel worse, because she was a reminder of how low I'd gotten, and her blue eyes looking back at me reinforced the absence of Matt's.

I'd tucked Stubby's letter under her when I brought it home from Fact & Fiction, and placed the photo of Matt and me next to them—all the heartbreaks I needed to let go of, together in one place.

After I left Thom in the bomb shelter with his letter, I lit some candles and sat on my windowsill, breathing deeply of the night air that smelled, luckily, more of ocean than pulp mill. My eyes moved from the shadows outside to the envelope, thick and narrow, under Pixie. I bit my thumb, my curiosity doing battle with my anxiety.

"I'm sorry it took so long to find your letter," I whispered into the darkness outside. "But if I read it now, I'll never hear from you again. Will I?"

I scanned the shadows outside, waiting for an answer. Every fibre of my body tensed.

Silence.

I swallowed the lump rising in my throat, reasoning with myself. What had I expected? An owl? That kind of magical thinking had caused so much of my trouble. I couldn't expect it to save me, now.

A breeze kissed my cheek, fluttering the lace curtain and filling the room with a warm, summer smell. My eyes moved to Stubby's letter, and my heart started to pound. The letter was pulled out from under Pixie, almost dangling off the wardrobe. And the candle flames around my room were dancing wildly, longer and brighter than I'd ever seen in my life.

I got up and reached for the envelope.

July 1987
My darling Kitten,

    I had a dream last night telling me that I should write you this letter. I hope I'm just being silly. If you find this in your book and I'm still downstairs, talking about birds with Howard Barker, just put the letter back in the envelope and tuck it away until I'm gone. I hope that won't be for a long time, but death comes when it wants. Nothing anyone does or doesn't do can stop that.

    I want Fact & Fiction to be yours, my sweet girl, because I've seen you learn and grow so much here over the years and I know you'll love the store, and the magic each book holds, as much as I have. I hope it'll be a safe harbour for you, but not a place to hide. You'll need to come out of the attic now and then.

    Be kind to your mother. We tease her about her end of the world preparations, but she's doing her best. She's spent too much time imagining the absolute worst that could happen to us, after what happened to Nerida. Her grief is as deep as her love, but I'm not sure she knows how to do one without the other anymore. I guess since you're reading this letter, you might understand that kind of sadness. I hope you come to know how the wounded bits of your heart can grow back bigger and stronger. And do you remember what I told you that day when you and Tiny snuck off to the beach? You can't spend your life thinking of bad things in the past, or worrying about things that might happen. The only place you can control and find joy is right this minute. So don't spend time thinking about what's lost, Kitten. Go find something even better.

    Now, I know you think it's a secret, but I know about your magic. I've heard you and Tiny giggling and chanting, and I can tell which books are missing from the shelves. I think you've hidden it from me because you thought I'd be mad or think it's silly, but it might surprise you to learn that I believe in magic, too. I know it's real. It's in the smell of a new book when you first open it. It's in opening a used book and seeing tiny notes made by people who read it before you, giving you a window to someone else's thoughts. It's in driving to the beach on a summer day and rolling down the windows to let in that warm, salty air. There's magic in hearing your favourite song on the radio, and suddenly your day is a whole lot brighter. There was so much magic, for me, in holding you for the first time, and loving you so much more every day after that. There's big magic in falling in love, and I hope you find that magic in abundance, with someone who appreciates how magical you are. The magic is in living. It's all magic, Kitten. Every bit of this world. And that includes you. Every bit of you. I hope you never lose sight of that.

Go find your magic. Go find your treasure.
With all my love forever,
Dad

Let's Live for Today

Dear Kitty,

I wish I'd thought of leaving a letter. It would've been nice to tell Queena and Bunny that it wasn't their fault, but Queena would've accused Bunny of writing it, and Bunny would've accused Queena, and they'd both flip their wigs.

Still. At least they'd know. We weren't big on saying "I love you" in my family, but if they had a letter, they'd have something permanent from me. I could've written letters to everybody, telling them not to forget me and not to take their world for granted. I can imagine their faces when they found them. It'd be far-out.

I've been thinking about what your dad said about living in the present and not getting stuck in the past. Do you think that's what I've been doing? Well, not the living part. Ha. But maybe there's more to life than death. Or more to death than not being alive. Whoa. That was deep.

I picked the Judgement card for you today because it's about transformation and healing, like a phoenix rising from the ashes. It's also about a big decision that could alter your life's course. I know you're not great at decisions, so I wanted you to be prepared.

I put a rose quartz on top, so you'd know it wasn't just the wind blowing a card over. I'm a little insulted you thought that, after all the work I put into moving it (it's not easy, you know. pushing stuff around with transparent fingers). I'm pretty sure this falls under Haunting and not Interfering. I guess I'll have to wait and see if I get blasted by a lightning bolt or whatever. Ha.

Love,
Nerida
xoxo

True

I had the weirdest feeling someone was watching me.

Another card was flipped over when I woke up that morning, with a crystal placed on top. I really wanted to ask Bunny if she knew anything about it, but if I told her that tarot cards were magically appearing in my room, she'd probably cart me off to the doctor again.

The attic was dim. I hadn't turned on any lights, but I'd lit a whole bunch of candles—not only for atmosphere, but to watch their flames. If there were big flickers, it might be a sign that there was a spirit present.

I heard a knock, and the door at the bottom of the steps opened.

"Can I come up?" Ed called.

I shifted to cover the tarot cards with my black peasant skirt. Paired with an electric blue off-the-shoulder T-shirt I'd found in my wardrobe, I looked as much an '80s artifact as anything else in the attic.

Ed looked around at all the candles. "Bunny said I should come on up. I didn't mean to interrupt."

"It's okay. It's just for atmosphere. I'm not doing any weird stuff up here."

Ed lowered himself, a bit awkwardly, into the beanbag chair.

"I just came by to let you know I won't be able to meet for coffee on Monday and Wednesday. I'll be back for Thursday, though."

We'd been spending the afternoons together after my therapy

sessions for the past few weeks. We'd grab a coffee from the café and take it to the beach and spend a couple of hours walking the sand and talking. I'd come to look forward to it. When he wasn't around my brother, Ed was funny and charming, and he gave such good advice that I told him he was like Yoda. But in the evenings, when Thom was around, I'd sit next to Ed on the sofa and say things like "Pass the chips, twat-waffle," so that Thom wouldn't get suspicious.

"I've got an interview for a position in Ontario. It's just for the academic year. I'm flying there on Sunday."

"Ontario? You never mentioned anything about this."

"I applied ages ago. I didn't think anything would come of it. It still might not, but now that Mum's doing better, I should probably focus on my career. If I stay here much longer, I might end up stuck on the sofa forever, like Thom."

I laughed the way people do when something isn't really funny. My stomach felt twitchy and the floor under me felt shaky, and my fingers grasped at my long skirt, searching for something solid to hold on to. I focused on my breath like my therapist had taught me, confused by my reaction.

"That's great, if you want to go." I tried to smile brightly. "I mean, great for your career. If you want to leave. It's just, I mean, I didn't think you wanted to." The heartbeat in my ears was as loud as Queena's wallpaper.

"It's not that I want to. I could try to pick up classes in Elgin if I really wanted, and maybe it'd lead to something more permanent, but..." His voice trailed off, and he stared at the floor between us, his finger tracing a shape like an infinity symbol along the floorboards. He stopped, looking at the edge of my skirt, where the tarot deck was peeking out. "Maybe you should do a reading for me. You know, give me an idea of what I should do, or how the interview will go."

I scoffed and tucked the deck further under my leg. "No way. You don't believe in this stuff. You'll laugh at me."

"Why would I laugh? Maybe I don't really believe in it, but I always thought you were good at it." He leaned forward and pulled the deck from beneath my skirt, his hand brushing my thigh. I kept my head down as he handed me the cards, so he wouldn't see how flushed my face had become.

I glanced over to the five cards that had mysteriously shown up in a layout. I didn't want to put them back in the deck until I understood how they'd gotten there. In fact, I was kind of scared to touch them.

"Some cards are missing. It won't be accurate," I said.

"I don't mind. I won't even know."

"You promise you won't tell Thom? He's such an arse about this stuff."

"Pinky swear," he vowed.

I linked my pinky with his, and told him to think of a question. "You don't have to tell me what it is if you don't want. And I won't tell Thom. Pinky swear."

"I don't really have a question. I just want to know what I need to know, I guess."

"Okay, I'll do a simple past-present-future spread then. Just three cards."

I got Ed to split the deck in three, and then shuffled and drew a card, placing it on the floor between us. The familiar, faint scent of ocean filled the room. I was coming to associate it with tarot.

"This is the Hermit, and it represents your past. Maybe you needed to remove yourself from the world, or maybe you felt stuck. The Hermit tells us that sometimes the best way to learn or grow is to be patient, and to be on your own for a while, so you can block out all the noise and listen to your inner voice." I tucked a curl behind my ear and smiled. "Do science-y people listen to their inner voices?"

"Maybe if they set up an experiment to test its validity." Ed reached for the Hermit card to have a better look just as I put down the second card, and our hands touched. I bit my lip and tried to stay focused.

"Okay, this is the Ace of Cups, and it's in the present position. It means the start of a period of strong emotional health. All kinds of joy, happiness, and success, and a big change might be happening." I glanced up at him. "I think this is a positive sign about your job interview. Let's see what the future tells us."

I turned over the last card, the Nine of Cups, and smiled at Ed.

"You got the wish card! It's a sign that you're going to get exactly what you wish for. Although, you should be careful about that. Be specific about what you want beccause the Universe is listening." I laughed. "Okay, now I sound woo, so you've probably had enough of this." I felt my smile fading, and busied myself with picking up the cards.

Ed handed me the Nine of Cups. "So I can wish for anything I want? And I'll get it?"

"Maybe not eternal life or omniscient power, but yeah, just about anything. Choose wisely." I sighed. "You know, I've always been so bad at choosing things. Even if someone told me I could have anything I wished for, I'd probably be too scared to figure out what I wanted. My therapist says the decision I've made most is deciding to do nothing at all, because it seems safer. Isn't that sad? I probably missed out on so much happiness."

Ed ran a hand through his hair, leaving it sticking up in tufts. "Like prom."

"Prom? What's prom got to do with anything?"

"Neither of us went. We could've gone together, but we both ended up sitting on the sofa watching *Star Trek*, feeling sorry for ourselves."

I blinked at him, trying to understand. "You never asked me to the prom."

"Bunny told me to, but I knew you'd say no."

"Well, I didn't do stuff like that after Stubby died. And who's to say I'd have been happier going to the prom? Maybe watching *Star Trek* was the better choice."

"Maybe."

"Prom's stupid anyway. I hear it's nothing like in a John Hughes movie." I scooted over to the milk crates of mixtapes and sifted through until I found what I was looking for. I put the tape in my boombox and stood up.

"C'mon then." I held out my hand. He looked bewildered, but he gave me his hand and I pulled him off the floor as Spandau Ballet's "True" started to play.

"Here?"

"Yes. Here. Your tarot spread said you had a chance to make one big goal a reality. Here it is. Your chance to go to prom with me." I took a step closer and put my arms around his neck, and he stepped closer to put his arms around my waist. We started to sway awkwardly.

"Congratulations," I said after a minute. "This is just as awful as the few junior high dances I went to."

"If I'd known we were going to do this, I'd at least have brought you a corsage or taken you out to dinner."

"Well, then Queena would warn me that you might 'expect things.'"

Ed had come over straight from work, and his crisp button-up shirt was cool against my cheek, with a faint scent of clean laundry and textbooks. It was comforting, and I settled against him a bit more, leaning my head on his shoulder. He held me just a tiny bit closer. The candle flames grew longer and flickered wildly, but I figured maybe we were stirring up the air with our dancing. Little points of colour spilled onto the attic floor as the sun broke through the clouds and hit a jar of sea glass on my windowsill. If I squinted my eyes, I could pretend it was a glitter ball.

I wished I'd spent a lot more of my teen years dancing to Spandau Ballet in attics, and a lot less time worrying that I was cursed. Maybe it wasn't too late to start.

The song ended. We kept on swaying for a moment before pulling apart, and then stood awkwardly. I didn't know what to do with my hands, so I folded my arms, and then put my hands on my hips before quickly shoving them in my skirt pockets.

Ed ran a hand through his hair again. "I guess we should get downstairs. We don't want Thom to get suspicious."

I busied myself with blowing out candles. "Yeah. Well, anyway, good luck with the interview. If you believe the tarot reading, you've got a good chance of getting what you want."

"Thanks. Sometimes it feels like it all comes down to luck."

"Take this, then." I went over to the jar of sea glass and plucked out a small blue piece. "The blue ones are the hardest to find around here, so I always feel like they're lucky."

He smiled and tucked the tiny piece of glass into his pocket. "I promise I'll give it back next week, when I get home. I mean, if you still want to meet for coffee."

I smiled and blew out the last candle. "You know where you can find me. I'll meet you at the beach."

PART VIII
Those Who Influence You

Crying Over You

Thom and I only ever had real conversations during game shows. Maybe it was because when we were little, that was the only time Queena left us alone and we could talk freely. She always left the room when *The Price is Right* came on after supper, because she said the Showcase Showdown did in her nerves. She'd once seen someone lose the Showcase after overbidding by just one dollar and she never recovered.

"Just think of it—if he'd only decided to bid one dollar less, his whole life could've been so much better," she'd said. "He would've had that new trailer and a trip to Cancun. Maybe he would've met a nice girl there, on vacation, and they would've gotten married and had a family. And maybe one of their children would've cured cancer or something, and now people are going to die because he made the wrong decision!"

I think my therapist would've called this catastrophizing. I called it Average Tuesday with Queena.

"*Wheel of Fortune*?" I suggested, flipping through the channels. Ed wouldn't be back from Ontario for another two days, so it was just me and Thom. The sofa felt a lot bigger.

"Can't watch it anymore. I've gone off Vanna."

"What did Vanna ever do to you?"

He grabbed a handful of Cheezies and popped one in his mouth. "I had this dream I was on *Wheel of Fortune*, except Pat Sajack was the devil, and when I spun the wheel the only prize on it was 'DEATH.' Then this big neon sign drops down over my head and it blinks *DEAD* in big red letters. And then Vanna turns into a demon and drags me into a pit of hell, and Stubby and all the other guys in our family who've died young? They were looking up at me and waving from their graves."

"Wow," I said, after a pause.

We watched *Jeopardy!* until the first commercial break, and then I turned down the volume and shifted to face Thom.

"So hey, when you and Kim broke up and you kept calling her, did you know what you'd say to her? I need to figure out how to get Matt to talk to me."

Thom shovelled Cheezies into his mouth and glared at me. "You're asking me for relationship advice?"

"Yeah. That's how desperate I am."

"I sure as hell don't know how to get someone back. Look, Puss, it's done. If he hasn't called after all this time, he's a dickhead and you shouldn't be wasting your time crying over him."

"He's not a dickhead."

"You've been here, what, a couple of months?"

"Seven weeks and four days."

He snorted. "Yeah, if he wanted you back, he would've called the day you left. Would've flown out here to find you."

"He didn't know I'd gone to the airport. And besides, it's hard for him to get away. He's a doctor. He doesn't sit on his arse all day like you."

Thom stretched out on the sofa and pushed his feet against me. I kicked him away.

"Stop making excuses for him, Puss. He's moved on. Probably has someone else now."

The Cheezies felt like lead in my belly and I shoved the bowl at Thom. "Just because Kim went off with Dickhead doesn't mean it happens to everyone."

He set the empty bowl on the coffee table. "Face it. It's over. You're just mad at me because you know it's true."

"Shut up!"

"You shut up."

"Fuck."

"God."

Jeopardy! came back on, and we went back to watching TV in silence.

Tiny and I had been hiding out in the Smutty Paperback room for half an hour while she cried and I handed her tissue after tissue. Rodger had brought Nicholas into the store, along with a new girlfriend.

"He knew I was here today. He did this on purpose, to make me feel like shit," Tiny said.

"He's shit. He's the shittiest ball of shit. He doesn't deserve you."

Angel walked in carrying an enormous diaper bag covered in teddy bears. She pulled up a box of books and sat next to Tiny, giving her knee a quick, sympathetic squeeze.

"Bunny told me where you were hiding. This is the biggest bag I had, and it's spill-proof." Angel pulled out a big thermos and three plastic cups and started to pour. "It might only be 10:30 in the morning, but this sounded like it required fake margaritas."

"It's just not fair," Tiny said. "I spend all my time taking care of Nicholas or working here. There's no time for me to meet anyone else. He's having the time of his life, and I'm always going to be alone."

"You guys should put a spell on him!" Angel said. "Make his wiener fall off or something."

Tiny laughed, and I smiled at seeing her happy, even for just a moment. "Oh my God, Ang. Who the hell says wiener?" She looked at me. "Do we know any wiener-shrivelling spells?"

"I wish."

Tiny gave me a long look as she blew her nose. The pile of used tissues at her feet was a mob of soggy little ghosts.

"What's up? You seem jittery."

I took a long swig of my mocktail. "I think I should call Matt to say goodbye. You know, tell him I'm sorry things ended up like this, and that I should've gotten help earlier, and I wish he could forgive me."

Tiny kicked at the tissue ghosts. "Why are you putting this on yourself? What about the way he acted? He just let you go off across the country without even calling to see how you are."

"After living with you for six years. And almost having a baby with you," Angel added. "That's cold. Like, candidate for the wiener-shrivelling spell."

"I mean, he's a doctor," Tiny said. "He should get that you needed help, but instead he lets you leave and ignores you? That doesn't exactly scream 'I love you.'"

"I'm with Tiny. Sorry, but no matter how hot he was, I think you're better off without him."

I looked out the window at the grounds crew tending the flower beds at the bandstand across the street. It'd been early spring when I left BC, and now it was almost summer. February seemed like a lifetime ago.

"Maybe you're right. But we had a whole life together there. A house. Everything I own is there. And memories. It's not like he can just walk away and never talk to me again." My voice was barely a whisper. "I thought I'd be there forever."

"What if you write to him?" Angel asked. "That way you can think it through and say everything you want to say. Tell him how he's made you feel and let him know you don't need that shit. You're moving on." She gave Tiny a stern look. "We're all moving on."

———

"When you and Sara ended things, did you talk to her afterwards? To try to get closure or something?"

Ed busied himself with adjusting the old red beach blanket. It was covered in little blue lobsters, which drove me bananas because obviously, it should be the other way around. Honestly, I got pissed off every time I looked at that blanket. Ed looked like he wanted to throw the blanket over his head to avoid having this conversation.

"We don't have to talk about it. It's just, I've been talking to my therapist about it. Closure, I mean. I asked Tiny and Angel about it, too. Even Thom. So, I guess I just wanted your opinion..."

Ed handed me my coffee and a chocolate croissant. I'd mentioned they were my favourite, so he always got me one. "She wasn't really in the mood to talk to me for a long time, after I called off the wedding. Obviously. She went away for a while, and by the time she came back it seemed better just to let it be."

A seagull marched down the beach towards us, eyeing our food. I held my croissant protectively.

"Thom thinks Matt's probably found someone else. Tiny and Angel think I should write him so I can at least have closure. What do you think I should do?"

"I don't think you should be asking me or Thom for relationship advice, for one thing."

"But, I mean, if you were a guy—"

"I *am* a guy."

"Right. But if you were the guy in this situation, would you even listen to anything I had to say?"

Ed threw some croissant to the seagull. It snatched it up and hopped joyfully down the beach. "I'd always listen to you."

"I think of how he used to look at me when we first met, and how he looked at me the day I left...it hurts so much. I'm such a goddamn mess."

I fell back dramatically on the beach blanket and looked at the clouds. I saw one that looked like a cat, and one that looked like a Rockaberry cooler. "Therapy's helping me understand everything a lot better, but I feel like how I handle things with Matt is the final exam."

"I hope you do better on this exam than you did in Grade 12 chemistry."

I sat up and threw a handful of sand at him.

"You've got this. But if he's horrible to you, Angel and Tiny will bring buckets of margaritas. And I'll be right here on your lobster blanket."

"Will you? Or will you be in Ontario?" Ed had been back for two days and hadn't mentioned how the interview had gone. I hadn't asked. The subject chafed between us like sand in a wet bathing suit.

Ed half-smiled at me and looked away. "I haven't heard anything. But you know you can always talk to me, wherever we end up."

Something inside me deflated, and I realized I'd been hoping the interview hadn't gone well. I turned my head away to wipe my eyes, getting sand all over my cheek. Ed reached over and brushed it off with a napkin.

"It's the salt air. Makes me tear up," I said as I took the napkin to blot my eyes. "Anyway, I guess I have to call him. Or write him. I have to get it over with."

"I forgot your lucky blue sea glass," he said. "I'll try to bring it over tonight when we watch TV with Thom. You might need it, for courage."

I stood up to shake the sand from the lobster blanket. "It'll take more than sea glass to fix my life. I need some kind of divine intervention."

Don't Let Me Be Misunderstood

Dear Kitty,

I have a confession to make: when they gave me my options about staying here with the Living or moving on to the Afterlife, I wasn't really paying attention. I was checking out how my hands flowed right through things. It was trippy. But I think I might've missed some important stuff.

See, the way it works is that not long after you're on this side, someone you know comes to walk you through what happens next. It's usually someone really close to you who went on ahead, but the only person there for me was my great-grandmother, who I'd never even met. I'd heard she'd been a witch, so I thought it might be cool. It wasn't cool. She looked me up and down and seemed a little uptight about my bikini top.

So anyway, my great-grandmother basically rattles off stuff about how the Afterlife works and all the stuff you can do, and she said to reach out if I had any questions, but I never did. Now I'm wondering if I should've listened better. It can't all be sitting around waiting for everyone else to show up, right? I feel like I'm missing something. I'm doing death wrong.

Shit. This is like when I walked into my biology test and realized I'd studied all the wrong stuff.

Anyway, the card I'm leaving for you today is pretty important. The Moon. All about betrayal, and people and things not being what they seem. I'm really hoping you'll get the message, because this is the only way I have to make you pay attention.

And I'm trying not to be jealous that you're thinking of writing to Matt instead of me.

Love,
Nerida
xoxo

Don't You Want Me?

Queena was sitting at the kitchen table reading the *National Enquirer* when I finished watching *Who Wants to Be a Millionaire?* with Thom and Ed.

"That stuff's trash, Mum, you should really stop buying it."

"Some of it's true, dear. It's just hard to know which bits, sometimes." She set the paper down and peered over her reading glasses at me. "You look perkier tonight."

I backed away so she couldn't start fussing with my hair. "Where's Bunny?"

"She's in the bath and then she said she's going to bed."

"Oh. Are you going to bed soon, too?"

Queena raised an eyebrow. "Why are you so interested in bedtimes?"

I opened the fridge and glanced inside, trying to look casual. "I might call Matt later. Just wanted some privacy."

Queena's brow furrowed, which she generally tried to avoid because of wrinkles. She patted the seat next to her. "Come sit with me, Kitten. I need to talk to you about something."

I dropped into the chair, perching stiffly on the edge like I used to when she was about to lecture me.

Queena fiddled with the edge of the tea cozy. She seemed to be struggling for words, which was unusual for her. I waited, running my finger over the place where I'd carved my name into the table with a pencil when I was five and learning to print: *K I T I N*. Finally, Queena cleared her throat.

"Now, I didn't want to tell you this because I know it will be upsetting. Matt called earlier."

I sprang to my feet to go to the phone, but Queena placed a hand on my arm to push me back to the seat. "No, Kitten. Just wait." She avoided my eyes and stared at her copy of *Soap Opera Weekly*. "He told me that he wanted to let you know that he...he's going away. On vacation. With someone else. A woman he knew from before. Someone he was serious with."

"What do you mean? Who?" My gut twisted. It must be that woman who broke his heart before I met him. I'd found a picture of them together, once, in his closet. Maybe I'd just been a really long rebound.

"All he said was he's going away, and he doesn't want to talk to you." Queena folded her hands on the table and rubbed her thumbs together. "I was waiting for the right time to tell you, because I know it's not easy to hear."

My heartbeat pounded in my ears. I couldn't believe she was sitting there so calmly, hands folded and face placid, when she'd just plunged a knife into me.

"Why didn't he ask to talk to me? You must've misunderstood."

Queena patted my hand sadly. "I'm afraid not, Kitten. That's what he said. You weren't home, and he didn't want to call back. He asked me to tell you that you shouldn't call him."

I pushed back from the table and went up to my attic without saying a word to her, holding my hand to my chest and barely breathing. My body shook with pain and panic. Maybe it was the Love Heart. I hoped it was.

I hugged my Care Bear and stared up at the poster of Sting. Matt had probably found some nice, rational person who never talked to dolls and had never been cursed.

I rolled over and looked at my tarot cards. I'd already felt in my heart that it was over, but Queena's news and The Moon confirmed it.

———

I kept my sunglasses on to cover the dark circles under my eyes when I walked into Fact & Fiction the next morning, but it didn't fool Bunny.

"Is this an attempt at old Hollywood glamour, or are you hungover?"

I climbed on the old red stool behind the cash. It was so high and brightly coloured that when I'd sat on it as a little girl, I'd imagined I was a parrot on a perch. "Neither. I didn't sleep. I was up writing a letter to Matt, to say goodbye and try to explain things."

Bunny poured some tea and slid the cup toward me. "What kind of things?"

"I told him that he never knew the real me. I tried to be someone else with him and leave all the sadness behind, but it didn't work. The person he knew was a fake."

"You're not a fake. And not to say 'I told you so,' but didn't I warn you running away from things doesn't work?"

I held up a hand. "Please. Not now." I took a breath and carried on. "Anyway, I went out to mail the letter before the sun came up, and then I just walked around town for a couple of hours. I guess I was trying to convince myself I can deal with living here forever, since I have nowhere else to go."

"There's always somewhere else to go. You just have to decide what you want."

"You say that like it's such an easy thing."

"You're the only one who can find your path forward, sweet thing. Listen to your heart."

I pictured my heart, punctured by swords like on the tarot card. I wasn't sure I could trust anything it said.

———

Four days later, Thom and Ed were on the sofa when I came in from Fact & Fiction. Thom turned down the TV's volume.

"Package came for you, Puss. From Kelowna. On the kitchen table."

I stood motionless, staring down the hall through the kitchen door at the package as though it were a bomb. Thom turned the volume back up. Ed looked at me and raised an eyebrow. I shook my head and walked down the vinyl runner to the kitchen.

The package was postmarked well before I'd mailed my letter to Matt. Maybe he'd mailed it before he left with his other woman. I peeled the paper off slowly to delay seeing what was inside.

He'd sent a bundle of all the Valentines he'd ever given me, and a small box I'd filled with petals from flowers he'd given me through the years. He'd sent my Magic 8 Ball, and I held it against my chest hoping it might transmit some answers. At the bottom of the box was a little envelope tucked under some tissue paper. It held one of the ultrasound photos, and a note that said, *I thought you might want these. I'll send the rest of your things later. Love, Matt.*

I set down the Magic 8 Ball and placed the cards, the photo, and the note next to each other on the table. My eyes moved from one to the other, trying to understand. Why did he write, *Love, Matt*? If he loved me, why was he going away with someone else? He obviously didn't want me going back to Kelowna, since he said he'd send the rest of my things. Maybe he wanted all signs of me out of the house, so he could move the new woman in.

I put the lid on the box and carried it up to my attic. I couldn't look at these things. I didn't want these things. I slid the box under my bed like I was sliding the remains of our relationship into a crypt.

Lies

I woke up clutching the Magic 8 Ball, with the ultrasound photo on the pillow next to me. Misery sat on my chest and pinned me to the bed. I was supposed to be at Fact & Fiction, but that wasn't a good enough reason to get up. Bunny or Tiny could manage without me. Plenty of people managed without me.

I didn't get out of bed until late afternoon. Thom and Ed were in the kitchen when I came downstairs. I took a knife from the drawer, grabbed the Cheez Whiz out of the fridge, and started eating it directly from the jar.

"You okay?" Ed asked.

"Dandy."

"You look like shit," Thom said. He was wearing a pair of sweatpants with the crotch torn out and an Expos shirt with holes under the arms. At least I'd put on a fresh pair of pyjamas.

I took my Cheez Whiz and went out to the deck, slamming the door behind me.

Thom and Ed came out twenty minutes later, joined by Bunny. She sat down across from me and lit a cigarette.

"Thom called and said you were acting weird, so I closed up a little early."

"Acting weirder than usual," Thom clarified. "Thought you might be hitting the Rockaberry coolers again."

268

"The coolers were just a gateway to the heavier stuff." I nodded down at the empty jar of Cheez Whiz. "I don't need another intervention. I'm fine." I leaned back in my chair and closed my eyes, hoping everyone would be gone when I opened them again.

"What was in the package?" Ed asked. I opened one eye to give him a dirty look but stopped myself, remembering we were friends now. I gave him the stink eye anyway, just so Thom wouldn't get suspicious.

"He sent some sentimental stuff. And a note signed, *Love, Matt*, whatever that means. He said he'll send me the rest of my stuff later. Probably after he gets back from vacation with this new woman of his."

"What new woman?" Ed sat down next to me.

"I think it's someone he was with before he met me. He told Queena he's going away with her, and he doesn't want to talk to me ever again. So that's that."

"What do you mean he 'told Queena'?" Bunny asked.

"The other night, she told me he called and told her all that stuff. He told her I shouldn't call him."

Bunny took a long drag on her cigarette. "Matt told Queena this?"

"Yeah."

"And did you phone him anyway? I'd want to hear it from him."

"Yeah. I got the answering machine, so I guess he'd already left." I slid lower in my chair. "I didn't want to leave a message in case the new woman heard it. I wrote a letter instead. Remember, I told you I wrote a letter?"

Bunny nodded. She put her cigarette out in the ashtray and watched the tendrils of smoke rise and fade.

"Ed, honey, would you go phone The Memory Garden and ask Queena to come home? Tell her we've got a situation here."

"What's the situation?" I asked, as Ed went inside.

Bunny looked out into the yard, toward the spot where Stubby had died. "I don't know. I think your mother does."

We heard the shaggin' wagon pull into the driveway about fifteen minutes later. Bunny got up and went inside.

"Do you know what's going on?" I asked Thom.

"I never know what's going on."

"No duh."

Bunny came back out to the deck, followed by Queena, just as the mill's horn blew to mark the end of the day shift. It startled the crows in the nearby trees, and they swirled overhead in a dark cloud before settling down again.

"What's wrong? Ed said it was an emergency. Is someone bleeding or vomiting?" Queena's voice was shaky.

"No," Bunny said. "It's not a medical emergency."

Queena sank into a chair and some colour came back into her face. "Oh, thank goodness. I was worried it was the Love Heart." She reached over and patted Thom's hand. "It's never far from my mind, you know."

"Neat," Thom muttered.

Bunny leaned forward and folded her hands in front of her on the table.

"No, it's not the Love Heart. But Kitten here does have a broken heart, and I think you might know something about it."

"I don't know what you mean, Bunny."

"Queena, tell the truth: did Matt phone the other day to say that he was going away with another woman?"

Queena opened her mouth and closed it. Then she opened her mouth and closed it again. I had a fleeting memory of the time Stubby took me fishing and I'd watched the mackerel flap around and gasp for air while I sobbed in horror.

Queena twisted her wedding ring, sliding it off and on her finger, and I worried she'd drop it between the deck boards. She finally looked up, glancing at each of us until her eyes landed on me, but then quickly looked back down at her hands.

"Kitten, there are some things I probably should've told you for a while now, but I thought it was best not to. It was for your own good, really. You see, when you first got here...well, Matt called quite a lot. Every day, really. He wanted to know how you were. He wanted to come, but I told him he needed to give you space."

I couldn't move a muscle except to blink.

"You were so fragile," Queena continued. "You didn't even get out of bed for that first little while. I was so scared you were going to be like you were that time in high school, after your father.... I didn't do a good job at protecting you then."

I looked over at Bunny, but Bunny's eyes were firmly on Queena.

"You wouldn't tell us what had happened, but it was clear to me that you wouldn't be back here, all upset and staying in bed, if Matt hadn't done something horrible."

"What did Matt say about it?" My voice was cold and flat, just like it had been that night at the hospital when I'd been avoiding the ultrasound screen. And just like that night, words and thoughts ran frantically through my head.

Queena's eyes were lowered, but I could see them darting under her dark lashes. She put her hand to her throat to fiddle with the collar of her blouse.

"Oh, he said you were having a hard time after the miscarriage. That you weren't yourself and the two of you had fought and he thought you needed some help. I figured there must be more to it—something he'd done that made you leave. So, I protected you from him."

"Protected me?" The sun sparked off of Bunny's cut-glass ashtray, and I squeezed my eyes shut against the light. I felt like I'd walked out of a cave after months in the dark: I wanted to see the world again, but it hurt.

"It was good to have you back here. Things felt right again. And soon, you got up and out of bed and started seeing that doctor, and you had friends. You were back at Fact & Fiction. I didn't think you needed him anymore. I decided you'd be better off staying here, where I can take care of you. So, I told him not to call."

"And that was it?" Bunny asked, her voice dark. "You told him not to call so he just...stopped calling?"

Queena shifted her body away from us. "Well, no. Just around the time you started seeing that doctor, Kitten, he called and said he was at the airport and was getting on a plane. I thought that would only upset things, so I told him you were gone. I told him you'd reconnected with an old boyfriend and you'd gone away with him, and that Matt should just forget it. He was upset, but I guess he accepted it. He stopped calling. He knew you were mad at him." She said this as though it was the most reasonable thing in the world.

I remembered the sadness in Matt's eyes, that first night we met, when he told me how someone had broken his heart—how she'd left him for an old boyfriend. And now he thought I'd done the same thing.

The crows flew to the roof above us, their caws echoing through the yard. Probably giving all the other crows in the neighbourhood the play-by-play of the shitshow unfolding below them.

Queena drew herself up and folded her arms. "After all, you're the one who came here. It was your decision, Kitten. If you'd really wanted him, you would've stayed there with him. All I did was help make your decision easier."

Her eyes, dark and defiant, locked onto mine. I looked away first. My stomach twisted—what she was saying was true. I'd decided to come to Paradise Valley. I could've stayed with Matt. It had been my choice to leave.

My head was so hot it made me queasy, and I could feel a vein pulsing at my temple. But then a thought pushed through the noise in my head, certain and solid, and spread through me with cool clarity. I opened my eyes.

I hadn't been in a place to make any choices. I'd been broken. Queena had seen that. She'd seen that, and she'd done this anyway.

After months of condemning myself, I realized, in that moment, I wasn't guilty.

"This was *not* my decision," I kept my voice low so Queena would have to listen to every word. "I didn't *choose* this. I needed help. Any idiot could see how upset I was. Even Thom could see that!"

Thom shrugged and nodded.

Bunny let the long ashes from her cigarette fall onto the deck. "Queena, this is too far, even for you."

I pushed my chair back and stood with my back to my mother, biting my thumb as I collected my thoughts. The crows yelled at us like the studio audience on *Jerry Springer*. I turned to face her.

"This isn't one of your soap operas or scrapbooks. This is my life! Me, your daughter. Christ. You can't lie and pretend to make things the way you want."

Queena looked up at me, her face as haughty as it was in the picture of her being crowned prom queen. "Why not? You did."

Even the crows went silent.

"There's no other woman, then?" I asked, once my breath returned.

Queena wiggled her shoulders as she sat up straighter. "Well, I don't know that, Kitten. He didn't say so, but I suppose a man like him won't be alone for long."

I turned my back on her. I didn't want to give her the satisfaction of seeing me cry. I fully expected to cry. I mean, I'd been crying for months. But my eyes stayed dry and burning, my shoulders still and steady. I was solid, and I wasn't going to dissolve because of her.

"Kitten? Kitty? Talk to me." Queena's voice became a whimper. "I thought we'd be together. That's all. Like we used to be."

The whimper grew into a sob, and then became a full-on wail. Bunny led her inside, swearing as she closed the windows so the neighbours wouldn't hear us go batshit.

Ed got up and wrapped me in a hug. I sank into it just long enough to let my shoulders relax and to take a deep breath, then I pushed myself back. I couldn't melt; I had to fix this.

Thom was sitting with his head in his hands, his mouth gaping open. With his scruffy hair and stubbly chin, he looked like Shaggy from *Scooby-Doo*. Appropriate, since we'd just unmasked the villain.

"You!" I said. "You're always around. You must've heard her on the phone. Didn't you know who she was talking to?"

Thom held up his hands in defence. "You know how she is. Talks about the weather and shit to anyone who calls, just to be polite. I don't pay attention. Just grab my beer and go."

I wiped my eyes with the backs of my hands as I stormed into the house and grabbed the phone, stretching the curly phone cord into the dining room. It was only early afternoon in Kelowna. Matt was probably at work, but maybe he'd come home early, like he had the day he'd found me in the baby's room.

It rang six times, then the answering machine cut in. I forced myself to hold it together as I listened to his recorded voice and waited for the beep, and then I rushed to tell him everything before the machine cut me off. I had to call back three times to get everything in.

My voice sounded old and hoarse. "I never imagined my mother would do something like this. You probably don't want anything to do with me at this point, but I wanted you to know the truth. I was never off with someone else. Please call me. Please."

I dropped the receiver, slouching against the wall for support as I tried to catch my breath. Queena was still crying. I couldn't be in the house with her. I wanted to kick her down to her goddamn bomb shelter and lock her in it, forever. I wanted the Russians to drop a bomb directly on top of her.

I slammed the receiver back into its cradle, grabbed the keys to the shaggin' wagon, and left. I had no idea where I was going, but I never wanted to see my mother again.

PART IX
That Which You Long For or Fear

Emotional Rescue

When we were fifteen, Tiny and I made lists of the top twenty things we wanted to do before we died. We probably got the idea from something we'd read in *Seventeen* magazine or a *Sweet Valley High* book. I don't remember most of the things I put on my list, but I know that one of the top items was "Sleep on a beach." At fifteen, this seemed bohemian and very romantic—not to mention Queena would hate it. This goes to show that my grasp on romance has always been slightly dodgy.

I drove around aimlessly for over an hour before I went to the beach. I walked farther than usual, far past the spot where Matt had proposed to me, and found a spot to spread the infuriating blanket with the blue lobsters.

The pressure in my head was so strong that I sat with my head in my hands to try and contain it. It felt like I was going to shoot off like a firecracker. My face twisted in anger. When I was little, Queena told me not to make faces because I'd freeze that way. Well, if that happened now, it would be her fault. Everything was her fault.

I'm not sure how long I lay numbly in the damp sand on the lobster blanket, but eventually I realized it was getting dark.

Not only did I not have a coat, but I was still wearing my pyjamas. The prospect of spending the night alone, on this beach, in thirteen-year-old Pee-wee Herman pyjamas, did not now strike me as the least bit romantic. I really needed to break this habit of dramatically running off and figuring out the logistics later.

Someone was calling my name. I flattened myself against the lobster blanket and played dead.

"Kitty!" Ed called. "Are you here?"

Maybe he wouldn't see me. Maybe he'd mistake me for a big pile of seaweed, or a large, dead jellyfish.

"Kitty?" He crouched down next to me. "Are you okay? I came by earlier but you weren't here. I couldn't think of where else you'd go."

I pushed myself up to sitting and looked past him. "That's where Matt proposed to me," I said, jutting my chin toward the spot on the beach. "Right over there. I sure as hell never thought things would end up like this."

"Yeah. Well, no one would've predicted this—all your troubles, and what Queena did."

"All my troubles," I echoed. My face crumpled and I finally cried, the sobs spilling out in hiccups and gulps. Ed sat down and pulled me toward him, keeping his arm around me while I struggled to pull myself together. He was being so sweet. I hated it. I didn't want anyone being sweet. I wanted to be alone.

He shrugged off his sweatshirt and wrapped it around my shoulders, leaving his arm there to shore me up. I tried to wipe my nose discretely on my shoulder when he wasn't looking, but then I remembered that his sweatshirt was there, and therefore I was wiping my nose on *his* sleeve.

"Everyone's worried," Ed said. "I told them you probably just needed to be alone."

"I'm cursed. It's true. All the McQuinn bad luck is mine. I'm one disaster after another."

"It's not a curse, Kitty, it's just life."

"Well, I want a do-over. I want to go back and make different decisions, or at least make *some* decisions on my own, and cut out all the bad parts."

Ed adjusted his sweatshirt around my shoulders. "Things might not end up any better, though. Maybe whatever decisions you made would just screw things up in a different way. Or maybe it'd mean you'd miss out on something wonderful that hasn't happened yet."

"Whatever, Yoda."

Ed scooped up a handful of sand and let it run through his fingers before he spoke again.

"Matt's an ass. He should've ignored Queena and come here right away. I don't know why he'd even hesitate."

"He probably thought what she said made sense. I was really upset when I left."

"You're making excuses for him. Seriously, Kitty, nothing Queena said could've kept me away from you."

The fog was becoming a drizzle, and I wondered if I should give Ed his sweatshirt back. Just as I started to shrug it off, he cleared his throat.

"You're not a disaster," Ed said softly. "From the time I was twelve—you've always been the most beautiful, most magical girl I've ever known. This for sure isn't the right time to say this, but no one's ever compared to you."

His voice trailed off and he ran one sandy hand through his hair. He left it there, half-shielding his face from my view. "Shit, never mind, okay? I shouldn't have said that. You've got enough to deal with right now."

This was something that wouldn't have been on my list when I was fifteen: sitting on a dark beach with my brother's dorky friend as he declared his lifelong love for me. But almost a lifetime later, what surprised me most was not what he'd said but the realization that I'd always known it, and that I'd wanted to hear him say it.

I took Ed's hand away from his face and turned his face to look at me.

"Thank you." I pulled him close and kissed him. I felt his initial shock melt as he wrapped his arms around me.

When the kiss finally ended, we were both breathless and covered in sand.

"I guess we should get you home. Everyone's worried." He looked into my eyes. "I'm not so anxious to leave, though, honestly."

I pulled away and tried to shake some of the sand from my hair. "I'm not going home tonight. I can't face Queena. I'll murder her with a fucking scrapbook."

"Where will you go?"

"I'll sleep in the shaggin' wagon, maybe. I'm already in my pyjamas, anyway."

"Look, my cottage is just up there. Let's go have a drink and dry off, and you can figure out what to do."

I got into the shaggin' wagon, and as I followed Ed's tail lights, I met my eyes in the rear-view mirror. I was a mess. What the actual hell was I doing, kissing Ed on a beach in my Pee-wee Herman pyjamas, for God's sake? I mean, *Ed*.

Ed was turning on the porch light when I parked my car behind his. I walked around the porch to the front door, waving off the moths that zigzagged to the light. I hesitated in the doorway—I remembered standing in this exact spot as Mrs. Fraser propped me against her while she opened the door, after she rescued me. I could feel those waves pushing me down. I shook my head.

Ed held out some sweaters. "Something warm. There are towels in the bathroom if you want to dry off."

Seeing the chipped pink bathtub brought such a visceral rush of memories of the day I'd tried to end my life that I leaned over the toilet thinking I'd be sick. The feeling passed, but the memories didn't. I braced my hands against the sink and stared at my reflection in the mirror, surprised to see an almost thirty-year-old woman and not a seventeen-year-old girl. I'd lost almost half my life to this darkness. I couldn't do this anymore. And I couldn't let Queena decide whether I'd be happy or miserable. I twisted my hair into a damp braid, slipped an old argyle cardigan over Pee-wee, and tried to breathe away the nausea.

Ed was waiting for me out on the creaky porch swing. I sat down, hoping he wouldn't notice I was trembling.

"I thought this would help warm us up." He handed me a tumbler of Scotch. He'd brought an old plaid blanket, too, and spread it over our legs. We sat in silence for a few minutes, until the damp air quelled the last of my nausea.

"You know, I was here once with your mother. A long time ago." I took a tentative sip of Scotch and felt myself relax as its warmth spread through me. "She gave me a blanket, too. I think it looked like this. I don't really remember. Maybe it's the same one."

"When were you here with my mother?"

"A lifetime ago." I hesitated. "A few months after Stubby died, I hitchhiked to the beach and...I walked into those waves, and I didn't intend to walk back out. I took some poison. One of the plants I grew. I was done with everything."

"Oh, Kitty." Ed reached for my hand and gripped it tightly.

"Your mother found me. She pulled me out, just as I was giving up. She brought me back here to get warm and called an ambulance. I was in the hospital for weeks. She never told you?"

"She never said anything about it. God, Kitty, I'm so sorry. When you didn't go back to school that year, Queena and Thom said you had mono."

"Queena didn't want anyone to know. I'm not even sure Thom knows what really happened. Your mother knew the truth, though.

I always felt like she was keeping an eye out for me, after that."

We were silent for a few minutes, drinking our Scotch and listening to the rain and the creak of the porch swing. Ed was still holding my hand. I didn't try to move it.

The rocking and the Scotch and the adrenaline from the emotions of the day were making me sleepy. I closed my eyes, just for a moment.

"I got the position in Ontario. They called to offer it to me yesterday," Ed said.

My stomach dropped and my eyes opened. I was wide awake now.

"Really?"My voice sounded bright but felt strangled, and I took another sip of Scotch to soothe it.

"I guess your lucky sea glass worked. I keep forgetting to give it back to you." He pulled it from his pocket and held it out to me now, barely visible in the dark.

"Keep it." I waved it away, wishing I'd never given it to him. But it was too late now. The sea glass had worked its magic and he'd be gone soon. Just like Matt.

The swing wobbled as I sat up straighter. Everything inside me wobbled, too. Maybe it was the Scotch. I bent to set my glass on the porch, but didn't let go of Ed's hand.

"I have to call back after the weekend to let them if I'm accepting the offer."

His words kindled a spark of hope inside me. "You haven't said yes already? Why not?"

Ed hesitated. "I don't know." He let his hand slip away from mine.

My hand tingled with electric connection, even without his touch. I spread my fingers on the blanket, feeling the soft wool and the heavy mist and the cool evening breeze. All at once, I realized that nothing felt right, or would ever feel right, without his hand on mine.

"I don't want you to go." I let the words rush out. "I don't want to be here without you. I'll miss our coffee dates. I'll miss you."

Once again, I leaned in to kiss him. Ed pulled me against him and kissed me back—tentatively at first, then deeper and more urgently. I had a split second of guilt as I thought of Matt, but then remembered that part of my life was over. Queena had made sure of it.

It started to rain harder, and the porch didn't offer much protection. "We should go inside," Ed whispered. I nodded.

He pulled me off the porch swing and we made our way into the cottage, still wrapped in the blanket. As I stumbled backwards, tangled in Ed's arms, I banged into the corner of the huge old sofa. My ankle gave out under me, and I fell arse over teakettle (as Bunny would say) onto the floor.

"I think that's a sign," I said, once I stopped swearing. "I don't think we should do this."

Ed looked away. "You're right. I wish you weren't."

"I'm not, usually."

"You can stay here tonight if you want," Ed said. "I'll go back and tell everyone you're okay."

"No. Maybe I'll go to Fact & Fiction. There's a little couch in the back room where we make tea."

"Will you be okay?"

I smiled. "Tonight, or in general?"

"Both?"

"I'll get through it. I have friends, right?" I gave him a kiss on the cheek.

When we got to our cars, Ed started to open my door for me but paused.

"Do you want to go for dinner tomorrow night?"

I was sure I could see him blush, even in the dark.

"Like an actual date?"

"Yeah. A date. I'll pick you up at your mother's house, and I'll get you home by curfew."

I waited a second to see if he was teasing, and if my brain and heart were in agreement on my answer.

"On one condition."

"What's that?"

"You're the one who breaks it to Thom."

Light My Fire

⭐

Dear Kitty,

My friends and I wanted to be cool and wild, like the hippies we saw on the news—the girls with long hair and skimpy clothes that got my parents all bent out of shape. We talked a pretty good game about sex—who we'd made out with at parties and stuff, what we wanted to do and with who—but to be honest, I didn't have a lot of experience. My Good Girl Catholic upbringing held me back, you know? And we didn't have stuff like the Pill. At school, they'd separate the boys from girls and show us these horrible filmstrips about VD and teen pregnancy and all the other ways sex could ruin our lives. Maybe I'd have had a lot more fun on your side if sex hadn't been so damn terrifying.

This one guy I was going out with—the one who dumped me the day of the Spring Formal—he was really pressuring me to go all the way. We'd come pretty close the week before, and I almost didn't get him to stop. I had to fight him off and get myself out of the car, and he was really mad and called me a tease and made me walk home. I know he stood me up for the dance just because I wouldn't put out. I told Bunny, but not Queena. Queena would've flipped her wig and snitched to our mother.

You're older now than I was then, but even when we were the same age, you had some freedom that I never had. I'm not sure how much you took advantage of it, since you only wrote song titles in your diary and sometimes I couldn't figure out what had happened. At least now you're giving me some details. So, in the hopes that you'll have a REALLY good letter to write me next time, I'm giving you another card and a crystal for inspiration. The Lovers, for sexual attraction and choosing between two paths. And the crystal is a carnelian, to give you a little boost of sexual energy. I think you see where I'm going with this. Ha. More sexy bits, please.

No offense, but your clothes are really square. Too much black. You look like you're in mourning or an old lady. It's such a drag. So, I'm giving you a little help with that, too, because I haven't gotten in trouble for any of this, and I'm pretty sure "encouraging" isn't the same as "interfering."

Consider me your Fairy God-Ghost.

Love,
Nerida
xoxo

Slow Burning Fire

I t was six o'clock, a full day since I'd left the message for Matt, and he hadn't called back. I felt like I'd gone on the Tilt-a-Whirl after eating three cones of cotton candy, but otherwise, I was curiously numb, with a weariness in my soul—a kind of acceptance that this is how it ends.

I tossed the Magic 8 Ball from one hand to another before I decided on the question I wanted to ask.

"Is it a good idea for me to go out with Ed tonight?"

Without a doubt.

I looked through my wardrobe, wishing something would appear that wasn't black and two decades old. I turned back to my suitcase in case I'd missed some article of date-appropriate clothing under the flannel and sweatpants. There was a tarot card on top of it—The Lovers—held down by a carnelian.

I sat on the edge of my bed and looked from the suitcase to the deck of tarot cards, over on the other side of the room. They were in a neat stack where I'd left them, with my crystals above them on the windowsill. Goosebumps raised on my arms, and I twisted my hair around my fingers, trying to understand what was happening. Maybe Bunny was right about attics—maybe they really were haunted.

"Stubby?" I whispered. I heard nothing. I felt nothing, other than a bit foolish. I looked back at Nerida's tarot cards.

"Nerida?"

The room was silent. The curtains didn't even flutter in the breeze. But the scent of the ocean was back.

Whatever was happening was just my imagination. Maybe I needed to have my medications adjusted. Maybe the stress of the past few months combined with Queena's bomb shelter food was causing some kind of hallucinogenic panic attack that made me see tarot cards where there were none. I ran down my steps and stopped in front of Nerida's door, my hand shaking on the doorknob. Something compelled me to go into her room.

The evening light through the yellow curtains made the room glow. It was cool, like a breeze had just blown through. I wasn't sure why I'd come in. I felt a bit foolish. I turned to leave, but then I saw a shimmer in the closet.

Nerida's closet was stuffed full of clothes, so that you could only see fabrics and colours. I'd noticed this dress before, because the fabric was fancier than anything around it. Now it was front and centre. Everything else was pushed to the side, as if someone wanted me to see it. I peeked out the door to the hall, to see if Bunny was out there, pranking me. I knew she'd never joke about anything to do with Nerida, though.

It was a simple silver brocade sheath, sleeveless and thin. It didn't look like it'd been worn—there was still a price tag inside. I doubted that a dress meant for a seventeen-year-old would fit my almost thirty-year-old body, but I pulled off my sweatpants and T-shirt and lifted the dress over my head. It was a little tight in the chest and it was shorter than any dress I'd ever worn—I had t-shirts that were longer—but it looked amazing. I went back to the closet and found a pair of silver kitten heels—they were a little tight, but they'd do—and turned to look at myself in the full-length mirror. It was better than anything I had in the attic. In fact, it felt like the best thing I'd ever worn.

I was still admiring myself when I heard Bunny's voice in the front hall.

"Well, hello Ed. Don't you look dapper tonight!"

I grabbed a long white sweater from Nerida's closet and headed downstairs. Thom came bounding up the basement stairs just as I came down to the living room. Queena looked out from her chair in the kitchen, where she'd been sitting in exile.

"Hey man," Thom said to Ed. "Good timing. Jays game's about to start." He saw me coming down the stairs and wrinkled his nose in disgust at my dress.

Ed, on the other hand, was looking at me like I was a vision. I cocked my head slightly toward Thom to remind Ed of his side of the bargain.

"Actually, Kitty and I are going for dinner." Ed paused, watching pure incredulity spread across my brother's face. "Just the two of us."

Thom looked first confused, and then grossed out. He looked at my dress again and looked even more grossed out. Bunny leaned against the kitchen doorframe with one eyebrow raised, blowing smoke in my direction—goddamn Jiminy Cricket with a pack a day habit. And Queena, standing by her kitchen chair, watched me first with a look somewhere between wonder and heartache, and then as though she'd seen a ghost.

———

Ed glanced at me as he turned onto the coastal road that led to Elgin. "Open the glove compartment. There's something for you."

I leaned forward to open it, hoping it was donuts. I hadn't eaten much all day. I took out a little plastic box that held a spray of pink roses.

"I was going to bring you flowers, but it's prom night, and I ended up in the flower shop with a bunch of teenage boys who were picking up corsages. Some guy got dumped and was cancelling his order, so I bought his corsage off him."

"Aw, that's sweet! Well, not the getting dumped part, but the flowers are sweet. Thank you."

"It kind of goes with your dress."

I smoothed the small bit of fabric covering the top of my thigh. "It was my aunt's."

"Bunny wore that?"

"The other one. Nerida."

"Oh, wow. It looks great. On you. I mean, you look great."

My cheeks got warm. "Well, you look good, too." He was wearing khakis and a mossy green button-down shirt that matched his eyes.

I raised the roses to my nose and looked past Ed to the ocean beyond his window. We weren't far from his cottage. I thought about the night before and my heart started to beat faster. I'd been thinking about it all day.

I took a deep breath and kept my gaze firmly on the corsage in my lap.

"Would you mind very much if we didn't go to dinner tonight?"

From the corner of my eye, I saw disappointment flash across Ed's face.

"I guess...yeah, maybe this is all a little weird, huh?"

I shifted to tug at the hem of the minidress. "It's just, I was thinking...maybe we could just go to your cottage, instead? You know."

As soon as the words were out of my mouth, I felt like an idiot. Ed was still looking straight ahead, and at first, I thought he was going to ignore my awkward attempt at propositioning him. But then a faint blush crept up his neck, and a smile twitched around the corners of his mouth.

"Okay," he said, like it was no big deal.

In a matter of minutes, he pulled into the lane that led to his cottage and hastily parked the car on the lawn. I swung myself out of the car, hoping I looked devil-may-care, while struggling to keep the minidress from riding up to my waist. Ed glanced at me over the car roof as he locked the door, and then dropped the keys in the ankle-deep grass. He swore.

"Leave them," I said. "It's not like anyone's going to steal your car out here."

"But it's the key to the cottage, too."

I stared at the grass. I hoped it wasn't a sign.

He kicked at the grass until he found them and then, keys in one hand, he grabbed my wrist with the other and we laughed as we sprinted to the cottage.

We both hesitated at the bedroom. Everything seemed really quiet—or maybe my heartbeat just drowned out any other sound. I kicked off the kitten heels and stepped toward him, putting my arms around his neck, and he pulled me against him and kissed me. I fumbled with the buttons on his shirt and reached to undo his belt, but suddenly his hand was on mine, stopping me.

"What's wrong?"

Ed rested his forehead against mine and shut his eyes, taking a few breaths before he answered.

"I want this more than anything," he opened his eyes and looked into mine, "But—"

I interrupted by kissing him again, but he pulled back.

"I don't want you to regret this."

"I won't. Ed. Please." I pulled Nerida's dress over my head and dropped it to the floor as I pulled Ed onto the bed. He started to explore my body, and the world became nothing but the two of us: the sound of our breath, the touch of skin.

And then, his cellphone started to ring.

"Ignore it," he whispered. I was barely noticing it, honestly.

The ringing stopped, and for a while it seemed like the whole world stopped. My anger was gone. My sadness was gone. I gave in to a joy that I hadn't let myself fully experience before—not just his hands on me and his body moving in and with mine, but also the joy of knowing what I wanted and the power of having someone want me so much. I tasted so much life there, in the same cottage where I'd once been so close to death.

And then the ringing started again, annoying and persistent like a mosquito in a bedroom at night, falling silent only when we did and leaving an uneasy stillness in its wake.

I looked across the pillow and smiled at Ed as the world slowly came back into focus. His hair was even more rumpled than usual.

"Are you okay?" he whispered, brushing my hair off my face.

"I'm way more than okay." I nestled closer against him. "Are you okay?"

"I've never been so okay," he laughed. "This is the best prom night ever." We giggled as though we were, in fact, in the backseat of a car after the prom.

The little crinkles around his eyes melted away, though, and his face became serious. He looked into my eyes so deeply that I shivered, and he tucked the quilt around us.

"Remember when you read my tarot cards, and you said I could have one thing I wanted more than anything? It was you." He buried his face in my hair. "It's always been you."

"You mean my magic actually worked, for once?"

"Your magic always works on me." He pulled back and looked deep into my eyes again. "I love you. I always have."

And then the phone started ringing again.

"Goddammit," I muttered. I untangled myself from Ed, and he leaned over the bed to fish the phone out of his pants. He flipped it open and checked the tiny screen.

"I think it's Thom."

"If he's calling to tell you the score in the baseball game, I'll kill him."

Ed answered, and then handed the phone over to me. "It's Bunny. She sounds upset."

The bed springs screeched as I sat up to take the phone from him.

"Kitty, you need to come home. No, to the hospital actually—right away," Bunny said when I answered. "It's Thom. It's his heart. The ambulance just left, and the paramedics are working on him. That's all I know. Get to the hospital as soon as you can."

"Oh my God." I sank back onto the bed, which squeaked loudly again. I bit my lip and hoped Bunny hadn't heard. "We'll be right there."

I flipped the phone shut and looked over at Ed.

"It's Thom." I clutched the quilt against me. "It's his heart. They just took him to the hospital."

Ed was already out of bed and reaching for his pants. "It's the Love Heart," he said, forgetting that he was too science-y to believe in it.

I looked at our clothes scattered on the floor and remembered the shocked look on Thom's face when Ed and I had left together.

"Oh shit. We did this. We killed him!"

(Don't Fear) the Reaper

aradise Valley's hospital was a foreboding Victorian building. When I was little, I was sure it was really a laboratory where mad scientists collected body parts from the people of Paradise Valley. Somewhere in that creepy old building, there were probably rooms filled with jars of pickled tonsils, gallbladders, and hearts. What mad scientist wouldn't want a mystical, cursed Love Heart for their collection?

The hospital looked no less menacing tonight. Ed and I ran through the over-waxed hallways that dipped and warped with age, until we reached the double doors into the waiting area of the emergency room. Bunny sat in a chair in the corner. The half-dozen or so people waiting to see a doctor all looked up at us, glancing from our panicked faces to Bunny's. The room buzzed with the hum of the fluorescent lights and rumours: another Love meeting his fate.

"Where is he?" I struggled to catch my breath.

"Down there, in the exam room." Bunny jutted her chin toward a closed door down the hall. "Your mother's waiting down there, too. You'd better go to her, honey. I stayed out here to wait for you, but she shouldn't be alone."

"I'll wait here. I've got nothing to say to her."

"Kitty, she's your mother, and she's scared. Your brother might be dying. Come on."

Bunny led the way and Ed walked beside me, his hand on the small of my back. People were still staring. I gave the whole lot of them the stink eye, and the eyes quickly snapped away.

God, I hated how this place smelled. The odour of disinfectant and the crackling PA system took me right back to the night I'd lost the baby. Those memories blurred with the ones of me on the "special ward," wishing Mrs. Fraser hadn't pulled me out of the water. A blackness started to spin behind my eyes, and I squeezed them shut. *Not now.* I was here for Thom.

Queena sat in a metal chair, staring at the examination room door. Her back was ramrod straight and she held her hands tightly on her lap, but her face was crumpled, soft and dissolving like a dark cloud blown away in the aftermath of a thunderstorm.

I crouched next to her at a safe distance and touched her arm. Her eyes looked down to meet mine. She looked so old. Old, and defeated, and tired.

She motioned to the door and reached for my hand. "They won't let me in. Oh, Kitty, I don't want to lose him, too!"

I pulled my hand back. "We're not losing anyone. Tell me what happened."

Queena gulped down a sob and patted her bosom for a tissue. "He was downstairs in his room, and then he came upstairs and said he felt kind of funny. But I didn't think anything of it. Oh, why didn't I do something?" she wailed.

"Calm down. Take a breath. Then what happened?"

"And then...and then I went upstairs to put the laundry away, and he was in the bathroom being sick, and then he was on the floor clutching his chest, and he was gasping for breath and saying, 'Oh Mum, it hurts!', and then he—he fainted, I guess. And I screamed, I think, and Bunny called the ambulance. And those doctors won't tell me anything! They shoved me out here, even though my baby's dying in there, all alone!"

"You don't know that, Queena," Ed said. "They likely just needed room to work."

"It's been ages! Why haven't they told me anything?"

No sooner had the words come from her lips than the door to the examination room opened. The four of us turned, preparing ourselves to face a doctor and hear the worst. Instead, we faced our Thom—fully dressed, looking pale and sheepish.

"Thom!" Queena screamed and flung herself at him. Heads poked around the end of the hall, no doubt certain they'd see Queena in the throes of grief. Seeing that her scream was out of relief, they looked away, uninterested.

Bunny rubbed Thom's arm as I gave him an awkward hug. "What happened?"

Thom leaned against the wall and looked down at his feet. "Sure as hell felt like my heart. Never had pain like that in my life."

"What was it?" Ed asked.

Thom kept staring at his feet. "Probably heartburn."

I shoved him, hard. "HEARTBURN? You had us thinking you were dead because you had gas?"

Queena caught my hand. "Now dear, don't carry on like that. People will think we're riff-raff. Thom, are you sure? There's nothing wrong with your heart?"

"Geez, Queena, you sound disappointed. No, it's not the Love Heart. Just need to lay off the spicy pepperoni, I guess."

Queena crossed herself. "You've been blessed, Thom. Destiny has given you a second chance."

"For fuck's sake, it's not like he rose from the dead. He just needed to fart." I was already tired of all the attention Thom was getting.

"Language!" Queena warned.

"It's not destiny. And it's not my heart." Thom finally looked up from his shoes. "My head's what's messed up—listening to all the people telling me I was going to die young. The Love Heart thing is bullshit. Sorry to disappoint you, Queena."

Queena's eyes widened. "Well Thom, I never—"

Thom cut her off. "When the doctors had me hooked up to those machines, I thought about what I've done with my life. Nothing. Haven't done a thing. Kim was right. I haven't been living. Just been waiting to die." He shrugged off Queena's arm. "It's all a crock of shit."

"Just because you escaped it this time, doesn't mean it's not real! Your father didn't believe in it and look what happened to him!"

"You can go on believing this family is doomed, if you want, but I won't. You've pretty much ruined Pussy's life with your bullshit. Not me. I'll die when it's my time, but until then, I'm going to live."

"Does that mean you're getting off the sofa, then?" Bunny asked.

"I am. I had a shock tonight, and the doctor thinks that might be what made the heartburn so bad."

I looked nervously at Ed out of the corner of my eye. He was looking nervously at me out of the corner of his eye. I braced for Thom to call us out for almost killing him and pulled Nerida's long sweater to cover the minidress.

"Pussy gave me a letter she found from Stubby. I finally read it tonight."

I let myself breathe. Ed's shoulders relaxed.

Thom pulled a piece of paper out of his pocket and cleared his throat.

"*You may find it strange, or even disappointing, that I left you my hockey card collection,*" Thom read. "*I'm leaving it to you for two reasons. One—you and I spent so many good times looking at the cards together. I hope you'll remember those times when you look at them after I'm gone. And two—there are cards in the collection that are incredibly valuable. Remember how I'd never let you touch the 1966 Topps USA Test #35 Bobby Orr rookie card? Well, I had that card appraised this year. It's in mint condition, and it's worth over $150,000.*"

"What the hell?" I cried.

"Kitten, language!" Queena clucked, sucking in her breath.

"I have a collector interested in buying it when you're ready to sell. His information is at the end of this letter. I put that card and a couple of other valuable ones in the little safe in the bomb shelter. The code is at the end of this letter, too. I want you to sell those cards and use the money to start living your life to the fullest. Do whatever it is that will bring you joy.

"Maybe it's true about the Love Heart. Sometimes I'm not sure. I hope you'll live a very, very long time. But whether you live until ninety or die next week, live so that when Death meets you, you'll have no regrets, and you won't think back to what you might've done."

Thom stopped reading and looked around at us.

"Some other stuff, too. More hockey cards that are worth something. Then you know, I love you, blah blah blah."

Queena had to sit down. Ed and I were stunned into silence. Even Bunny couldn't think of anything to say.

"I'm going to sell the cards and use the money toward opening a restaurant here in Paradise Valley. Been thinking about it for a while, but I thought I'd never be able to save up."

Queena looked confused. "You're going to get rid of things from *my* house? You know I like to keep things just as they were when—"

"It's been thirteen years," Thom said. "Keeping that stuff won't bring Stubby back. Look, getting rid of it will help me get my arse off your sofa."

"Sell everything fast," I said to Thom. "Get as far away as you can, before Queena decides to lock you in the bomb shelter or something."

Queena looked from me to Thom to Bunny to Ed. "Could you all excuse Kitten and me for a moment, please? I'd like to talk to her alone."

"Not now," I protested. "I have nothing to say to you."

"Now." Queena turned her back and walked to the metal chairs in the hall.

I widened my eyes at Bunny, but she ignored me and walked off. Ed reached for my hand and gave it a squeeze before he headed off to join Bunny and Thom. When Thom saw Ed take my hand, I thought he might need to be hooked up to the EKG again.

Queena patted the metal chair next to her. I perched on the very edge of the seat.

"I remember that other time you were here. After you tried to drown yourself."

"Shh, not so loud!" I hoped the nurses walking past hadn't heard.

Queena reached for my hand. "I did wrong by you, Kitten. You needed much more help than I gave you. I had a time like that myself, you know. After Nerida died, when you were a tiny baby, I had to go away for a little while. I was so worried someone would find out. It broke my heart that it was happening to you, too. I felt like I'd passed that on to you, just like the curse."

I pulled my hand back and shifted away from her. I felt bigger than her, somehow, as if I'd grown into myself in the past few hours.

"Why didn't you tell me about that when I had to stay in the hospital? It might've helped. I thought you were ashamed of me."

"I was ashamed of myself, I suppose. I didn't want you or anyone else to think of me like that. I just wanted to move past all of it, like none of it had happened."

"But that's the problem. You're always pretending stuff didn't happen. And considering how you lied to me and Matt, you'll do just about anything to keep on pretending."

I was clenching my jaw so hard I thought I might break some teeth.

Queena lowered her voice, probably hoping I'd lower mine, too. "I hope you can forgive me. I just thought I could protect you, and that's not a bad thing, is it?"

"Jesus Christ. It's just like when Stubby died and you locked yourself away for months and left Thom and me alone, as if our feelings weren't important. You wanted your make-believe world more than you wanted us..."

My words trailed off as I remembered holding Pixie while Matt accused me of wanting my make-believe world more than I wanted us. I stared ahead, unseeing, as my brain had a tug-of-war between anger and compassion.

Queena was crying, but not her usual histrionics. She was sobbing noiselessly, as if her sobs were too big for this world and could only be heard on some non-human frequency. Every dog in Paradise Valley was probably howling along with her. She looked confused, and scared, and desperate.

I knew how that felt.

I stood up and shrugged off Nerida's long white sweater. Fury made me warm.

"Maybe I could call Matt and explain?" Queena's words were raspy and staccato.

"I called him. It's been a day, and he hasn't called back. It's over."

"I'm so sorry, Kitten. I promise, I'll make it up to you. I'll change. I'll get help. I just...I don't know where to start. It's been so long. It feels like so much." She put her face in her hands and sobbed.

I walked in a little circle in the empty hallway, biting my thumb and trying to wrestle my emotions to a place where they made sense. I was torn between hating her and feeling sorry for her. I settled somewhere in the middle—a sort of drained irritation.

"Listen. Maybe we could do this together. I mean, maybe we should. Things aren't like after Nerida died, you know. You can talk about stuff like this now."

"Oh, I know, love. I've seen *Oprah*. Oh, Kitten. It would be so much better if I knew you were there for me."

"Let's talk about it tomorrow. I don't think any of us are thinking clearly after all this, and Thom's fart attack, and...what?"

Queena's tears had stopped, and she was staring at me.

"That dress. It was Nerida's."

"I got it from her closet. I wanted to wear something that wasn't black, for a change."

She touched the hem like she was touching a butterfly wing. "She never had a chance to wear it. It's lovely on you. Looking at you, I can imagine what she'd look like as a grown woman."

I waited for her to start crying, but she didn't. She looked calm, almost grateful, and then bemused.

"Did you have a nice time with Ed this evening, dear?"

"Yeah. It was fine." I kept my eyes on the floor.

"Good dinner, was it? Until we interrupted?"

"Yeah." My cheeks blazed. I turned my face away from Queena and looked toward the waiting room. "We should go. Bunny's probably croaking for a cigarette."

Queena rose out of her chair as though every part of her body hurt. "Yes, let's get home. I need tea. And you should put your sweater back on, love. I'm not sure you're dressed appropriately for an emergency room."

———

Ed pulled into the driveway and turned off the car. I put my hand on his. I suddenly felt shy.

"Are you okay?" he asked.

"I'm relieved we didn't kill Thom. And I'm worn out by Queena, but that's nothing new."

Ed leaned back against his headrest and looked over at me. "You're the most beautiful thing I've ever seen. I want to kiss you so much right now."

"So do it. I double dog dare you."

"I can't! Thom's watching!"

Everyone was waiting in the driveway while Bunny searched her purse for her keys. Queena was occupied with giving Bunny helpful suggestions, but Thom kept stealing glances at us.

"I guess we shouldn't mess with his heart again," I said.

"This'll have to do for now." Ed lifted my hand and kissed the inside of my wrist, just above my witch's ladder, sending little shivers through me.

"Kitten! We need your key!" Bunny yelled. "Where the hell is the jeezlus thing?" She dumped her purse on the ground and stood over the contents, hands on hips, a cigarette dangling from her lips.

"After we get some tea into them, we can talk. Maybe the beach?" I suggested. "Or somewhere more private?"

He answered with a smile and leaned across to open my door.

I handed Bunny my key while everyone talked over each other. The happy chatter stopped abruptly when a car door shut on the street in front of our house and footsteps fell on the dark driveway. Thom stood up. I looked over my shoulder. An owl hooted from the trees behind our house, demanding, "Who? Whooo?"

He stepped into the light from the street light.

"Hi, Kit," Matt said.

Bizarre Love Triangle

ime passed as I stood in shock in the driveway, staring at Matt. Glaciers melted. Galaxies were discovered. Regimes crumbled. Céline Dion probably released at least two albums. My heart did not beat once.

"I got your letter when I got home from work yesterday. Your phone messages, too." Matt held something out to me. "I brought this for you."

I took a careful step toward him and reached out my hand.

"It's a cassette?"

"A mixtape."

"You flew across Canada to bring me a mixtape?"

Matt cleared his throat and glanced at my family. And Ed.

"I promised I'd make you a mixtape someday, remember? This says everything I've wanted to say since you left. Everything I should have said."

He turned his back on my family (and Ed) so that he was talking only to me. "When you didn't come home, I called the police, but they said it was too early to file a missing person report. So, then I phoned here, because I couldn't think of where else you'd be, but your mother said you weren't here. I spent a day imagining the worst. Then I got your message telling me to water the plants. I phoned back right away, but your mother said you wouldn't talk to me."

"It wasn't true." I moved a step closer. He took half a step closer, too, like we were playing a very emotionally charged game of Mother, May I?

"The plant in the dining room died, by the way. Sorry."

"It's okay. You're a GP, not a plant doctor."

Matt took another step. "I wanted to come here but your mother said you'd met up with some guy you used to be in love with and left town with him. She sent me proof." He reached into his pocket and held out a photo. It was me, talking to Rodger at Fact & Fiction the time he'd come in, when Queena had been walking around taking photos.

I swallowed my anger and took a step closer. "She told me you'd called to say you were back with an old girlfriend."

"I should've just gotten on a plane. I don't know why the hell I didn't. But I believed her. I mean, why would she lie?"

I glanced toward my family (and Ed). Queena was standing behind everyone else now, turned away from us, staring into the rose bushes.

"Kit," Matt said, his voice breaking. "I'm so sorry. For everything."

I took another step forward, into his arms.

———

Bunny set the tea on the outdoor table and discretely went back into the house. No one in my family was known for being discreet. I had a feeling they were all watching from behind curtains.

(And Ed. Oh God.)

I turned the mixtape over and over, not trusting myself to talk until I was confident I wasn't going to cry. I wanted to stay in control.

"You should've called to let me know you were coming," I said.

"I called a few hours ago from Toronto, but no one answered."

I thought back to what I'd been doing a few hours ago.

He pulled me onto his lap, and I buried my face in his shoulder, drinking in his scent. It smelled like everything I thought I'd lost, but maybe a bit like something I thought I'd left behind, too.

"God, I've missed you," he said. "I wish you'd told me how you were feeling all this time. I wish I'd known."

I wiped my eyes with my sleeve. My sweater smelled like Ed. I shivered, wondering if Matt could smell it, too. He ran his hand down my body, but it made me think of the way Ed had touched me. I'd been happy. I'd made that decision, and I didn't regret it.

The thing I regretted was that Matt hadn't called earlier to tell me he was on his way.

"Everything will be okay now," Matt said. "We'll find you a great therapist in Kelowna and get you away from your mother. We'll put all of this behind us."

I looked at the bug light to avoid looking in his eyes. I was going to have to make another big decision. Two in one night, and I was still reeling from the first. I waited, counting as five bugs flew to their sparky deaths before I spoke.

"I can't go back to Kelowna with you. As much as I missed you and as much as I felt shitty about how I acted, I was pretty mad at you, too. Because if the tables had been turned, Matt, I would've gone across the country right away to find you. I wouldn't have left you alone."

Matt pulled back. "That's not fair! You know I can't just pick up and leave. I have patients. It's not that easy."

I let another three bugs sizzle while I gathered my thoughts. "But, the thing is, I've been seeing a great therapist here, and I don't want to start over with someone else. She gets me, and I trust her. I have a lot more work to do. And I have family and friends here to support me."

"Haven't I always supported you?"

"Of course, you have." I tugged at the hem of Nerida's dress, trying to pull it lower. "But, I mean, they know me. You only knew part of me, I guess. What I wanted to show you. Maybe you won't even like the real me. Whoever that is. I'm not even sure yet. That's why I'm in therapy." I laughed awkwardly. Matt was silent. I took a deep breath and kept talking.

"And also, I've been working at the bookstore since I've been back. My bookstore. I love it so much, Matt. You know I've always had a hard time deciding what I want to do. This is it. This is what I'm supposed to do. So...I don't think I can go back to Kelowna. I've always made fun of this place, but it feels like this is where I belong."

Matt's eyes were wide as they searched mine. "What do you mean, you're not coming back? I don't understand." His voice broke. "I thought you belonged with me."

I blinked back tears and looked away. "Right now, I need to be here."

I was sure he was bewildered. Paradise Valley wasn't a place you chose to stay. It was a place you stopped to pee and refuel on your way to somewhere better. I didn't know how long I'd need to refuel, and I didn't know if Matt would understand. I fiddled with a button on his shirt, nervous to continue. "The thing is, I need to stay for Queena, too. I know what she did was awful, but she needs help."

Matt dropped my hand. "You want to help her, after she lied to us?"

"Matt, I know. It's not like I can forgive her. But in her own twisted way, she was doing it from a place of love."

"How does lying to us have anything to do with love?"

I slipped back to my own chair. "Lying doesn't, but grief does. That's why she lied. I think maybe love and grief are both so strong that when they meet, it's like pouring gas on a bonfire. It can get dangerous and out of control. And my mother's been burning like that for years. Turning my back on her isn't going to make anything better."

"You're choosing your mother over me? After what she did? Kit, if you stay, you let her win." There was an edge of anger in Matt's voice that reminded me of my last day in Kelowna.

I squeezed my eyes shut. I didn't even know who I was angry with anymore. Maybe everyone. "So, who would win if I left? Queena'd probably get worse. I'd never deal with my stuff. In some ways, what she did wasn't so different from what I did. It was wrong and I'm angry, but she's my mother. Are you saying that I have to choose between you?"

"I just thought you'd want to get as far away from here as possible. I have plane tickets for us for tomorrow because I wanted to get you home."

"But maybe I am home." I spoke quietly and slowly, wrapping my hair tightly around my fingers.

Five bugs incinerated in the bug light before Matt spoke again. "Take the time you need here, and I'll come back. I'll move here." He reached to pull me back onto his lap. "I'm not going to leave you to deal with all of this alone."

"You can't just move here. You said you couldn't even come here to make sure I was okay because you've got patients and a practice. And your family's there."

"My life is with you. I want to be with you. So, let's do this: you stay here a couple of months to do what you need, and if you decide you don't want to go back to BC, then I'll come here." He ran his hand through my hair, looking relieved that he'd solved the problem.

It would've been so easy to just go along with his plan, to slip back into our life together. But the idea of it felt like trying to slip into a favourite sweater that'd shrunk in the wash.

"You don't have to make decisions for me anymore, Matt. And there's a lot of other stuff we need to talk about..."

And then he kissed me. I forgot what I was going to say.

"We'll talk tomorrow," he said. His hand moved up my thigh, under the high hem of my dress. "I can't remember the last time I saw you wearing something other than black. And what's this?" He held my wrist up to inspect the witch's ladder.

"Oh, this? I joined a gang."

Tempted

I took Matt to get settled in the attic, and came back to the deck. Ed was gone, and there were so many competing emotions in my head I felt dizzy. I took a swig of Rockaberry cooler to make myself even dizzier.

Bunny joined me, closing the sliding door with her hip to keep her tea from spilling. "So. Is everything fixed up between you two, then?"

"There's a lot to talk over. A lot's happened." I tugged Nerida's sweater lower on my legs. Sixties minidresses weren't made for cool Nova Scotia nights.

Bunny picked up her pack of cigarettes and started to take one, but then set it back down. Her chair legs scraped as she turned to look at me directly.

"Okay, tell me: just what happened between you and Ed tonight?"

"Why? What do you think happened?"

"You were a little dishevelled when you got to the hospital."

I grabbed my hair and started to weave it into a braid. "We walked on the beach. It was windy."

"I thought you were going out for dinner?"

"We changed our mind. Geez, Bunny."

Bunny looked me up and down and then looked away. "Your dress is inside out."

Flames leaped up my face. "It is not!"

"It is."

I loosened my sweater and peeked at the dress. The seams were out, and a small tag stuck out on my hip. The sweater had been covering it. Maybe since it was dark, no one else had noticed. Maybe Matt hadn't.

"We were at Ed's cottage." I didn't meet Bunny's eyes.

"Jesus Mary and Joseph. Did you sleep with him?"

I rolled my eyes like I had when I was a teenager and Queena caught me doing something I shouldn't. "No. We didn't...sleep."

"Kitty, for chrissakes!" She set her cup down on the table, hard, and leaned forward. "Did you actually?"

I shrugged and bit my thumb. I expected her to tease me or make some ribald comment, but she looked furious.

"Don't you hurt Ed!"

"Trust me, I didn't hurt him."

"That boy's been crazy about you for years. Honestly, Kitty! Going off when you're upset, using that poor boy to make yourself feel better..."

"Stop calling him 'that poor boy.' It's not like I tortured him. God."

"If it was anyone else you'd done this with, I'd have a good laugh at you for the mess you're in. But not Ed." Bunny lit her cigarette and inhaled from it deeply before she spoke again. "Kitten, it was Eileen Fraser. The one I was in love with."

I pictured my aunt with Mrs. Fraser and my understanding of the universe shifted, again.

Bunny sat back in her chair and folded her arms, staring up at the night sky. "You brought us together again, for a bit, after she found you at the beach. She phoned me from the hospital. Before you woke up, we talked about everything. But then Queena arrived, and I saw the way she looked at us. And everything was such a mess. The moment passed, I suppose. Then she got sick. Oh, I've wanted to go to her so many times. But maybe I deserved to be away from her. Maybe it's punishment."

"Punishment for what?"

Bunny crossed and uncrossed her legs. "The day Nerida died, I was supposed to go to the beach, too. I bailed on her because Eileen and I had a chance to be alone, at her family's cottage."

"At...the cottage."

"And then we heard the sirens, and saw a crowd of people on the beach, and ran down. I should've been there. So maybe Eileen and me being apart is a kind of atonement."

"If I said that, you'd tell me I was being ridiculous. Besides, you and Eileen staying apart won't bring Nerida back. I bet she'd want you to be happy. Did she know about you two?"

Bunny blew a smoke ring and smiled. "She knew. She used to cover for us."

I leaned over and took her hand. "Listen, I got a letter from Stubby, too. He told me to look for magic. To not get stuck thinking about the past or worrying about what might happen, but to be happy, right now, and find my treasure. I think that's what you should do. Stop punishing yourself for something you didn't do. Be happy."

She patted my hand and gave me a weak smile. "Oh, sweet thing. If only it was that easy." Her voice wobbled. In the dark, I couldn't tell if she was crying.

"Is that why you're always so nice to Ed? Because of Eileen?"

"Well, Ed's a nice boy. He deserves to be treated better than you've always treated him."

"I treated him pretty well tonight."

Bunny burst out laughing and stood to go inside. "Kitten! Sweet merciful Jesus. I'm not going to lecture you, but you need to fix this mess. People are going to be hurt, and you can't blame your mother for this one. This is all you."

As Bunny closed the door behind her, a moth flew into the bug light with a spectacular, prolonged sizzle. I feared I was headed for a similar fate.

PART X
What Will Be

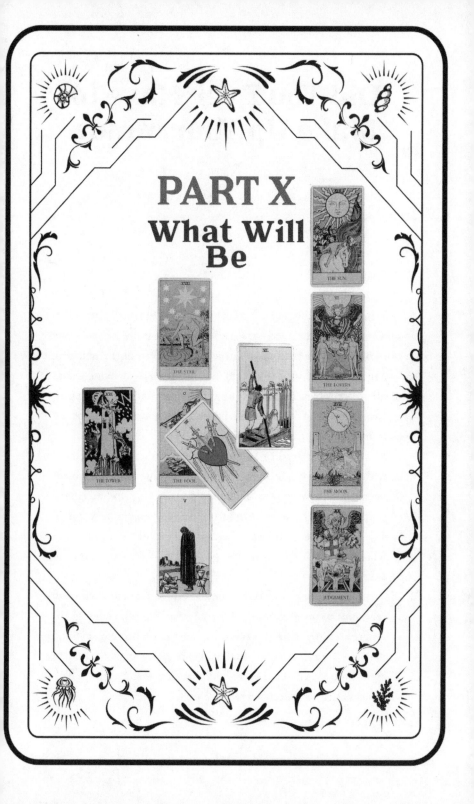

Did You Ever Have to Make Up Your Mind?

Dear Kitty,

Whoa. Shit. Judging from the state of my dress, the carnelian worked. Glad the dress got some action, even if it wasn't with me in it. But Matt's here now? Guess I'm kicked out of the attic. Ha. Maybe I should stick to pulling tarot cards and knocking things off coffee tables, because being your Fairy God-Ghost seems to have unintended consequences. I guess this is why I'm not supposed to interfere.

I was going to pull a card for you, but another one jumped out of the deck: the Page of Cups. It's telling you that you're a different person now. How you felt about things and how you reacted in the past was the old you. You can forgive and move on to new things.

But you know, because the card fell out like that, I've been wondering if it's also meant for me. Maybe I need to leave the old me behind.

I gave your dad's letter some more thought, and decided to reach out to my grandfather for some clarification about all the Afterlife stuff. He was always really sweet to me on your side, and man, was he ever happy to see me! He hugged me for the longest time. I was never a big hugger, but wow, it was so far-out to have someone see me and touch me again.

It turns out, I should've paid better attention when my great-grandmother was going over stuff, because there's a lot I've been missing out on. It's called the After*life* because there's life there. It's not like you go and sit quietly in a dark corner and wait for everyone else to show up. Stuff happens. You learn things. You meet people. YOU CAN GO TO CONCERTS. Jesus Christ, do you know who's on that side, now? Janis Joplin. Jim Morrison. Jimi Hendrix. Cass Elliott. All doing shows every damn night! Grandpa said it's like Vegas, without any cover charge. He says there's lots of people my age, and unlike high school, no one's a dick. He claims he's met some nice boys my age he wants to introduce me to, although some of them are technically a few centuries old. Ha.

He says I can go anytime I'm ready. But it means I can't come back here. I won't be able to see you, or Bunny and Queena. Like you, I guess I have some decisions to make.

Love,
Nerida
xoxo

If You Leave

Ed opened the door just enough to peer out, but he made no move to invite me in.

"I brought you a treat." I held out a coffee and shook the brown paper bag that held chocolate croissants.

He opened the door a bit wider. "Where's Matt?"

"I imagine he's somewhere over Manitoba by now. He left this morning."

Ed opened the door wider. "He left? That was fast."

"He didn't see any point in staying. Look, can I come in so we can talk?"

Ed stepped outside and closed the door behind him. "My mum's got company. Let's go around back."

I followed him into the backyard, where we settled into two swings hung from a big oak tree. Ed took the coffee I held out without looking at me.

"Did you tell him about...us? Last night?"

"I couldn't figure out what to say. I'd already told him I wasn't going back to Kelowna, so it felt like I'd only be making things a thousand times worse."

"Not going back—ever? Or just not today?"

"Maybe not ever."

Ed kept his eyes on his coffee, turning the cup in his hands without drinking it. "I don't get it. I've spent weeks listening to you talk about how you wanted him to call. Why wouldn't you go back?"

"It's complicated." I set my coffee down in the grass and plucked a daisy growing next to the swing, pulling off petals and watching them twirl to the ground. "When I saw him in the driveway, I knew in my gut that I didn't want to go back. It's not home. This is. Remember when you visited last year, and you were really irritating and asked me why I haven't done anything with my life?"

"I don't think that's exactly what I said."

"Close enough. I think it was because deep down, I knew what I wanted, and I wasn't going to find it there. I wanted the bookstore. My magic. The stuff I always wanted was here, but I thought it was gone."

Our swings moved slightly out of synch, stirring the air between us that was so heavy with everything we weren't saying.

"Matt's pretty upset. I mean, I would be too, if someone chose a farty small town over me. I think he thought that when I woke up this morning, I'd have changed my mind. But this is one of the rare times in my life when I know what I'm doing."

"So...that's it?" I could hear the hope in Ed's voice.

I leaned back and pushed to make the swing go a little higher. "I told him let's see how we both feel after a couple of months. Maybe he'll get back there and get used to things without me, anyway."

"Last night, it didn't sound like he was going to feel different about things. I saw the way he looked at you."

I slowed the swing again, keeping my eyes on my feet as they skidded through the worn grass. "He loves me. Or the version of me he knew about, anyway."

"And you love him."

"I mean, we've been together six years. I fell in love with him so fast. Maybe not just with him, but with the idea of who I could be with him. I don't know. Maybe not every love is supposed to have a happily ever after."

"Yeah. I guess I know that one."

I brought my swing to a full stop. "So. About last night."

Ed's swing came to a stop, too. "You don't have to say anything."

"I wanted last night to happen. I'd thought about it all day. And I thought about you all last night. How you had to stand there and watch me and Matt together."

Ed's eyes looked like he hadn't slept much. "Maybe I shouldn't have let anything happen between us. But I'd give anything to have stopped time in that cottage last night."

"I wouldn't change a thing, apart from everything that happened after your cellphone rang. Right after you told me you love me." I shifted so that I was facing him directly and reached for his hand, trying to synchronize the sway of my swing with his.

"I probably shouldn't have said it. It's always been true, though," he said.

"Oh, Ed. Maybe you're in love with some bitchy teenage version of me. You barely know the grown-up me. I barely know me."

Ed reached over to still my swing. "I know who you are, Kitty. I've known you since we were kids. I've been sitting on that beach with you since you came back, and I've seen who you are now. I love all those versions of you—even the one that's kind of bitchy. Maybe even especially that one, because I know her best."

I turned my head slightly to blink away tears. If I looked at him, I might break into a thousand pieces. "Well, God knows you've seen me at my worst. If you love me even with all that, you must be crazier than all of us Loves combined."

Ed touched my cheek and turned my face to look at him. He looked older than he had even a few days earlier—wiser, maybe, and more self-assured. Which was funny, because I felt about two years old and really stupid.

"I always seem to be there at the worst times in your life. Just once, I wish I could be there for your best."

"Last night with you was pretty close to the best. What happened between us—not just last night..." I struggled to find the right words, and then I dug deep to find the courage. "The thing is, Ed, I...love you too, and that's so messed up. I don't know where Matt fits into this, and I don't know what's happening, and..." I couldn't finish. Even if I'd known what to say, my throat had closed up.

Ed studied my face as though he was committing it to memory. "Like you said, maybe not every love is supposed to have a happily ever after."

"I didn't mean *us*, butthead." I looked away, fighting the urge to take him by the hand and lead him to the backseat of the shaggin' wagon. "So, what do we do now?"

Ed took a deep breath. The look on his face was the same one he had after he scored on his own net when he and Thom played peewee hockey.

"I'm leaving, Kitty. If I'd thought there was any chance for us, I would've stayed, but when Matt showed up last night...well, I called first thing this morning and accepted that job in Ontario."

I stared, unseeing, at the shimmer of ocean in the distance. The pressure building in my chest kept me from saying anything.

Ed got off his swing and leaned against the tree. "You need to figure out what's happening with Matt, and I'd only complicate things. Maybe you need to be on your own to figure out what you want."

"Why are you always so goddamn right about things? Damn, it's annoying," I wiped my eyes on my sleeve and stood close to him against the tree. "The job's only eight months, right? If you leave, will you come back?"

"Do you want me to come back?"

"Do you want me to want you to come back?"

222222

He caressed my cheek. "I want you to be happy, Kitty."

I leaned my head against his chest, listening to his heartbeat, wondering how it could sound so steady and strong when mine was performing some kind of unrehearsed halftime marching show.

"Remember that old movie Tiny and I made you guys watch once? *An Affair to Remember*? Where Cary Grant and Deborah Kerr agreed they'd meet in a year's time at the top of the Empire State Building if they still wanted to be together?"

"I remember. Thom bitched the whole time because there was too much kissing and no explosions."

I looked up at him. "Maybe, when your contract is up in April, if this is still what we both want, we'll meet on the beach, okay? I mean, it'll be like our Empire State Building."

Ed wrapped his little finger around mine. "Pinky swear." He leaned down to kiss me, but I pulled away when I heard laughter coming from the house.

"I could've sworn I heard Bunny," I said.

"Yeah, she came over just before you got here. I wanted to give them some privacy."

I scrutinized his face. "Do you know why they'd want privacy?"

"Do *you* know why?"

I nodded.

"When Mum was sick, she told me that she'd once been in love with a beautiful woman, but things ended badly. She only told me it was Bunny a couple of months ago, after I told her how I felt about you."

Bunny and Mrs. Fraser stepped out the back door into the garden, holding on to each other as they laughed at some private joke. They spotted us under the tree and headed over.

Bunny looked younger than I'd ever seen her, and she giggled like Tiny and I had in the fairy tale section when we were little.

"Imagine meeting you here," I said.

Bunny beamed at me. "Well, as you can see, Eileen has accepted my apologies."

"And Bunny has accepted mine," Mrs. Fraser added. "Better late than never, right?"

"It was you and Thom who led me to come here, Kitten," Bunny said. "Seeing Thom's face at the hospital after reading that letter, and what you said last night about Stubby telling you to seize joy or whatever. Carpe diem. Carpe Eileen."

She and Eileen stood, smiling at Ed and me. We were still holding hands. Ed loosened his grasp, but I held on tighter. Carpe Ed.

Bunny pinched my cheek. "I'll see you at home later, sweet thing. Don't wait up."

She and Mrs. Fraser walked back through the garden, their arms wrapped around each other like they'd never let go again.

———

Bunny came up my attic stairs just after seven the next morning. Her face was as bright and sunny as Nerida's room.

"Well, seeing as you're wearing the same clothes you had on yesterday, I guess I don't have to ask if you had a good night," I said.

Bunny put her hands on her hips. "It looks like I could say the same about you, Miss Kitten. I very reluctantly came home to make myself presentable for work. I didn't think my boss would give me a day off just because of shenanigans."

I patted my bed for her to join me. She sniffed as she sat down.

"Why does it smell like the beach up here?"

"It's been like that since I moved back."

Bunny looked over her shoulder as though she'd seen something. "Attics give me the creeps. I don't know why you like them so much."

"Well, if I tell you something super creepy, do you promise not to drag me to a psychiatrist?"

"Tell."

"Stuff's been happening. Tarot cards showing up in different parts of my room. Crystals moving. And that dress I wore, of Nerida's? I felt something drawing me to her room, and when I went inside, the dress was in the closet with all the other stuff pushed out of the way, like someone had put it there for me."

Bunny shivered. "Sweet Jesus. You know, sometimes, over the years, I've thought I'd heard Nerida laugh. She had such an infectious laugh. But then I'd give my head a shake and tell myself I'm just imagining it because I miss her so much. Or maybe I'm cracking up."

"Maybe we're both cracking up."

We looked around the attic, listening to hear something through the silence.

"Well, if she's listening to us, at least she's being well entertained," Bunny said with a wink. "Look at us! Such debauchery. I don't even know where to start, sweet thing. I didn't think I'd ever feel this kind of happiness. I don't quite trust it."

"You deserve happiness."

"You do too. You were glowing when I saw you with Ed."

"Are you going to lecture me again about hurting him?"

Bunny took my hand. "I'm more worried about him hurting you. Eileen told me he's leaving."

I fell back onto my bed. "This isn't the way '80s movies said things would work out. At the end, I'm supposed to walk out with some guy as a power ballad swells in the background. But maybe Matt will decide to stay in Kelowna. Maybe Ed will never come back. I'll end up a crone, handing out love tea and practising witchcraft in my bookshop."

Bunny fell back next to me and stared up at Sting. "That sounds delicious, actually. You should do that regardless. Look, just remember what your father told you in that letter—about magic and finding your treasure."

"But what if I found the treasure and let it go? What if I've made all the wrong decisions?"

"My darling girl. What if the treasure is you?"

Here Comes the Sun

Dear Kitty,

Next time we talk, it'll be in person. Or in ghost. Ha. Maybe I'll get to be the one to show you the ropes. We could even go to some concerts together, because some of those bands you like will probably be over on my side by then. I think that Prince guy and Jimi could really rock out together someday. It'd be groovy. Or like you and Tiny used to say, it'd be totally awesome.

It wasn't hard to decide to go, in the end. You're all living your lives, and I've got to live my own, you know? Or die my own death, or however you explain it.

I did want to stick around and find out how things will turn out for you, but you know what? I've done all I could to help. I think you'll listen to your gut now, even without my tarot messages. You can fill me in when we see each other again. It'll be ages for you, but it'll be just a few minutes for me.

I left one last card on your pillow. The Sun.

Truth. Illumination. Joy. Fulfilment. The dawning of a new day. Here comes the sun, little darling. We're going to be all right. See you on the other side.

Love,
Nerida
xoxo

The Best of Times

Wednesday, May 2, 2001

I woke up and didn't immediately know where I was. The room smelled like cardboard and fresh paint. The pale-yellow walls were bare. I stretched a leg across the bed, relishing the crispness of the new sheets, the cool expanse of empty bed, and the hush of the flat.

I was alone.

I giggled at the deliciousness of it and rolled over into a patch of early morning sun, watching dust motes dance in a sunbeam, and dreaming of all the living I'd do here.

The mill's horn blared to start a new day. At the same time, the doorbell buzzed, insistent and annoying, like a hornet trapped in a jar. I rolled out of bed and tripped on a box, stubbing my toe, and cursed all the way to the front door, because no one was there to reprimand me for swearing.

Thom kept pushing the buzzer even after I'd opened the door.

"Frig off." I swatted his hand away from the bell. "God, I can't get away from you, even in my own place."

Tiny squeezed past Thom and handed me a large take-out cup of coffee. "I told him we should bring some, because I figured you probably haven't unpacked a coffee maker yet."

"I'm not your personal damn barista." Thom kicked off his shoes and made himself at home on one of the few spots in the living room not covered with books or boxes. "Seriously, you guys act like my restaurant is your own friggin' kitchen."

Thom had opened his restaurant on Valentine's Day. We'd all been bracing for it to fail, frankly, because we're Loves and failing's what we do, but it was a success. Burgatory had a menu featuring gourmet burgers (to attract the locals) and locally sourced seafood (to attract the tourists). It had a patio with ocean views, and a bar that was much more popular than Paradise Valley's tavern. The burgers all had names, like the spicy DevilBurger and the vegetarian AngelBurger. The kids' menu had TinyBurgers. Thank God, there weren't any PussyBurgers or BunnyBurgers.

Tiny snuggled next to Thom on the sofa. He gave her a kiss on the cheek and they rubbed noses. I couldn't stop myself from making a face. They'd been together for months now, and I was happy for them, but, I mean, ew.

Tiny pulled away from Thom and turned serious. "So, Kitty, listen. Last night—"

The angry-hornet buzzer interrupted her and the front door opened before I even moved off the box I'd perched on.

"Good morning, Miss Independent Kitten!" Bunny came down the hall like she owned the place. "This is so exciting. You're just like Mary Tyler Moore. And Tiny lives downstairs, so she's your Rhoda."

"You might just make it after all," Eileen sang. She and Bunny put their arms around each other's waists and laughed like they'd said the funniest thing in history. I laughed, too; I couldn't help it with their infectious happiness. It'd gotten me through our trip to BC the month before, when we'd packed up my things and I'd signed the papers to sell the house I'd shared with Matt.

Bunny plunked herself on a box, and I moved some books so Eileen could sit down next to Tiny. Tiny had an odd expression on her face—kind of a cross between excitement and angst—but I figured it must be a by-product of dating Thom.

Queena trailed in behind Bunny and Eileen and stood in front of the living room's big bay window, clutching a package to her chest and sucking in her breath.

"Oh my, we need to get curtains up here right away, Kitten," she said. "Your neighbours could look right in here and see you walking around undressed."

Thom snorted. "No one wants to see that."

I punched his arm. "Shut up."

"You shut up."

"Ed's on his way home," Tiny blurted. All eyes zipped to her face, which turned bright pink, but she kept her eyes on mine. "He called Thom last night. And he said—" She bit her lip, remembering the exact words. "He said he'd bring your sea glass back, if you meet him at the beach Friday night."

All eyes now turned to me. I took a step back to support myself against the wall, but I bumped into a box and sent a stack of books clattering onto the hardwood floor. The marching band started up in my chest again as I bent to pick them up.

Eileen cleared her throat. "He called us, too. He's already on the road. I wasn't sure if I should say anything. I know you two haven't spoken since he left."

I was intent on stacking the books and making sure they were perfectly even, but my hands were shaking. I went to shove them in my pockets, but my robe didn't have any, so I ran them through my hair and then crossed my arms tightly in front of me as I shifted from one foot to another. My mind unravelled an endless loop of cautions. Maybe he truly wanted to return the sea glass. Or maybe he wanted to say goodbye for good, in person. That seemed like an Ed thing to do.

I wished—not for the first time in recent months—that tarot cards would start magically turning up again to tell me what was going on.

"Oh?" I tossed my hair and feigned disinterest, but avoided making eye contact with Bunny or Tiny. They always saw right through me.

For once, it was Queena who came to my rescue.

"Oh! I have something for you!" She handed me the package she'd been holding—bulky and covered in twenty-year-old Smurf wrapping paper. "A little housewarming gift."

It was the enormous, ugly orange macramé owl that had hung on the wood-panelled wall in our living room.

"Wow. Awesome." I unfolded the owl and held it in front of me. It stretched from my neck to my ankles. "You know where this would be great? Up in The Sea Witch."

The Sea Witch was our new magic boutique, in Fact & Fiction's attic. We had bookcases filled with books on witchcraft and folklore, displays of crystals, and shelves filled with the candles and spell jars Tiny made. The rough plaster walls were peppered with framed pictures of nereids and sea goddesses, and we always had steaming cups of Love Tea available for customers. And twice a week, in front of the window with the view of the ocean, Tiny and I offered tarot readings.

Queena looked slightly put out. "Well, that's fine, dear. I can find lots of other things from home that you could bring here, so that you'll have memories around you." Although she'd started updating the house, Queena hadn't truly been getting rid of things. She just gave stuff to us, or used it to decorate the bomb shelter or The Memory Garden.

Bunny frowned. "She's trying to get away from the '80s, Queena, not bring it with her." She got up from her box and looked authoritatively at us. "Now, Kitten, go get dressed so we can get this show on the road. You can come with me and Queena in the shaggin' wagon, and we'll meet the rest of you at the beach. We have a birthday to commemorate."

The gulls had the beach to themselves until we showed up, and they coasted over our heads, showing their displeasure at the interruption.

The sandbars stretched out forever, and since there was barely a breeze, the ocean beyond was unusually calm for this time of year.

Queena hadn't been to the beach since the day Nerida died. It'd taken months of therapy before she felt ready to finally visit. She'd decided she wanted to go on May 2nd, Nerida's birthday, so we could celebrate Nerida's life, and not think only of her death.

Eileen, Thom, and Tiny were already sitting on the lobster blanket with a picnic basket. Bunny and I each took Queena by an arm and led her down the stairs toward the water. Our steps were halting, and the tension in Queena's arm made me wonder if she might turn and run. I could hear her breathing, fast and shallow.

We took off our shoes—Queena fussed with hers, lining them up neatly on the pebbles—and set out to cross the sandbars. None of us spoke as we skirted tide pools and crossed the cool sand to reach the waterline. Queena's arms trembled and tears tracked down her cheeks as she scanned the water, raising her head and breathing deeply, as though trying to catch Nerida's scent.

"It was right over there." She nodded to the right. "That's the last place I saw her. But she's not here. I don't feel her here." Queena's voice was a mixture of relief and surprise. "I really expected I would. This'll sound crazy, and I probably shouldn't even say it, but sometimes I've felt her in our house. Just every so often, over the years, I felt like she was there, and that if I turned around quickly, I'd see her. I could smell her suntan oil and Breck shampoo. I know that sounds crazy. I haven't felt it for months."

"It doesn't sound crazy." Bunny stared at the horizon with unfocused eyes. "If she was going to be anywhere, it'd be here. She loved it here. We all did."

Queena nodded, taking a tissue from her bra to dry her cheeks. "We did. I shouldn't have stayed away so long. Not just from here, but from…everything. So many years, I've made my life small. Nerida wouldn't have wanted that, would she? Not Donny, either. They'd be so disappointed in me." She started to cry harder and sank against Bunny's shoulder.

"Not at all." Bunny's voice was gentle as she stroked Queena's arm. "They'd be proud of you. Because you've come through it all, and you got help, and that's a very hard thing to do. And look at you now! So much stronger, and wiser, and you've got way better hair. Nerida would be amazed by that."

Queena laughed through her tears. She'd finally gotten rid of the long bangs and centre part she'd worn since I was born. The new shoulder-length waves made her look ten years younger.

I squeezed Queena's arm. "You've changed so much this past year. Not just how you look. All the changes you've made to the house, too."

"Now if we could just tackle the bomb shelter," Bunny teased. "You could make it a nice scrapbooking room, maybe, since you don't need to protect us from global annihilation anymore." She spread her arms and raised her face to the sun. "Look at this glorious world! Only beautiful things can happen."

"Oh, for goodness sakes, Bunny. Ever since you and Eileen got back together, it's like you're smoking dope or something. Nothing's ever completely safe. And I think the bomb shelter adds to the house's market value, if I ever thought of selling it."

I reached into my tote bag and pulled out a bunch of flowers wrapped in cellophane. I handed Queena and Bunny each a pink rose, keeping one for myself. I stepped into the water and turned to reach my hand back for Queena. Her eyes widened.

"Come on in. It's okay. We're with you," I said.

Queena clutched the neck of her shirt and looked from me to Bunny, who nodded encouragement. Taking my hand, Queena stepped into the sea. She wobbled a bit, as though she was leaving Earth's atmosphere and walking into space, but the three of us linked arms and took tiny steps until the water was above our ankles, squealing as the cold North Atlantic numbed our feet. Then, nodding at each other in agreement, we threw the roses as far as we could, out into the sea.

"Happy birthday, sweet Nerida," Queena whispered. The roses sank beneath the surface.

"Hard to imagine she'd be forty-eight today. I can't picture it. I don't know how it's possible, when I'm only twenty-six," Bunny said, laughing at her own joke.

Queena didn't laugh. She cocked her head, listening to the silence. "There's nothing. No ghosts."

"No," Bunny said. "Not bad ghosts, at least. Maybe ghosts of all the good times we had here."

"But they are here, really, aren't they—Nerida and Donny? There's always here. With us. They'll never leave."

I leaned my head on Queena's shoulder. Bunny snorted. "Who sounds like they're on dope now—eh, Queena?"

Queena shook her head, a gentle breeze lifting her hair in a cloud around her peaceful face. "Never mind, Bunny. Let's go sit on the rocks like we used to. Pretend we're sixteen again."

"But I *am* sixteen!" Bunny laughed.

"You've got underthings older than sixteen." Queena took Bunny's hand, and they turned toward the beach.

I walked behind, lifting my long boho skirt to keep it out of the water. Something sparkled up at me from below the sun-dappled ripples, just a few inches away: a handful of tiny pieces of blue sea glass. I'd never seen so many in one place, all together like that.

I bent down and took one piece, but left the rest. I thought someone might need them more than me, and I made my own luck, now. I held the sea glass up to the sun and wondered how long it takes to go from being a broken bottle on the shore to a beautiful, smooth, polished sea jewel. It would be a lot of tossing in the waves, years of friction and sea salt. It would take ages. Maybe a lifetime. But figuring out how long was probably one of those practical uses of math I was no good at.

The breeze lifted Tiny's laughter to me, and I walked across the sandbars to the shore to join my mother and aunt, who were sitting on the sandstone boulders like sirens in the sun.

The Magic Mixtape

- Cowboy Junkies. "Sun Comes Up, It's Tuesday Morning." *The Caution Horses*. RCA Records, 1990.
- The Cure. "The Lovecats." *Japanese Whispers*. Fiction Records, 1983.
- Duran Duran. "Is There Something I Should Know?" *Duran Duran*. Capitol-EMI Records, 1983.
- Spirit of the West. "Home for a Rest." *Save this House*. WEA Records, 1990.
- The J. Geils Band. "Love Stinks." *Love Stinks*. EMI Records, 1980.
- The Zombies. "She's Not There." *Begin Here*. Decca Records, 1964.
- Morrissey. "Every Day is Like Sunday." *Viva Hate*. HMV Records, 1988.
- Fleetwood Mac. "Sisters of the Moon." *Tusk*. Warner Bros. Records, 1980.
- Siouxsie and the Banshees. "Spellbound." *Juju*. Polydor Records, 1981.
- Violent Femmes. "Gone Daddy Gone." *Violent Femmes*. Slash Records, 1983.
- Oingo Boingo. "Dead Man's Party." *Dead Man's Party*. MCA Records 1985.
- Norman Greenbaum. "Spirit in the Sky." *Spirit in the Sky*. Reprise Records, 1970.
- Bananarama. "Cruel Summer." *Bananarama*. London Records, 1984.

- The Association. "Never My Love." *Insight Out*. Warner Bros. Records, 1967.
- Eddie Murphy. "Party All the Time." *How Could It Be*. Columbia-CBS Records, 1985.
- The Go-Gos. "Our Lips are Sealed." *Beauty and the Beat*. IRS Records, 1981.
- Tears for Fears. "Mad World." *The Hurting*. Phonogram Records, 1982.
- Howard Jones. "Things Can Only Get Better." *Dream into Action*. WEA-Elektra Records, 1985.
- Janis Joplin. "Little Girl Blue." *I Got Dem Ol' Kozmic Blues Again Mama!* Columbia Records, 1969.
- Naked Eyes. "Always Something There to Remind Me." *Burning Bridges*. EMI Records, 1982.
- Rough Trade. "High School Confidential." *Avoid Freud*. True North Records, 1980.
- Kool & The Gang. "Ladies Night." *Ladies Night*. DeLight Records, 1979.
- Pixies. "Here Comes Your Man." *Doolittle*. Elektra Records, 1989.
- Peter Gabriel. "In Your Eyes." *So*. Geffen Records, 1986.
- The Bangles. "Eternal Flame." *Everything*. CBS Records, 1989.
- Strange Advance. "We Run." *2WO*. Capitol Records. 1985.
- The Guess Who. "Undun." *Canned Wheat*. RCA Victor Records, 1969.
- Prince. "1999". *1999*. Warner Bros. Records, 1982.
- Kate Bush. "This Woman's Work". *The Sensual World*. EMI Records, 1989.
- Guns and Roses. "Sweet Child 'o Mine." *Appetite for Destruction*. Geffen Records, 1987.
- Joni Mitchell. "Both Sides Now." *Clouds*. Reprise Records, 1969.
- Ramones. "I Wanna Be Sedated." *Road to Ruin*. Sire Records, 1978.
- The Four Seasons. "Big Girls Don't Cry." *Sherry & 11 Others*.

Vee-jay Records, 1962.

- Information Society. "Tell Me What's on Your Mind (Pure Energy)." *Information Society*. Tommy Boy Records, 1988.
- The Psychedelic Furs. "The Ghost in You." *Mirror Moves*. Columbia Records, 1984.
- The Monkees. "A Little Bit Me, A Little Bit You." *Headquarters*. RCA Victor Records, 1967.
- 10,000 Maniacs. "Trouble Me." *Blind Man's Zoo*. Elektra Records, 1989.
- The Police. "Message in a Bottle." *Regatta de Blanc*. A&M Records, 1979.
- The Grass Roots. "Let's Live for Today." *Let's Live for Today*. Dunhill Records, 1967.
- Spandau Ballet. "True." *True*. Chrysalis Records, 1983.
- Platinum Blonde. "Crying Over You." *Alien Shores*. CBS Records, 1985.
- The Animals. "Don't Let Me Be Misunderstood." *Columbia*. Gramophone Records, 1965.
- The Human League. "Don't You Want Me?" *Dare*. Virgin Records, 1981.
- Thomson Twins. "Lies." *Quick Step & Side Kick*. Arista Records, 1983.
- The Rolling Stones. "Emotional Rescue." *Emotional Rescue*. Rolling Stones Records, 1980.
- The Doors. "Light My Fire." *The Doors*. Elektra Records, 1967.
- Skydiggers. "Slow Burning Fire." *Restless*. FRE Records, 1992.
- Blue Öyster Cult. "(Don't Fear) The Reaper." *Agents of Fortune*. Columbia Records, 1976.
- New Order. "Bizarre Love Triangle." *Brotherhood*. Factory Records, 1986.
- Squeeze. "Tempted." *East Side Story*. A&M Records, 1981.
- The Lovin' Spoonful. "Did You Ever Have to Make Up Your

Mind?" *Do You Believe in Magic?* Kama Sutra Records, 1965.

- Orchestral Manoeuvres in the Dark. "If You Leave." *Pretty in Pink: Official Motion Picture Soundtrack.* A&M Records, 1986.
- The Beatles. "Here Comes the Sun." *Abbey Road.* Apple Records, 1969.
- Styx. "The Best of Times." *Paradise Theatre.* A&M Records, 1981.

Acknowledgements

Thank you:

To Whitney Moran and the whole team at Vagrant Press, for everything that happened after Whitney said yes.

To my editor, Stephanie Domet, for standing up for my characters when I wasn't doing right by them, and for her brilliance in casually suggesting, "Why not structure it like a tarot reading?"

To my children, Ainsley and Elliott Boyd. Poor you. So many dodgy meals. So much '70s and '80s music in the car. Thanks for putting up with me. And a special shout out to Elliott for being a crappy sleeper as a baby. Rocking you to sleep every night gave me time to invent a whole world in my head—a world that eventually become Paradise Valley.

To my sister, Patricia Morash, whose love and dark humour got us through two parental deaths in two months, and who appreciates crustless asparagus funeral sandwiches and funeral playlists as much as I do.

To my therapist, Angela McKay. Thank you for helping me find my way back to myself.

To Judy Donato, Kathryn Reeves, and Renée Hartlieb, who read much earlier versions. Your feedback and enthusiasm prodded me on.

To my friend and MFA mentor, Kelly S. Thompson, for helping me recover my writing mojo.

To the universe, for sending such a hideous 2020-21 that I essentially had a breakdown—yes, I'm thankful, because staring at the wall for weeks helped me understand Queena in a way I hadn't, and convinced me to give the manuscript just one more try.

To all the artists whose music inspired me as I flipped through the K-Tel Record Selector in my head to find just the right song.

To David van Zoost, my eighth-grade English teacher at Amherst Regional High, who once told me, "If you become anything but a writer, it'll be a waste." His words hung over me like a curse for several decades, but teenaged Michelle was so happy he said it.

To my cats, Smudge, Ivy, Rory, and Freddie Purrcury, for occasionally sitting on my keyboard and deleting entire paragraphs that I guess I didn't need, anyway.

And to my dog, Pippa, for forcing me to go for walks when all I wanted to do was stare at the wall. Entire scenes appeared in my head during those walks, so even though you can't read and might even eat the book, thank you.